not your *mama's* mambo

a SULLIVAN'S CREEK *novel*

BARBARA BARRETT

Previously published by the Wild Rose Press

First Champagne Rose Edition, 2016

Republished January 2024 by Barbara Barrett

Sullivan's Creek Series, Book Three

Published in the United States of America

This book is dedicated to families, large or small, close or dysfunctional. They tend to play a significant role in shaping who we are, what we aspire to become and clearing away the obstacles we face getting there. In particular, I dedicate this book to my family; you are so important to me.

CHAPTER 1

"Rutting season. So much for that sale." Mike Woodley stuck his cell back in his jeans pocket. Too bad he didn't still use a landline so he could slam down the receiver. Hadn't felt this level of frustration in years.

His partner, mega-entertainer Jake Bonneville, known to friends and family as Ned Collier, stuck a stack of music in his briefcase. "Excuse me?"

"It's late October. Now that the fields have been harvested, bucks are out in droves trying to score. The potential buyer ventured out to Sullivan's Creek around dusk to take one more look at the property she was considering before signing. On the way back, she ran over one of those sex-starved creatures and now can't get past the shock."

"That's it? Deer are all over the place these days. She could've met one on any street in town."

The growing herds had increasingly infringed upon suburban and even urban areas of Iowa in recent years, in part because people like the two of them were turning rich farmland, forests and wilderness into housing developments like Sullivan's Creek.

Mike fished the client's file from his pending folder. "On the other hand, I suspect it was more a case of presale jitters. Much as she said she wanted that property, as purchase time neared, she lost her nerve, but rather than say so, she invented this deer story."

"Seems a bit far fetched rather than just say no."

Mike closed the folder and slammed it into the top right drawer of his mahogany desk. "Not the first time someone's backed out by inventing some flimsy excuse."

Ned settled into one of the Woodley den's two cushy leather chairs. "I had no idea we were losing folks. Why haven't you mentioned it before?"

Because Mike hadn't wanted to damage his image as the white knight who'd come to his friend's aid a few months back. Ned had stretched his considerable financial resources to the limit and needed help to keep the project from going under. "Dismissed it for a while as the nature of the beast. Figured with time and more finished homes promoting the venture, there'd be less back-tracking. Besides, when you haven't been on the road reviving your singing career, you've been with Shae. Didn't want to disturb."

Throat nodules had sidelined Ned's concert and club appearances for several months. Only recently had he been able to perform again and generate more revenue for the project.

"Should we call that woman back?" Ned asked. "I could give her the star treatment."

Ned usually kept a low profile when it came to his celebrity status, but he wasn't averse to pulling out the charm when needed. "Save it, for now," Mike replied. "I'm learning the hard way about people who sell themselves a bill of goods that they really want to build here. When it comes down to it, they just want to be part of the perceived glamour of living in Jake Bonneville's little town. Better to weed them out early rather than later when we've invested so much time on them."

"Guess you're right. But I don't like you having to deal with all this negative stuff while I'm off rebuilding my career. What can I do to help?"

"Stop feeling guilty. I signed on for this when I agreed to be your partner. You had the property and the investment in the infrastructure, and I had the new capital and business experience. But if you've got some ideas how to find additional buyers and market this place better, I'm all ears."

"I could do a concert out on the grounds, if you think that would help?"

Mike cringed at the thought of scores of looky-loos besieging the property. Plus, considering the dusting of frost on his windshield yesterday morning, the days of outdoor concert weather were fast coming to a close this year. "Let that one germinate a bit. Not sure a concert would net the kind of customers we're after."

"Am I interrupting?" an unfamiliar but surprisingly seductive female voice asked. "The woman who answered the door said to come right in."

Ned recognized her first, though Mike was just a split second behind. "Darren? You're Darren Williams, the artist, right?"

She turned toward Ned, offered a killer smile. "That's me. I'm surprised you recognized me, Mr. Bonneville. It's been a few months since my showing at your mother's gallery."

Mike took in their visitor while Ned made chit-chat. A tad below shoulder length, her black hair was slightly longer than the last time he'd seen her, but she still looked damned good, especially in her white leather jacket and tight navy jeans, which revealed a slim but curvy figure. Something about her had registered that night at the showing, enough for him to hassle her to gain her attention, but business and later his partnership with Ned had prevented him from following up. "Come in, Ms. Williams. Ned and I were just finishing our discussion."

She made her way into the room. Only then did he notice she was carrying a package, which she rested against the side of the empty den chair. She removed red knit gloves and then undid the red plaid scarf protecting her neck from the day's chill. "I've finished the seascape you commissioned last summer."

Right. He vaguely remembered calling her afterward and placing the order. God, had this project taken over his brain so much he'd forgotten about a looker like her?

Ned's phone pinged. He shot it a brief glance. "Gotta go. Wish I could stay for the reveal, but Shae—Shae Harriman, our general contractor and my lady, who you met that night, too—needs me back at my house. The special synthesizer I ordered for my music room just arrived, and I have to approve it before it's installed. Nice to see you again, Ms. Williams."

She nodded. Unlike most people who met Ned, she didn't appear intimidated by the superstar. "Please call me Darren. Both of you."

"Then I'm Ned, not my alter ego, Jake Bonneville, and he's Mike," Ned called as he grabbed his jacket and slipped from the room. "Catch you later, man."

"You arrived just in time," Mike told her. "My bud there wanted to discuss a subject I'd rather put off."

She lifted a brow. "Oh? What would that be?"

"How to promote our housing development so we can sell the remaining lots. He wants to do a concert to raise interest."

"There's no denying his name could be a draw. It certainly helped at his mother's showing."

"True. But we want to attract bona fide buyers, not just his fans. I was trying to figure out a diplomatic way to tell him when you appeared."

"Maybe his mother could share with you how she was able to draw actual patrons to her showing rather than just those who wanted to meet her son."

He studied her with new appreciation. Gorgeous, talented *and* smart. "Good idea. Thanks."

"Glad to help." She hefted the package and held it toward him. "Would you like to do the honors?"

His parents and the rest of his siblings lived in various parts of the country, so he had the old homestead, one of the town's major mansions south of Grand Avenue, to himself. Except for Ned. At his invitation, Ned was staying with him while his new home in Sullivan's Creek was going up. It was almost finished.

Mike also had a place under construction in Sullivan's Creek, but he was less anxious to move in than his pal. He'd purchased the home Ned had been building for his mother, Janice, when she decided to remain in town. Mike had purchased it more as a favor than as an intent to settle in the country. The shell was done, but he never seemed to have time to deal with the interior. He'd get to it. Sometime. Right now, his focus was on selling more lots.

He came out of his reverie to find Darren staring at him, still holding the package. "Don't you want to unwrap it?" A tinge of hurt underlay her tone.

"Uh, sure. Sorry. My head's still back in my meeting with Ned." He made a big deal of taking the parcel from her and ripping off the brown paper. He propped it against the end table and stepped back to examine it. Something didn't equate. This was supposed to be a picture of the Pacific Ocean as seen from his beach house in Malibu. He'd emailed her several shots he'd taken at sunrise. He'd expected shades of gray, blue, mauve. Maybe even some morning mist. Instead, reds and yellows dominated this seascape.

"You did receive the photos I sent you, didn't you?" he asked.

Her eyes narrowed. Apparently she hadn't expected his question. "Uh, yes. They helped me get a feel for what you see daily when you're there."

"A feel?" His voice rose. "I intended to see one of these scenes replicated in your work. Not this, what should I call it, *impression* of my view."

"I, uh, I'm an artist, Mike. I interpret what I see. I don't *replicate* views." She bit out the last sentence.

Neither spoke for a few seconds. Was nothing going his way

today? As pleasing as she was on the eyes, he couldn't deal with her artist's temperament at the moment. "Look, uh, no offense. You're a good artist. This picture just isn't what I anticipated." Hell, five minutes ago, he hadn't even remembered the painting, but now that it was here, it wasn't what he wanted. Go figure.

Her chin jutted out, and she seemed to grow two inches taller. "But I spent considerable time on this, even though I wasn't able to get started on it right away. Perhaps I could make a few alterations that would be more to your liking?"

"Yeah. Do that." What was with him? Why was he sending this beautiful woman away, her tail feathers in a bunch? Because he was that discouraged. Not with her. But with the latest loss of a sale. He needed to strike out at something. She was closest to his force field.

"I don't want a storm at sea. I want something peaceful, calm, tranquil," he said, attempting to soften the blow. "Come back when you can make it look like that."

Coffee-brown eyes now wide, Darren grabbed the painting, her gloves and neck scarf and headed out, leaving the paper behind. Within seconds, the front door slammed.

"What was all that about?" the lilting voice of another woman asked from almost the same spot where Darren had stood minutes earlier.

"Mom? What are you doing here?" Mike went over to her and gave her a perfunctory hug and peck on the cheek.

Frances Woodley, still wearing her black wool jacket, stepped out of his embrace and eyed him with surprise. "I came home. To my own house. Is that so surprising?"

"It is when you haven't been here in ages. Why didn't you let me know you were coming?"

"If I had, I might have missed the little scene I just witnessed. Who was that and why did you send her away nearly in tears?"

"She's a local artist delivering a painting I commissioned a few months back. What you heard was me telling her I didn't like it and asking her to change it." Asking? Okay, demanding. The painting wasn't all that bad. In fact, it was pretty damned good. He'd taken out his frustration on her.

"What I heard was no request. You were bullying her, Michael."

She'd used his full name. Home less than a minute and she'd already reverted to mom mode. "She's a professional. Should be used to critics and clients taking issue with her work."

Her still-firm brow furrowed. "There was nothing personal going on?"

"No," he spit out a little too fast. "I've met her for all of a few minutes at her showing last summer. I bought an Iowa landscape that night and called her a few days later to order a seascape. That's all."

"I thought I sensed stronger vibes."

"Then your sensors are off. There's nothing going on between us, and after what I said to her, I doubt there's much chance of it happening in the future." Then he remembered his mother's surprise appearance. "What brings you back to Des Moines? Just stopping through on your way to some more exotic location?"

She waved away his comment. "Heavens, no. I'm back for an indefinite stay. Your father will be here later this evening, as well as Joey. We're not going to leave you here to fend for yourself any longer. Your family, at least some of us, are moving back. How about that?" She laced her slim fingers in front of her and offered a fait accompli smile.

Was she serious? "You're moving back? Just like that?"

"Actually, your father and I have been discussing the possibility of relocating for some time. We didn't mention it, because we didn't make up our minds until a few days ago. "

"I don't get it. You never liked this town. Only stayed here because Dad grew up here. What changed your mind?"

His mother twisted around. "Where's Tammy? The ride share driver only brought my things as far as the front door."

"She's grocery shopping. I'll get your bags. Jay's moving back, too?"

"Uh, yes. He's had it with condo life in the same town as Alicia, when she barely lets him see his own children. He's driving down, but he shouldn't arrive for several more hours."

"Alicia's idea?"

His mother breezed past him and straightened several items on the room's large desk. "No. Your father and I thought he needed a change of scenery. He's still reeling from the divorce. Maybe he can regain his bearings back in his hometown."

"It's been over two years." Joseph Woodley Jr.—Joey to his mother, Jay to Mike and his senior by a couple of years—had never displayed the leadership qualities one might expect of the oldest child. But that hadn't stopped their dad from bringing Jay into Woodley Industries and handing him a top-level job. To no one's surprise except Jay's, his wife, Alicia, had married him for his name and the money. She'd given him two beautiful children, probably to guarantee her continued access to the family wealth, and then thrown him out of the house. Jay hadn't fought her, even when her alimony demands far exceeded what she was due.

Though Mike suspected it was the lack of funds bringing his brother home to the fold, he stayed silent. Neither his mother nor his father tended to see Jay's faults, including his inability to manage his own money.

So the old homestead was gaining more occupants. Mike could manage. He'd just move into the east wing with Ned. Neither needed much space. Just a room and en suite bathroom for each. His parents and Jay could have the west wing. As for the rest of the house, Ned would be moving out soon, and both of them could just start eating out more to avoid family meals.

DARREN STORMED into the living quarters of her studio west of town. She held her anger in check long enough to place the painting along the wall before she dumped her purse and outer garments on the table. "Not what he expected, my eye!" She'd put in extra hours on this piece, trying to get the light just right. His patronage was important to her career. She'd daydreamed about dazzling him so much he'd recommend her to all his business associates.

So much for that fantasy.

Though he'd been curt the night of the showing, she'd later learned his attitude had resulted from a disagreement with Janice's famous son, Jake Bonneville, uh, Ned Collier. But today his behavior bordered on insolent and disrespectful. That didn't compute with what Janice had told her later, that though a driven businessman, he was also kind and reasonable.

"I don't need your support or your money, Mike Woodley." Someone else would buy this painting. She was an artist, not a technician. Forget about the changes she'd promised.

Decision made, she still felt as if she'd walked into a brick wall. She wasn't going to get any work done in this sour mood. Maybe a nice big piece of apple pie would sweeten it. Á la mode. Right. Only one place that made it like she liked. The Blue Iris.

"Darren. What a nice surprise." Her mother, Elise Williams, glanced up from replacing napkins in a holder on the counter as Darren entered the restaurant.

"I need pie, Mom. Got any left after the lunch crowd?"

"Apple, I presume? Let me check." Her mother returned shortly with a plate of the goodie. "Even found some cinnamon ice cream to top it off."

Darren settled on a round blue-vinyl counter seat and tore into her dessert. "You're a lifesaver. Want some before it's just a pleasant memory?"

Her mother leaned over the counter and shook her head. "Better not. I'm trying to lose a few pounds again." She straightened. "Now that you've taken care of your need for sugar, tell me what's bothering you."

Darren tilted her head. "That obvious?"

"You weren't exactly breathing fire, but you rarely go for sweets unless you're in a mood. Spill. Tell your old mom what's eating you."

"A client. Took me a couple of months to finish the painting he'd commissioned because I got so many orders following my showing at the Serenity Gallery a few months back. I even delivered it personally. He had the gall to say it wasn't what he wanted. Even asked, ordered, me to change it."

Her mother studied her. "Does that happen often? A client rejecting your work like that?"

"Not since school, before I'd developed my technique."

Despite her earlier statement, her mother ate the last two bites of pie, then removed the plate and fork and took them to the back room. "Want some coffee to wash it down?" she asked when she returned.

"No, thanks. I'm hyper enough already."

"Who was this client?" her mother asked, her eyes narrowed. "Someone I might know?"

"Michael Woodley."

"As in *the* Woodleys?" Her mother's voice rose.

"Uh, yes. At first, I thought he was Jake Bonneville's manager. That's how he was introduced at the showing. I didn't realize he was part of that family until later."

Her mother poured her own cup of coffee. At this time of day, midafternoon, there were no other customers. "So, he bought one of your finished pieces and then ordered another after that?"

"Yes. Why do you ask?"

"Maybe his purchases were just his way of seeing more of you."

Darren shook her head vigorously. "No, Mom. Don't start seeing orange blossoms and champagne glasses. He only bought them as a favor to Janice Collier, who not only owns the gallery but is Jake Bonneville's mother."

A tinkling sound came from the door, signaling the arrival of another customer. Darren's mother grabbed her pad, prepared to take an order, then stopped, smiled. "Darren? Does this Woodley guy have dirty-blond hair that looks like it hasn't been combed in a couple of days?"

"That's one way of describing it. Why?"

Her mother didn't reply but instead backed away and busied herself stacking clean coffee cups several feet away while the new customer took a seat at the counter.

"Hi," Mike Woodley said as he settled next to Darren and unzipped his windbreaker. "Looks like I'm too late to join you."

She attempted to cover her surprise as well as thank her lucky stars he hadn't arrived any sooner. "Hi, yourself. What brings you here?"

"Janice Collier told me if you weren't at your studio, you were most likely here. This a favorite or something?"

"That's my mother over there with the crockery, pretending not to listen. She's head waitress."

"Ah. Mystery solved. Hello, Mrs. Williams. Hope you're not closed. I could use a cup of java."

Her mother nodded and took care of his request immediately. After she placed the cup and spoon in front of him, Darren introduced him. "I hear you had some problems with the nice picture my daughter made for you. She's a good artist, young man. A great artist."

Darren groaned inwardly at her mother's temerity. But then when it came to defending her offspring, her mom could be a tigress.

Mike eyed her mother a moment and then turned to Darren. "That's what I came to tell her, ma'am. And apologize for my behavior when she presented it to me."

Her mother's demeanor immediately changed from protective

to solicitous. "In that case, why don't I get you the last piece of apple pie, on the house, while you tell her?" She was gone before Mike could protest.

"You don't have to eat the pie. My mom can be rather pushy at times."

"You think I'd turn down a piece of pie? I haven't indulged in a long time, but now that she mentioned it, it's all I can think about. Well, that and the apology I owe you."

Be cool, girl. Don't let him know how much he infuriated you. She faced him. "Okay. Let's hear it."

He stared at her a bit, as if he wasn't expecting such directness. "Uh, yeah. Well, here's the thing. Sometimes I can be too blunt. I say what's on my mind before thinking it through. Just before you showed up, I'd received bad news about a sale. Our sales have hit a few bumps in the road lately. I took out my frustration on you."

She didn't reply but instead waited for the rest.

Finally, he caught on. "So, I'm sorry."

"Thank you. Does that mean you're ready to accept the painting?"

He sat back. "Uh, no. I still have problems with it. But I could have turned it down with more civility."

Should she be pleased he'd tracked her down to apologize or continue being angry because he still didn't want the painting? She'd take the personal touch as a positive sign. He could've called or even emailed. Besides, she liked seeing him again. "Uh, okay."

"Great. I'm glad that's settled. You're really good at what you do. I just wasn't expecting those colors. But take your time. I want to hang it in the home I'm building at Sullivan's Creek, and it's far from finished."

"I didn't know there was a new home in the works. I thought you were happy at your parents' place."

"Have been, although that may change once my parents are there. My mother showed up as you were leaving and informed me she and my dad are returning to town. As for the new house, that was actually the one Ned was building for his mother, your friend Janice, but once she started seeing Shae Harriman's father, Tim, she preferred to stay closer to town, so I bought it from Ned."

Wow, the guy had a lot more going on in his life than just losing sales. Maybe she should cut him a break. She'd been introduced to Shae Harriman, the general contractor for the new housing development, at her showing. Shae's father owned the construction company.

"Would you, uh, like to see it? My new house. The exterior is pretty much finished except for the landscaping. The bones of the interior are done as well, but the rest awaits my decisions on colors and other stuff."

She hadn't expected such an invitation. She'd heard a lot about Sullivan's Creek from Janice, when her house was first under construction, but Darren didn't know Mike was the new owner. She'd been that busy with her work. Why not check it out? She doubted she'd get much painting done the rest of the day anyhow. "Okay."

As she rose and accompanied him to the door, she could feel her mother's eyes on her back. Without a doubt, she'd be receiving a call later that evening.

CHAPTER 2

The leaves, just recently luscious reds, oranges and yellows, had now fallen and laced the air with their crisp, burnt scent. Winter was soon to follow. Even though the day was overcast, Darren enjoyed the ride. Her own studio was also located on the outskirts of town, but farther south. This area was much more picturesque, the rolling prairie more pronounced.

Since Mike's house had originally been intended for Ned's mother, it occupied a prominent location, although it wasn't particularly impressive. But then, the original floor plan had been designed for Janice, who Darren knew to be conservative in her tastes despite her artistic leanings.

Since the front of the house was bare of landscaping and included no entry sidewalk yet, several boards had been laid from the street to the garage and front door, anticipating the arrival of appliances. Mike took her hand as they made their way to the door to keep her from sliding. Other than handshakes from customers, it was one of the first times she'd been touched by a man since her fiancé, Gordy, had been killed two years before. Mike's touch actually felt comfortable, maybe even a little exciting.

Before they entered, he held up a hand in warning. "Don't expect too much. It's a lot like a blank canvas."

"I can relate to blank canvases."

They emerged into a huge great room. In the back was what appeared to be a dining area. A stairwell led to the upper level.

"Not much to get excited about, huh?" he asked.

She left him to inspect the downstairs more closely. "A lot of space for just one person. But until you put your stamp on it, it's hard to say much more."

"Needs a good interior designer. The one I had didn't see eye to eye with me."

"Oh? *Had* as in you fired them?" Must have been another one of those days when he hit some bumps in the road. "What kind of look are your wanting? Contemporary? Traditional?"

"Can't really put my needs into those terms. Just know what I want and what I don't want."

No surprise, given his reaction to her painting. "Care to share?"

He strolled about the room. "I want to feel comfortable in my own home. Not cluttered with lots of heavy furniture. It should be welcoming to guests. I like wood, but not too much." He stopped.

"That's it?" He was right. He didn't know anything about decorating styles. If anything, he seemed to be grasping for feelings. "What about colors? You didn't like the reds and yellows in my painting. Does that apply to your house also?"

"Geez, I don't know, Darren. Guess my next decorator has their work cut out for them."

And she thought getting his painting right was problematic. His new decorator was in for the challenge of a lifetime.

At Mike's urging, Darren wandered from room to room, her footsteps echoing off the naked flooring. The room layout reflected Janice: a large kitchen, ample space for everyday and formal dining, a large main room for entertaining and a huge area that must have been intended for both a small office and gallery/studio. How would Mike take this skeleton and make it his own?

"What do you think?" he asked.

What kind of response did he want? "You were right about having a lot more to do before you can move in. On the other hand, what fun to put it together."

"Fun? My idea of *fun* is pulling off a financially beneficial business deal. Not picking out furniture."

"To each his own, I guess. The business side of my operation is a necessary evil to me."

"Want to see the upstairs? It's just a bunch of bedrooms, but since you're here …"

"Okay."

She followed him up the wide staircase on the interior of the great room. The master had to be twice the size of her own small bedroom. *And you said you'd kept everything within reason, Janice. Not here.* In the late fall afternoon, the room was rather dark until Mike flipped a light switch. Feeling somewhat ill at ease visiting what would eventually be his bedroom, she sought a neutral topic as she drifted over to three windows on one side of the room. "What direction do these face?"

He joined her and gazed out. "East, I guess."

"Nice. I like to wake up to the sun." Great. She'd meant to depersonalize their being in his room together and had instead set herself up. "Uh, I meant, my room at the studio gets morning light also, which makes it easier for me to wake up early and get to work." Could she sound more inane?

"Hadn't noticed that detail until you pointed it out. I need all the help I can muster getting out of bed in the morning."

"How do you stay on top of all your business ventures if you're not up before everyone else?"

He chuckled. "Two alarm clocks. But I'll deny admitting as much if you ever mention it to my competitors."

"It'll be our secret."

He reached over and placed a stray tendril of her hair behind her ear. "Deal."

Did he have any idea how this mere contact awoke the nerve endings behind her ear? Momentarily, she was glued in place, telling the rest of her body to ignore the shock waves rippling down her neck to her lower region.

Even in the room's dim shadows, she could tell when his eyes went smoky. "This room is giving me ideas I probably should ignore." He paused, stared directly in her eyes, giving her a chance to decide the next move.

He was coming on to her. No mistake. She'd never been propositioned by a guy she barely knew. Well, maybe at a rave when she was much younger, but that didn't count. Nothing from those days was real. Did he actually expect her to roll around naked on this wood subfloor? She couldn't help glancing down. "Uh …"

"Let's check out the other rooms." His voice had gone hoarse, urgent.

They headed toward the next bedroom.

"Mhrph."

"What was that?" Darren asked.

"Beats me. Sounded like it came from downstairs." He turned around and started for the stairs. "Stay behind me."

Halfway down, Mike jerked to a stop. Darren caught herself from bumping into him by a nanosecond. "What the …?"

A creature about two feet in length guarded the bottom of the stairs. A few feet behind it, four tiny balls of fur gazed up at them as if miffed by their presence.

"Raccoon?" she said in a whisper.

"Think so, but aren't they nocturnal?"

"Not if they've been disturbed." When her studio was being renovated, she'd experienced more than one irate raccoon that had been rudely awakened.

"How do we get rid of them?" he asked.

"Not sure. If you try to scare her off, she may go into defense mode to protect her brood."

"Do we wait them out, then?"

If it weren't getting so close to dusk, that might work, but the animal seemed comfortable in the house, as if she and her brood had been here for a while and didn't cotton to having company. Darren remembered the water she'd stuck in her purse earlier in the day. She eased her hand down over the clasp and carefully removed the bottle. "Our best bet is surprise," she said sotto voce. "I'm opening a bottle of water and will slip it to you. Step down and shout as many expletives you can think of while you pitch the contents at her. The second she backs away, let's run for the door."

Apparently Mike didn't have a better idea, so he followed her directions. As soon as he began shouting, the creature reared up and showed teeth, but when the water came her way, she twisted around and hustled away, her babies in her wake.

Meanwhile, Mike and Darren hustled for the front door. Once inside his car, they both released their breath and sank into their seats. "Whew. Didn't expect that. You okay?"

"Still … catching … my breath." Darren couldn't believe her idea worked. Some wildlife you're supposed to stare down, and others can be more readily scared off. But she couldn't keep them straight and prayed she'd been right about the raccoons.

"Quick thinking back there. Thanks."

"Glad you didn't quibble. I don't know what else we could've done."

He pulled out his cell and hit a number. "Shae? Mike. Looks like my house has been invaded by a mama raccoon and her brood. How do we deal with this?" He listened a bit, nodded. "Okay. Thanks."

He hung up. "Shae is on top of things. Apparently, we have an exterminator for such contingencies. Doesn't happen too much, but it appears something wasn't closed as tightly as it should've been and this enterprising mama wandered in. Seems to happen a lot this time of year as the temps dip. Shae's sending a crew member to seal up whatever was open."

"What about the raccoon family? Surely, the exterminator isn't going to ..."

"Nah. Shae assured me they get placed in cages and returned to the wild."

"Good to know."

At that, they both fell silent a few beats as the excitement of the last few minutes caught up with them. "Raccoons can be real mood killers," Mike said at length.

Probably for the best. She wasn't sure what she'd have done if things had heated up more between them. The mere idea she'd even considered having sex with this man she hardly knew suggested she may be ready to emerge from her two-year deep freeze. "Actually, mama raccoon added a bit of unexpected drama to the day."

"Drama I could do without. But I'm glad she didn't freak you out."

They returned to their own thoughts.

"Since our woodland friends cut our tour short, how 'bout I show you the rest of Sullivan's Creek? We're still finishing up Phase One homes, but the infrastructure is in for Phase Two, so we can drive through there as well."

"Sure," she replied a little too fast, some part of her apparently not wanting to end their time together.

The development featured wide sidewalks and just enough space between homes to make them neighbors but not on top of each other. The landscape was flat in spots and elsewhere melded into rolling prairie. A small stream, *the* Sullivan's Creek, wound through most of the property, and every few hundred feet was crossed by small bridges reminiscent of the one in the famous Monet painting of his home in Giverney.

They passed a home that appeared to be nearly done. A couple of vans were parked in the driveway. "That's Ned's house. Ironic.

He only promised to build one here to get his mom to sign on, and now she's staying in town and he's relocated to Iowa to be near Shae."

"They say love can make you do things you never dreamed possible." At one point, she'd been ready to put her art career on hold to be with Gordy. Another reason why, since his death, she'd totally thrown herself into her work.

"I guess. For some. Like Ned and Shae."

"I take it you don't include yourself in that category?" Interesting. She filed away the information.

"Uh, no. My siblings' dysfunctional marriages have convinced me of that. Three failures, although so far only one has resulted in divorce. Don't need that kind of trouble in my life."

He was warning her up front that marriage was not in his future, even though only minutes before he'd had no reservations about having sex. That made two of them. Getting past Gordy's death had taken too much effort and caused her too much pain. She wasn't ready to put herself out there again any time soon. Still, his feelings about commitment seemed awfully strong. What else was behind them? "What about your parents? They're still married."

"Staying married works to their mutual advantage, especially if they keep out of each other's way."

What more could she say? Her personal experience with happily married couples was cut short when her father died too soon, which threw her mother into a tailspin trying to put their financial security back together.

They headed for the main entrance once again, tour apparently completed. "This place is beautiful, Mike. Those who find themselves lucky enough to live here will really enjoy it."

"Would you like to stop on the way back to town for an early dinner?"

Again, she wasn't expecting the invitation, although she wondered if he was using their junket as a way to work off his negative feelings. "Sure, although I need to keep it light after that pie. I don't usually indulge in afternoon snacks, especially the sweet kind."

"Your experience with me forced you to eat pie?"

Had her dead to rights. "Our confrontation threw me off. I needed my mom's comfort."

"But we're okay now, right?" he asked, a wrinkle appearing on his forehead.

"Better. I still need to figure out how to proceed with your demands."

"Demands? That how you see it?"

"How else would you characterize the changes you want me to make before you'll consider taking possession of the painting?" After the tour of his house and the development and the accompanying activities, she probably should've used a less emotionally charged word, but this one just slipped out.

He gave it some thought. "Well, yeah, now that you put it that way, I guess that's what you could call them. But does this have to be an issue between us? I've already apologized for my mood earlier. They're just changes. Take all the time you want."

He had no idea what he was asking. A painting—at least originals like she did—wasn't like a word-processing document that could be revised with deletions and additions if the writer wasn't satisfied. She couldn't slap a totally different color palette over what she'd created. But it was obvious she wasn't going to convince him otherwise. She'd figure out how she was going to handle this later. Why ruin what had turned into a pretty interesting outing?

"Okay. Forget I said *demands*. Changes. That's what you want."

The next few minutes ticked by without either speaking. "There's Susie's," he said at last. He was quite the escort as he opened the car door and then the restaurant door for her and led her to a table, his right hand gently prodding her. She'd been on her own so long his attention startled her at first, but then, as memories of her times with Gordy flooded back, she just felt comfortable. And yet again stimulated at his touch. *He's just being a gentleman.*

The few seated patrons glanced up at their entrance and continued to stare. Couldn't be her. She rarely attracted a crowd. They must recognize Mike. Or it could simply be his presence. He did have a certain magnetism about him.

The place was cozy. Tables with one small white daisy in a vase flanked the center of the room and booths went around three sides. They chose a booth. "I've never been here, but my mom's spoken of it," Mike said once they'd ordered. "She checks out the competition whenever she has free time and reports back to the owners."

"It's just you, your sister and your mother?"

"Right. My sister, Colby, is in law school. Both Mom and I try to help out with her school expenses as we can."

"Sounds like you're pretty close."

Close? Her mother still blamed her father for dying too soon with little insurance, leaving them to fend for themselves. Over time, it had become much easier to lick her wounds than proceed to rebuild her life. Colby was so focused on studying, she didn't have time for either her mother or Darren, except when she needed something, usually money, which during this first year of law school was proving to be quite frequent. "We're all each other has."

"Interesting." He didn't say more because their meal arrived. He dived into his tenderloin and chocolate milkshake.

Darren took a few bites of her tuna fish salad sandwich and homemade applesauce. "Why do you call my relationship with my mother and sister *interesting*?"

He put down a french fry and considered. "I have two brothers, a sister, a brother-in-law, a niece and nephew, and both parents still living. I'd never characterize our relationship as all each other has. At least as I relate to them."

"You're not close?"

"No, we're not. Until today, my parents have lived in an upscale town in Michigan along Lake Huron. My brother lived there as well so he could be near our father in the family's business. My other brother lives in California with his wife and handles one segment of the corporation from there. My sister and her husband and kids live in Florida. I rarely see them." A few years back, he'd tried getting together, taking them out to dinner, offering them tickets to various team sports. Though Harper, his sister, seemed to enjoy these times, Dash, her husband, seemed bored after he realized Mike wasn't going to be much help advancing his place in the family business.

"It would be difficult for any family to stay close with everyone spread all over the country."

"Even when we're all together, we aren't close. My dad has always been busy building the business. My mother has taken her role as his hostess seriously, and my siblings spend their time staying in Dad's good graces. Me, not so much. I wanted to go out on my own. The rest of them couldn't understand. To top things off, I had the gall to pay off Ned's band contract in Europe when his dad was dying here in the States."

"They resented your helping him?"

"I used a large portion of my trust fund. Mine to do with as I saw fit, but my dad felt I'd let my feelings for my friend interfere with good business sense. The rest of the family sided with him."

"I don't know much about corporations and trust funds. When my mother, Colby or I need money, the other two pitch in and contribute what they can. Usually, it's sweat equity, like when Colby and Mom helped me clear out the old barn I purchased to set up my studio and living quarters."

"Sorry. Didn't mean to put a damper on our meal."

"Oh, no. You didn't. Your story is so different from mine, I find it fascinating."

"Perhaps another time. As much as the idea of my father and

older brother arriving today pains me, I should be there when they arrive."

"Of course." She finished her last spoonful of applesauce and wiped her mouth with a napkin. "I'd like to hear the rest. When you're ready."

"Then you shall."

Back at the Blue Iris, he accompanied her to her car. "Don't you want to fill your mom in about our trip?"

"Dinner shift is underway. I don't want to disturb her. Besides, she'll call as soon as she's on break."

"You know her pretty well."

She merely returned a smile.

He opened the driver's door. "Well. I, uh, guess I'll see you, uh, when you return the painting." They stood within a foot of each other, prolonging the moment. Before she knew what was happening, he bent and kissed her. One hand cupped the back of her neck. The kiss was firm, but he didn't linger.

"Uh, yes. Thanks for the tour."

"Where have you been?" Mike's mother asked as soon as he returned to the mansion. "We were going to wait dinner for you, but Tammy said you'd call if you wanted her to fix you something."

Tammy, their combination housekeeper and cook, was a jewel. She'd readily adapted to the irregular schedules of two bachelors living under her roof. Apparently, those days were over. He wondered if Ned had caught hell as well. "Glad you didn't. I ate something while I was out."

"Did you apologize to that young woman?"

"Yes, I did. You can check that one off your list."

As he anticipated, her response came out in a huff. "I do not have any such list." He visualized invisible hands stuck on her hips.

"Ah, Mom, that was just me unwilling to admit you'd been right and I'd been out of line to hassle her as I did."

"Is she married?"

"Not that I know."

"How about you? Are you seeing anyone?"

And here we go again. Wasn't enough to have three out of four of her kids married, even though one was already divorced and the other two seemed to be regretting their choice of partners. His mother wanted one hundred percent compliance with her version of a happy life.

"No. I'm not. I like my independence, and I'm super busy with Sullivan's Creek these days." Just because for two seconds his libido had come to life around Darren out at the house and he'd later kissed her good-bye did not in any way mean he was *seeing* her. He was attracted to the woman and wouldn't mind taking her to bed if she showed the least interest, but even if that occurred, it didn't mean they were headed for the altar. Settling down wasn't in the cards.

Unbelievably, mercifully, his mother let the subject of his marital status, or lack thereof, drop. Instead, she turned to the other topic. "Sullivan's Creek? That's the property your friend, Ned, is selling off, right?"

"One way of putting it, I suppose. Ned and I have gone into partnership to develop farmland he inherited from his grandparents into luxury homes."

"Once again, you helped him out of some poor business decision and spent your own money to do it."

"If you knew all that, why'd you make it sound like Sullivan's Creek was a big surprise?"

She put a hand on his shoulder. "You're a grown man, Michael. You've done quite well for yourself with your various business ventures. Maybe helping your friend was a good decision as well. I just don't understand the emotional hold he has over you when you'll hardly have anything to do with your own family."

"This is a great investment, Mom. Maybe you and Dad or Jay will want a place there?" He was playing her, but he was curious to know what reason she'd use to reject the idea.

But his question failed to trip her up. "As much as we'd like to support you, dear, I don't think your father would take to country living."

"You mean like living around a lake in Michigan?" Better stop. With his older brother and father slated to arrive soon, he needed her on his side.

She started to reply and then must have realized he was kidding. "Oh. I get it. Never mind."

"Never mind what?" Jay stood in the entryway, loaded down with various pieces of luggage. The expensive kind.

Mike took a breath, made himself think good thoughts. "Jay. Good to see you." He held out a hand to his brother, who after a few beats let his baggage tumble to the floor and accepted the handshake. "Heard you were spending more time at the old homestead rather than the coast. Looks like we'll be living together again for a bit. 'Til I find a place of my own, at least."

Mike opened his mouth to mention Sullivan's Creek but caught his mother shaking her head and closed it again. She was probably right. He didn't need his older brother as a neighbor.

Jay turned to his mother, hugged her briefly. "I stuck what furnishings I still had in the van Dad is sending. Figured we could find room for them somewhere in this mausoleum."

"Or we could put them in storage," their mother replied.

Jay considered. "That'd work also. Haven't really needed them, because the place I was renting in Michigan was furnished. Mainly kept them to stick it to Alicia."

"I took the liberty of having Tammy move you out while you were gone, dear," Mike's mother told him. "I assumed with the three of us moving in, you'd prefer to be in the east wing with your friend."

"You mean Ned Collier, aka Jake Bonneville?" Jay asked. "What's the big entertainer doing here when he can afford his own mansion these days?"

"I invited him. The place has more room for office space than at his mother's, and I appreciated the company. He's building his own home outside town and should be moving there in a week or two."

Their mother turned to Jay. "You must be famished. There's chicken and salad for you in the refrigerator. You just need to warm the chicken."

Jay hugged her again. "You're a doll, Mom. How 'bout showing me how to do that warming thing before you go in search of the maid?"

Their mother closed her eyes briefly. "It wouldn't hurt for you to learn your way around a kitchen. What did you do these past months in that furnished apartment?"

Jay held up his index finger. "Used this to call a few restaurants that kept me in food." He actually appeared somewhat proud of his prowess at ordering out.

Once both his mother and brother left, Mike decided to clear out himself and escaped to his new quarters while he tracked down Ned to warn him of the change in accommodations. He didn't want to be present when his father arrived. He'd put that one off until tomorrow.

It had been quite a day. He now had roommates. Not just roommates. Landlords. Life as he'd come to know and enjoy it was about to end. Already had with the arrival of his mother and brother and his mother's overly developed interest in his love life.

Love life. How ironic, since the day had also brought Darren Williams back into his life. Even contemplated sex with her. Not that he hadn't enjoyed dalliances with women he'd just met in the past, but those had usually been "two ships passing in the night" kinds of situations, not with someone he would be seeing again as her client. But something about Darren had awakened his libido. Immediate attraction, immediate desire. If his parents and brother were going to be underfoot, maybe Darren would be a welcome distraction.

CHAPTER 3

Darren entered the residence part of her studio in a much more positive mood than her last time here. Nonetheless, she was physically exhausted and headed immediately for her comfy couch, kicking off her shoes along the way.

"Hi, sis." A voice came from the small dining table across the room.

Darren pulled up, gripped her chest. "Colby? You scared me. What brings you all the way out here?"

"I, uh, needed to see you. You said I could drop by whenever and gave me a key ..."

"Of course. I just wasn't expecting you. What's up?"

Her younger sister rose slowly from the kitchen chair and took a seat next to her. Colby Williams, an inch or two shorter than Darren with lighter brown hair, took a deep breath and then met Darren's eyes with a breezy, confident smile. "Law school is a lot more expensive than I anticipated. And a lot more difficult. I've been working at the library but can only do a few hours a week and still stay up with my assignments."

"You couldn't be flunking out already. Or have you changed your mind about becoming a lawyer?"

"Oh, no. I'm still committed to law school. I just need more, uh, help with ongoing expenses than I estimated."

Her sister was a brilliant student and would make a very good attorney, yet apparently, she wasn't so hot at math and budgets. "Can't the financial aid office help?"

"Possibly. But increasing the amount of the small loan they've given me requires more paperwork. My rent can't wait until that's processed."

Darren had been prepared for Colby to hit her up for help, sooner or later. But this soon? A tiny warning bell sounded in the back of her mind. Probably had herself to blame. She'd rarely said no to her baby sister's needs, especially since their mother could hardly help. But now that Colby was an adult, it was time to start weaning her dependence. Nonetheless, it was important Colby retain that efficiency apartment. Sure, there was plenty of housing near the school, but most places required a roommate to make rent. Colby studied best on her own. "How much do you need?"

"Two hundred." The amount emerged quickly, as if no big deal.

Two hundred dollars? Not improbable for rent, but not something Darren could just pull from her purse, although her bank account had grown nicely since her showing at the Serenity Gallery. "I'll have to give you a check. Will that work?"

Colby rose. "Perfect. Can I get it now? I'll stop by the bank first thing in the morning." As soon as Darren wrote out the check, Colby hugged her, then made some excuse about having to finish a paper yet that night and disappeared.

What did she expect? For her sister to stick around and make small talk. Or for once to ask Darren how her day was going. No, neither reaction was in her sister's makeup. Colby was Colby. If Colby was to become less dependent, the initiative had to come from Darren.

Alone, Darren debated whether to paint with what little time was still left of the evening. Mike Woodley's refusal of her work followed by their unexpected trip and dinner had made for a full day. Now this. Nope, she didn't trust herself with a paintbrush right now, but she could still eye her work, discern where she wanted to go with a couple of items in progress. Maybe even consider how to handle Mike Woodley. Both the commissioned painting and the man himself.

Mike awoke the next morning with a sense of dread. His father supposedly arrived late the night before. Though Mike hadn't seen Ned, probably spending the night with Shae somewhere, Mike had texted him to warn of their new housemates, and Ned had confirmed receipt. Lucky guy. He had other places he could go during the day as well as night. Since Mike had made the Woodley home his main headquarters until he found an alternate solution, he was stuck here.

With that cheery thought in mind, he quickly showered, dressed and sought out breakfast, providing he could still eat. His father had beat him and was already sipping coffee and reading his newspaper.

"Those can be read online these days, you know." Stupid opening. Was he deliberately baiting the man?

His father glanced up, not the least bit surprised to see him. "So I've been told. But I still prefer the feel of newsprint in my hands each morning. Easier to find the continuations of page-one stories."

Mike reached out to take his father's hand. "Good to see you again, Dad."

His father shook his hand. "Same here. You just missed your friend Ned. Seemed in a rush to get going this morning. You know anything about that?"

"Several projects coming to fruition. Guess he was off to check on details." He kept his response general. Ned's projects could be his new album, a movie score or Sullivan's Creek. The guy was a modern-day Renaissance man.

"Sort of a turnaround from last summer when you flew back to California with me. You didn't want to talk about what had happened between you and Ned, which sent you back to the coast so fast, but I presumed it had something to do with his development project. Next thing I hear, you're back in Iowa partnering up with him."

Tread carefully. He's leading up to something. "Ned wasn't taking my advice. Figured I could make more of a statement by leaving."

"Must have worked, since you returned."

Hell, why not cut to the chase? "C'mon, Dad. With all your sources in town, you already know what happened. He got a loan from an unscrupulous shark, contingent on using the guy's heavy-equipment company for construction. The first crane that showed up was defective and could've caused a bad accident had the construction superintendent not caught it. When the authorities went after the creep, he demanded immediate repayment from Ned. That's when I stepped in."

"And once again dug Ned out of a mess of his own making."

There it was. No matter how financially smart it had been to become part owner of the residential development despite the present sluggish sales, his dad still saw Mike's action as rescuing his pal. Again. The issue had to be faced sooner or later. Why not today? "That really what's bugging you about this deal, Dad?"

His father put down the newspaper and stared at him, as if he couldn't believe the question. "I like Ned, and I like his singing. Back when you were struggling to be part of your high school basketball team, he's the one who showed you the ropes. But the man is a disaster when it comes to business."

"Ned was barely out of college when he signed that onerous contract in Europe. He wanted stability for his band but didn't realize it came with a price. Ned repaid my loan to get out of that arrangement as soon as his career took off. As for Sullivan's Creek, I've wanted to be part of that project for some time, but he kept putting me off. He didn't want to risk my relationship with you and the rest of the family, because he felt he'd been the cause of our earlier estrangement."

"Aren't you afraid that might happen again?"

Mike poured himself a cup of coffee and sank onto a chair across from his father while he pondered how to respond. "Maybe you're the one who's afraid. That's the real reason you apparently disapprove of this partnership, isn't it? You still want me in Woodley Industries, and this commitment causes a roadblock."

His father sat stock still. At one point, his hand shot out to his paper, but he retracted it, as if he realized his usual escape mechanism wouldn't come to his aid this time. "Of course, I want you in the family business. I've never hidden that desire from you or any of the family. I've bided my time as you've claimed your independence. Unlike your brothers, you needed to explore on your own."

Explore? That's how his dad perceived his career? Okay, maybe in some respects he had been exploring the numerous possibilities of where to invest his talents. He had a lot of interests. Every time he seemed to conquer one, another reared its head. "I like being my own boss. Or in the case of Sullivan's Creek, partner."

"Even if this Sullivan's Creek project was a good investment, surely you don't plan to spend the rest of your days here, doing what, selling lots?"

He attempted a reply, but his father's question, whether the old man knew it or not, cut right to the heart of Mike's current dilemma. Why had he involved himself personally in the sales phase when others with more realty and marketing experience could probably do a better job?

"Can't answer, can you?" For the first time since Mike had

joined him, his father sat back in his chair, crossed his arms. Just a hint of a smile, a broad one where his father was concerned, showed around his mouth. "Come join me in running the company. You can still play land baron. Just have others do the grunt work for you."

He'd almost been taken in by his father's words, until the old man said "grunt work." Was that what he'd been doing the last few months? He'd really enjoyed the first part, taking over for Ned to work with Shae, the acting general contractor, while her dad, Janice's new beau Tim, recuperated from heart problems. Along with Shae, he'd overseen construction of the homes in Phase One. But when they'd moved into the next phase, subscribing individual lots in Phase Two, the task had no longer been any fun.

"I appreciate the offer, Dad. And your confidence in me. But not now. You've already got Jay and Gardner plus Harper's husband, Dash, working for you. I'd just get in their way."

"Not necessarily." His dad glanced away, grabbed a slice of toast. "Don't rule out the possibility. Who knows? Now that your mom and I and your brother are back in town, maybe your perspective will change."

What in hell did that mean? Should he pursue it?

Before he had a chance to ask his dad to explain, Jay wandered into the room. "What's to eat? I'm famished."

Joseph Woodley gazed with hooded lids at his eldest child. "Surprised you made it this soon. Thought you might spend a day somewhere along the way catching your breath."

What an odd statement to make to the family's Golden Boy. "Coffee's in the carafe. Toast and eggs are on the warming plate. Juice is in the fridge," Mike said.

Jay turned toward his younger brother, something between a smile and a snarl on his face. "Haven't you become the little homemaker? Do you serve also?"

So that's how it was going to be with Jay. Resentment. Why? Mike was usually the one on the outs with their dad, and hence their mother, while Jay could do no wrong. "Nope. I checked in my apron a few minutes ago. Need to get to work, so you're on your own."

"Where's that cook?" Jay asked. "She sure makes herself scarce."

Tammy was one wise woman.

Mike retreated to his office in the den. He might have to face his dad across the breakfast table, dodge his mother's questions about his love life, and just plain avoid Jay, but here he was safe.

He called Ned. "How'd you escape the house so easily? I had to deal with my dad's first snipe of the day."

"Told him I had a meeting with a homeowner at eight and needed to run. I'm surprised you didn't come up with something similar. You can usually think on your feet a lot faster than I."

"Too focused on dodging whatever he threw at me. Was that just a story? Where are you?"

"At my house. Gets me out of town and away from the entourage at your place as well as lets me be Johnny-on-the-spot to wrap up the last details on Phase One houses. You really should've taken finishing your house more seriously. You could be doing the same."

"Too bad I wasn't psychic. Who knew they'd come back. Even Jay."

"The heating, ventilation and air-conditioning have been in for some time, so you could work there if you had someplace for your laptop."

"True, but the rest of the place is an empty shell."

"Wouldn't be if you'd stop firing decorators."

"Funny."

"Bet my mom knows a few. Want me to check?"

"Be my guest."

"In the meantime, I'm juicing up the finishing touches on my place. I'll be out of the mansion in a few days."

"Coward!"

"Make that homeowner."

Mike hung up and pulled out the folder containing his sales projections. Why, he wasn't sure, because he had it memorized. He set it aside and pulled up the financials on his laptop. Upon signing the partnership papers, he'd not only paid off Ned's debt to the loan shark, repayment he probably wouldn't realize for some time, but he'd also pumped additional funds into what had been a fast-disappearing operational fund. Now that it was reasonably healthy, he was loathe to tap it more than necessary. But if the salary plus commission of a top-notch realtor could sell those lots, it might be worth it.

He was about to go online when he heard a commotion outside the door.

"Put all that equipment in here." The door burst open, and Jay slammed in, followed by two guys in tan coveralls carrying what appeared to be every kind of weight machine in one. Jay scratched his chin. "Over there by the window, I think. Just stay clear of my brother on the other side of the room at the desk."

"What's all this?"

"Isn't it obvious? Brought what I could of my home gym with me."

Mike sucked in his lips. "This is a den. There's more room downstairs in the music room."

"Thought your buddy, the big entertainer, would be using it."

"Told you. Ned's moving out in a few days. Besides, his keyboard barely takes up five feet. In case it missed your notice, I'm using the den as my office. My *work* office."

The guys in coveralls had already set down their load and were on their way out. "Hey, wait," Mike said. "That monstrosity can't stay here."

The movers shifted their gaze to Jay. "Of course, it can. There'll be plenty of room for both of us in here."

It was a power play. Jay probably didn't even use this stuff. But Mike wasn't going to give his brother the satisfaction of either getting his goat or forcing him out. Though Ned's suggestion he set up quarters in his new home was appearing more appealing, he wouldn't give Jay the satisfaction of seeing him surrender his ground.

Jay and his lackeys departed, leaving the piece of equipment behind.

Ignoring the monstrosity as best he could, Mike returned to his sales review. How much would a superhot realtor cost? He didn't want to show his hand locally, so he put in a call to a guy he knew in real estate in L.A. The two markets had very little in common, but his friend could supply some insights he himself lacked.

"I'll give that real estate recruiter a call," Mike told him as Jay and his buddies returned with another piece of equipment, what looked like a stationary bike.

"There's more?" Mike couldn't restrain his voice from rising.

Jay stared at him as if he should know better. "I need more than that piece over there to keep in shape."

"This it?"

"There are two smaller machines. There's still plenty of room in here."

The place was starting to look like someone's garage sale. But before he erupted, Mike had an inspiration. Stay cool and let one of their parents fly off the handle. That'd get rid of it. Meanwhile, he could look like the cool one who tolerated Jay's narcissistic flaws.

Once all four pieces were in place, Jay reappeared one more time. He hung back near the door, hands in pants pockets. He wanted cash. Mike was sure of it. Mom and Dad had probably shut off their pipeline, and now Jay was forced to make nice with Mike.

"Uh …" Jay said.

"Yes?" Maybe floating him a loan, a small one, might improve relations between them. Yeah, sure. Who was he kidding?

"Did I hear you say something about a real estate recruiter?"

"You mean *overhear*? See, that's exactly why the two of us being in here at the same time isn't going to work. That was confidential information."

"We're family. I was going to say I might know someone, but never mind."

"You? You know someone in real estate?"

"Not exactly in real estate. Someone who'd do a great job selling all those lots in Sullivan's Creek."

How did he know about those? Dad. Jay had remained behind for breakfast with their father. Should've known. Their wavelengths were in synch. "At the risk of regretting it later, who?"

Jay removed his hands from his pockets, ambled across the room to Mike's desk, and leaned in, hands on the front. "Me."

"You?"

"Yes, me. I was assigned to the financial division of the company when I was in the rotational training program. Wasn't crazy about budgets and profit-and-loss statements, but when it came to marketing and real estate, I found my niche."

Interesting. Mike had never paid much attention to his siblings' roles in the company, because as long as their father was in charge, none of them would get a chance to flex their muscles. "If you liked it so much, why didn't you stay there?"

"Not in Dad's plans. He already had a couple of top-notch guys buying, selling and assessing. He wanted me ready to take over for him whenever that time came."

"How's the old boy doing? Any sign that time may be coming?"

"He's back in town, isn't he? Read what you want into that." Jay pivoted and headed for the door.

What in the hell was all that about? Jay wanted to be part of

Sullivan's Creek? In addition to preparing to step into their father's shoes someday? Didn't make any more sense than Jay's cryptic parting words about the reason behind their parents' relocation.

Something was definitely afoot. Did he really want to know what?

CHAPTER 4

Two days later, Darren stared at the piece she'd done for Mike Woodley. He said it wasn't calming. How could she redo this picture without totally destroying its spirit? The power of the ocean. The reds and golds and purples just didn't say "tranquility." She'd have to slather all kinds of blue over the red and get rid of the yellow, at least minimize it.

She couldn't do this to her own work, not when she was satisfied with the current product. Could she afford to paint a brand-new piece? If she pulled back on her usual time-intense process, she could maybe have something done in a week. She hated to put her other work aside just to appease the picky billionaire. But she couldn't afford not to. She wanted his future business. Maybe he'd talk her up with other members of his family.

Around ten, she decided her contemplation was getting her nowhere. She needed advice. Without further debate, she found herself visiting Janice Collier at her gallery.

"I'm glad you stopped by." Janice pushed a large frame to the side of her office to make more room around her desk. "I've had a nibble on that barn and pond piece of yours. Knowing this customer, it will take at least one more visit before he decides to buy, but I feel good about this one."

"Nice to know someone likes my work."

Her friend arched a brow. "Bad review? I advised you to pay those no heed. They're great for getting your name out, sometimes even the bad ones, but not as an ego boost."

"No. The reviews have been good. This is an unsatisfied customer." Without naming names, she described her experience when she delivered Mike's painting. "I don't accept many commissions. I prefer to do my own work and let others like them or not. I don't know how to react to this situation."

Janice tapped her chin with her forefinger, then made her way to her office chair. "Commissioned work can be tricky. You don't want to lose the customer if you ask for payment up front, but if you don't, you wind up in the pickle you've just described."

"Next time, I'll spell things out better. But that still leaves this particular customer and what I should do."

"The easy way out would be to do a completely different piece, but I sense your artistic integrity won't let you."

"That's exactly—"

"Mrs. Collier? Janice? You around?" a now- familiar voice called from the outer room.

Couldn't be. Last person she needed to see. She was still reacting to his kiss the other night, debating how it meshed with his refusal of her painting. Darren braced herself as best she could for their unexpected visitor.

Mike Woodley stuck his head in the door, then backed up a step. "Oh. Sorry. Didn't realize … Darren, Ms. Williams." His smile seemed to rest on her a tad too long. "Good to see you again."

"Mr. Woodley. Mike," Darren said. Good thing she hadn't told Janice the full story about her encounter with the billionaire. She resisted the urge to touch her face to check whether the heat she felt inside had made it to the surface.

Janice rose, her expression one of polite curiosity. "Mike! What a pleasant surprise. I hardly see you anymore now that Ned and Shae spend so much time together."

Mike crossed the room and gave her a hug. "Hope you don't mind my interrupting. Ned said you had some names of decorators for me. Thought I'd pick them up in person. Need to find someone soon."

While Janice searched the top of her desk and Mike waited, Darren covertly eyed the man. Mike Williams certainly did justice to a pair of tight-fitting black jeans, although at the moment she had a side view. From her seated position, she realized he was taller than she remembered.

Janice searched the top of her desk and from under a pile of brochures, pulled out a piece of notepaper. "Here you go. Two are immediately available. The third might be, if you're willing to pay more."

He stuck the note inside his tan windbreaker. "Thanks. Hope one of these works." He turned to Darren. "Since I last saw you, I've, uh, stepped up the time line on moving into my new home. I told you to take your time with my seascape, but if you could give it your immediate attention, I'd appreciate it. I'd like to include it in the design plan."

The man was an enigma. First, he didn't like her color scheme, and then he moved up her deadline to resubmit. The same man she'd considered going to bed with after their brief acquaintance. She kept her response noncommittal. "I'll see what I can do."

"Great. Stay in touch. I plan to line up one of these designers today so we can get the interior done soon." With that, he was gone, but not before she allowed herself one last glimpse of his tush.

Darren turned back to Janice, who'd folded her hands and sat watching her. "What?"

"Mike Woodley is your commission." It was a statement, not a question.

Darren nodded.

"I understand your dilemma now."

"Really? Then clue me in, because I can't seem to corral my thoughts."

"Anyone else you'd tell where to get off and refuse to make any changes. But for some reason, you don't want to offend Mike. He's wealthy, so I can see why you'd want to keep him as a future customer, especially now that he's decided to finish my house. Sorry, his house. Or you don't want him to badmouth you to other customers, not that he'd ever do such a thing. Then there's the fact he is quite handsome. Perhaps you noticed?" She smiled across at Darren.

Darren held her friend's gaze. *Give it up. She's on to you.* Probably why she'd made this visit in the first place, if she was honest with herself. "Of course, I did. He made quite an impression that night of my showing. But I don't tend to run in those circles, so I'll have to appreciate from afar."

"His *appreciation* of you seemed a lot closer. Or was I imagining things?"

Darren sloughed off her friend's comment with a chuckle. "When was your last visit to the optometrist? He was just being gracious, as well he should, considering the turpentine he's thrown on my canvass."

Should she share their visit to his new home? Why not? Although she'd skip the part about the scene the raccoons interrupted as well the kiss at her car. "If you must know, he tracked me down to apologize, after sending me home painting in hand, and as a sort of peace offering, invited me to see his new home." She gave Janice her best Mona Lisa smile. "You put together quite a nice floor plan, from what I could tell from the bare bones."

Janice leaned farther into her desk. "You've visited Sullivan's Creek?"

Darren's smile widened. "You gave up quite a nice place."

"Ned spared no expense to get the design the way I wanted it. But for now, I'm happy remaining in town at the old homestead."

"Which is a lot closer to Tim Harriman's house."

Now it was Janice who returned a smile reminiscent of *La Giaconda*. "For someone sharp enough to note the change in my social life, you seem just a tad underenthused about your junket into the country with the town's most eligible bachelor."

Darren shrugged. "What can I say? Other than this one outstanding negative, redoing the picture, I like him, at least what I know of him so far."

"So? What are you going to do about him?"

"Nothing. I've been in love exactly once in my life and lost him to a war too many miles from my understanding. A war he didn't need to be part of. My emotional system can't afford to go through falling in love and losing the man again."

"Mike's not in a combat zone. Nor am I aware of his involvement in other life-threatening activities."

"Maybe not, but I'm not in the market for an affair at the moment, and should your detection of his interest be right, that's all he'd want. He plays in a totally different league than me."

"And you want something more permanent?"

Darren sat back, rose. Paced around the room. "Not necessarily. It might be nice to have some fun for a change. Fun that doesn't involve a paintbrush. But like I said, we run on two different tracks."

Janice picked up a pen and doodled on a nearby pad. "Why do I suspect you're here to get my approval to go after that fun?" She held up a hand to ward off Darren's denial. "So do it. As far as how that decision plays into redoing the painting, I'd say take your pick. Any one of your options will elicit a response from him. And that's what you really want."

"What? No, you're wrong. I came here seeking your professional advice, not advice to the lovelorn."

Janice raised both brows. "Oh. My mistake. Professional

advice, huh? Well, then, forget about redoing the current piece. Keep it and sell it to someone later. Do a brand new seascape for him and bend over backward—no pun intended—to give him what he wants. Don't refuse. Even good guys like Mike sometimes have short fuses, so don't discount the possibility." She, too, rose. "Now, my dear, I must find a place to hang that piece I dragged out of our way when you arrived. I've given you what you wanted."

Darren chewed on Janice's advice on her way back to the studio. Janice was a smart businesswoman, so her words couldn't be taken lightly. Darren herself had been leaning the direction of doing a new piece, and in all honesty had probably visited her friend to see if Janice would agree. But was it worth her time and effort to appease this guy?

Colors and the vision of a new canvas streamed through her brain as she drove up to her barn conversion. What the …? Colby awaited her on the front porch. What appeared to be a somewhat-agitated Colby. "Two visits in one week? What's up?"

"Let's go inside," her sister said.

Darren unlocked the front door and held it open for Colby. "You look like you've flunked out or something. Oh my God! You haven't, have you? I thought you said your grades were coming along fine."

Colby wrung her hands, noticed what she was doing, and brought them down to her lap. "My grades are still in good shape. For now."

Ominous. Obviously meant as a hint. "Okay, I'll bite. Something is afoot that could hurt your grades?"

"I need money."

"Again?" Darren's voice rose involuntarily.

Colby had the grace to look away. "Yes." Unlike Darren, her volume decreased.

"But why? Did you miscalculate the other day?"

Her sister pursed her lips, didn't reply at once. "This is a new debt," she said at last.

Darren opened her mouth, but nothing came out. How could this have happened in the space of a couple of days?

"Like I told you, my school expenses mounted faster than I anticipated. A few weeks ago, some of my classmates convinced me I could earn a few bucks in a friendly game of poker. I came out a few hundred up the first night. Instead of stopping, I went back for more, and it's been downhill ever since."

"You need money to pay off a gambling debt?" Now she did let her voice rise.

Colby nodded but didn't gaze at her directly.

"How could you, Colby? Doesn't our family have enough money woes?"

Now Colby did stare at her, eyes narrowed, chin protruding. "Don't you think I know that? I'm supposed to be the money earner, once I'm practicing law. God knows, Mom's had to struggle enough to keep food on the table all these years since Dad died. And you've just started to make a living as an artist. But I need you now, or I'll be in big trouble."

Goose bumps streamed up Darren's arm. "What kind of trouble? With the school? The law? My God, Colby, you can't let yourself get picked up in an illegal gambling operation, or your career will be over before it begins."

"That's the only reason I'm back here. It's not easy coming to you for a handout."

"It shouldn't be. Gambling is serious business." She processed this latest revelation. "That's what the two hundred dollars was for the other day, wasn't it? If you paid off that debt, how were you able to get into another game so soon?"

Colby stared off into space, as if waiting for Darren to catch up. But Darren didn't respond. "I, uh, only needed a hundred and fifty. I used the remaining fifty to buy a stake in another game."

Darren gasped. "Colby! How can you expect me to give you

more money if you're just going to turn around and use it for another game?"

Colby grabbed her arms. "You've gotta help, sis. These people are serious. They don't take lightly to those who welsh on their debts. I'll use the money to pay them off. I'll stay away from the game from now on."

Darren didn't have much choice, but before she agreed to help, she had to make sure this gambling bug ended here. "How much this time?"

"Five hundred." Colby's voice was barely a whisper.

Darren gulped. "It will take a couple of days for me to get that much money together again. Can you hold them off that long?"

"I guess."

"I'll write a check but not to you. Get me a name."

"Uh, that's not the way it works. Everything has to be done in cash, because they don't want a trail."

Darren closed her eyes briefly, praying for wisdom. She wasn't a parent, nor did she know anything about gambling. But every instinct told her five hundred dollars, as difficult as that would be for her to come by, was not going to resolve her sister's issues. She needed a second team, but there wasn't time to put one together, let alone afford one. "Okay. I'll get you the money as long as you promise to end any and all ties with gambling. I'll have to take you at your word. Can I do that?"

Colby's arms went around her in a relieved bear hug. "Thank you, thank you. Yes, I promise. I'm cutting myself off from my gambling buddies as soon as I pay them off."

The occasion didn't seem to call for further socializing, so Colby cut out immediately, leaving Darren wondering how she could come up with that amount of money. She tried to swallow the bile that had forced its way into her throat and wouldn't go away. Over the years, she'd given her sister anything within reason she'd asked for, since their mother could barely support herself. Even then, she'd known she was walking a dangerous path, setting a bad precedent. She'd vowed to stop catering to the girl. Yet here she was again, caving to Colby's demands.

Times like this she wished she could go to her mother for advice and comfort. Her mom was there for her when she needed to share her successes, but Elise Williams didn't do problem-solving well. After Darren's dad died, it had been all her mother could do to keep herself going.

Darren had already used up her chips with Janice. At least for one day. As often was the case, she'd face this one on her own.

She no longer had to debate what to do about the Woodley commission. Time to get busy creating a piece the man would accept. Now she really needed the money.

THE NEXT DAY, Mike entered the breakfast nook after his morning run to grab his usual English muffin, fried egg white and cheese morning meal only to discover it wasn't in the warming pan. What was this? Tammy never missed a beat with his meals. He did a quick check of the buffet. Nothing. In fact, there was no bacon, scrambled eggs or fruit, either. The only thing he did see was about an inch of orange juice in the pitcher.

"What the ...?"

"Looking for something?" Jay asked from the chair Mike usually occupied.

Mike had been so busy seeking his food he hadn't noticed his brother. He took in the remains of his sandwich on a plate in front of Jay. "That egg-and-cheese sandwich was intended for me."

Jay wiped his face with a napkin. "Sorry. There was no label on it claiming it was yours, and it appealed to me this morning. Pretty good, too, as well as nutritious."

"Oh, c'mon, I've been having that combo for breakfast for years. You knew you were taking my food."

"Michael, old man, there's more food in this house than a

grocery warehouse. Surely, you can find something else? Or have that maid make you another."

"She's our housekeeper, and if I'm not mistaken, she usually does the marketing this time of day. Never mind. I'm on my way out as soon as I shower and dress. I'll catch something on the way."

Jay waved a hand dismissively. "Then there you are. No harm done."

Mike wasn't ready to concede. "Now that you know, that particular breakfast offering is mine every day. If you want the same thing, talk to Tammy."

"Got ya, brother. I'll keep that in mind, though I fail to see why something as mundane as a sandwich has got you so fired up."

In the shower, lathered up and cooling down, he had to admit he'd overreacted. Tammy's sandwich wasn't the issue. Jay's swiping it was. Probably not even that. He didn't like the impact sharing the house again with his parents and Jay was having on his lifestyle. He'd grown quite comfortable with things the way they'd been. He had a home, well, a house. Tammy kept the place clean, did his laundry, and kept him fed. He didn't like losing his sense of well-being.

The sooner he got himself out of his parents' home, the better. Good thing he'd made an appointment with one of the decorators on the list he'd received from Janice. Had to keep this project moving.

Lillian Cavanaugh was a tall, thin woman in her mid-forties. Mike had pictured someone who flaunted her artsy side like the bohemian-style outfits Janice used to wear at the gallery until she started seeing Shae's father. Instead, this woman wore a tailored pantsuit in a nondescript color between brown and gray.

"Nice place," she said as she glided into the great room. "Lots of space. Great light."

He ushered her around the room, then showed her the kitchen and dining areas. They wandered out to the patio off the great room and kitchen.

She held a hand over her eyes to view the backyard. "Terrific view of that stream down there. I assume that's Sullivan's Creek?"

"Correct. Just wide enough to be picturesque. Named for the guy who owned the property before Jake Bonneville."

"Jake Sullivan, his grandfather. I used to walk beans out here when I was a teen. One of my first paying jobs besides babysitting."

"You walked beans?" He couldn't picture this well-put-together woman out in a bean field in cut-offs and T-shirt.

She released a sort of surprised chuckle. "Yes. I grew up on a farm not too far from here. In fact, I know Jake Bonneville as Ned Collier. He's a lot younger than me, but his grandparents let him help out during bean-walking time."

"I grew up in town. Never had the pleasure, although in high school, when I met Ned, he brought me out here a few times. His grandparents were the best. That's why Ned's staying involved with this building project. He wants to assure the transition from farmland to residences respects the integrity of the place."

"I'd expect nothing less from him."

"How come you're not doing Ned and Shae's house, if you don't mind my asking?"

"Both of them have consulted me at times, but they wanted to remain in charge of their own décor."

"That's Ned. And Shae, too, now I think about it. They've had the luxury of time to consider what they want. Me, I've just recently decided to proceed with my place. Now I'm in a hurry to get it finished so I can move in. How fast can you work?"

She faced him, lifted a well-shaped brow. "That depends on your tastes. If you want something unique and high end, it will take time. If you'd be happy with whatever local dealers or online mass distributors can provide, your chances of taking occupancy sooner increase."

"What would it take to get the high end faster?"

The brow arched higher. "Money, which I'm guessing won't be a problem. But we'll also need to nail down your needs and desires immediately, and then, hope luck is with us."

"I can't afford to depend on luck. You'll have to be willing to pull strings and even lean on some suppliers. Are you up to that?"

The weather had grown nippy, so they strolled back inside. "I know how to make things happen, if that's what you mean. Let's discuss what you want."

He'd thought to bring a card table and chairs with him and indicated she should sit. He followed suit. "Okay, shoot. What do you need to know?"

"Let's start with this house. Were you involved in the design?"

"No. It was intended for Ned's mother, Janice, but she decided she wanted to stay in town. Why do you ask?"

"Now that the exterior is finished, is there anything you'd do differently, if you were designing it yourself?"

"Interesting question. Never thought about it. A house is a house, more or less, as long as it includes the necessary elements —bedrooms, bathrooms, kitchen, office."

"You didn't mention living room, or in this case, great room."

"Oversight, I guess."

"Maybe. But it tells me you don't tend to spend much time in your homes, mainly to sleep, eat and take care of your personal needs."

"Don't forget the office."

She sat back, tapped a fingernail on her chin. "Oh, I haven't. That detail says you're never very far away from your business interests." She reached into her valise, removed a book on design styles, and handed it to him. "Flip through here. Stop when you see something that appeals."

He did as directed, turned a few pages, turned more. Nothing jumped out at him. In fact, the more he viewed, the more things blurred. At length, he closed the book, shoved it back to her. "Sorry. Whatever these represent, nothing grabbed me."

Next, she pulled out a color swatch book and spread out the leaves. "Without thinking, point to the color that calls to you first."

He attempted to follow through but stopped, puzzled. "Strange. Nothing."

"That is strange. Okay, try this. I'll point to a color, and you give me thumbs up or thumbs down."

For the next few minutes, they played her game. With the exception of a very light beige, more like bisque, everything else was thumbs down. Finally, she shut the book a little too briskly. "This is a waste of time."

"That's what I thought, but I humored you with your exercise."

She shook her head. Her dangle earrings bobbled, the most action he'd observed so far from this buttoned-down persona. "Not what I meant. You haven't identified anything at all that you like. Nothing of substance, anyway, that would point toward colors or styles that appeal to you. The only thing you've told me is you like neutral. Bland."

This was a waste of time. Mike rose and pushed away from the table. "Thanks for coming all the way out here, Ms. Cavanaugh. But this is a waste of time for both of us since I don't know what I want in the way of furnishings." Was his experience with Darren's seascapes repeating itself? He didn't know what he liked until he saw something he didn't like?

The decorator remained seated, apparently not yet ready to give up this very lucrative assignment. "Let's not be so hasty, Mr. Woodley. Perhaps if we met in my studio, I could show you several sketches and mockups that would spark your interest. I'm sure with a little more input from you I could devise a design plan you'll love."

"Perhaps. But I don't feel we're communicating on the same wavelength. Thanks again for your time. I'll be happy to send you a check for your consultation."

Cavanaugh rose, gathered her purse and portfolio. "I'll send you an invoice. If you change your mind …"

He didn't respond but instead showed her to the door and watched her drive off in a silver luxury sedan. Damn! Why was furnishing a house so difficult? Why was this whole day proving so difficult? Had the stars gone into some bad orbit?

His mounting frustration surrounding his domestic situation prevented him from focusing on Sullivan's Creek. He needed to find a decorator pronto so he could get back to work. One name remained untapped on the list he'd received from Janice. No time like the present to proceed.

"You want this finished when?" the male voice on the other end of the line asked.

"In two weeks, sooner if possible," Mike told Jason B.

"No can do, man. I'm so buried in projects, I won't be able to take a breath until January. Call back then."

"That won't do. I need to get into my new home as soon as possible."

"Do you have any idea who you're talking to? I'm not like your ordinary repair guy or lawn-care company. I have a reputation here in town. I also have jobs in St. Louis and Omaha. I can't drop those clients just for you."

The gall! "Do you have any idea who I am?" Mike asked in return. He didn't resort to throwing his weight around very often, but sometimes the situation called for it. "The Woodley name means a lot in this town. Nationally."

"Yes, yes, I know. Your mother hired me once for a job."

"Good, then …"

"After I'd rearranged my schedule to redo a room for her that just 'had to be done' by some fancy gala she was planning, she canceled, saying she'd run into some big-name designer from Florida she was bringing in instead. Stiffed me on the bill for my consultation services."

Thank you, Mother. "I'm willing to pay a higher fee for your immediate services. A bonus if you get me in on time."

"Seems everyone in town wants their place redone for the holidays this year. If you find you can hold off until January, call back."

And that was that. Out of names. Might as well call it a day.

He was on his way up the front stairs at the mansion when his mother said. "Michael! I'm so glad you're home. Your father and brother have both disappeared."

Shouldn't do this. He was tempting fate. "What's up, Mom?"

She clapped her hands together. "I'm planning a party. A sort of 'welcome back to town' party for the three of us."

"Aren't your friends supposed to do that?"

"Most of our old gang now live elsewhere, have split up or died. It'll take too much time to reestablish myself in the organizations I was once part of, so I decided to short-cut things by doing it myself."

He didn't follow her logic. "If the *old gang* is no longer around, who are you going to invite?"

"Your father, Joey, and I may have resided elsewhere these last several years, but you've been here. That's why I'm glad you're home. I need your contact list."

"What contact list? My business acquaintances are far-flung. Most of the people I know in town are part of the Sullivan's Creek project or related to it. You think Dad really wants to rub elbows with the very people with whom he wants me to cut my connections?"

"Surely you know more people than that? Didn't you go to some soirée Ned gave this past summer?"

"You mean the gallery showing? That was his mother, Janice's party. I'm not going to steal her list." Besides, he'd already tapped her once this week.

"Perhaps I could ask. I haven't seen her in years. I'll just stop by her gallery."

"No, Mom …"

"Hello?" Darren stood in the doorway, a huge black portfolio under one arm. "Your housekeeper told me I could come right in, but once again, I seem to be interrupting something."

Thank God. "No, you're not. My mother and I were just discussing some social plans she's making. Mother, this is Darren Williams, a local artist. She's doing a seascape for me."

In an instant, Frances Woodley, whining mother, morphed into Frances Woodley, solicitous social leader. She extended her hand to Darren. "Ms. Williams. It's so nice to meet you. I understand you're making quite a name for yourself with your paintings. I'd like to see your work some time. In fact"—she stole a glance at Mike—"I was just telling my son it was high time I checked out the Serenity Gallery. I haven't visited Janice Collier in years."

Darren proved she could be just as convivial. "It's nice to meet you, too, Mrs. Woodley. I'm sure Janice would love to see you again and show you around her place. She renovated it this past year."

"All the more reason to drop by." His mother's tone oozed a warmth designed to charm their visitor.

Mike ground his fingernails into the fleshy part of his palms as he attempted to keep his cool while his mother prattled on. How soon could he get rid of her? His mother being in the same room with Darren made his stomach queasy.

"I understand she held a showing of your pieces a few months ago," his mother said. "I wonder if she'd ever consider doing such an event outside the premises. Like here, perhaps. I'm in the mood to throw a party."

Mike could almost see the wheels revolving inside that carefully coiffed head. Although her plan sounded halfway logical, he still didn't like it. His mother was trying to worm her way into his life more than he was comfortable sharing.

He'd been the object of her matchmaking efforts before. Once, she'd even handpicked a wife candidate who was supposed to apply to be his assistant. With an MBA degree from a prestigious school back East, the woman was well qualified. His mother had briefed her on his various likes and dislikes so the woman's interview responses were spot on, except when asked about her career aspirations. The applicant told him her greatest wish was to support the CEO of a huge family corporation. Though her response tipped him off, he gave her an opportunity to redeem herself by following up on her response. She still could have salvaged things by telling him how a family corporation differed from other corporate entities and why that was important to her. But she'd tripped over her answer. "Well, isn't that your career plan as well?" Could it have been more obvious she'd been coached?

How was he supposed to stop this runaway train without appearing to be an ogre?

"That's an intriguing idea, although the advantage to staging the showing at the gallery is the greatly reduced liability of transferring several works of art to this house."

His mother tapped her lips with a recently polished nail. "True. But surely she's not a stranger to offsite showings. I'll bet she's never done one of these galas in one of the town's more prestigious residences."

Darren shot him a look that asked how he expected her to answer. He rolled his eyes but still gave it a shot. "Look, Mom, Janice is probably seeing clients throughout the day. It wouldn't be a good idea to just show up."

His mother pulled up, appeared to consider his comment. "There is that. I know. I'll call first." She dashed out of the room.

Mike threw a frantic glance at Darren. "My phone's in my office."

She quickly retrieved her own and slipped it to him. "Here. Go for it."

Hallelujah! She got the message. Just so he'd beaten his mother to a dial tone. To his relief, his call went through and Janice answered. He warned her what was about to happen. "Please don't feel obligated to agree. I don't know why she feels the need for this party, which it is to her, before she's barely unpacked, but don't let her bulldoze you."

"Thanks for alerting me, Mike, but actually, I find the idea of a showing at your house intriguing. Would you mind it that much?"

Wasn't expecting that response. How did he feel? "Uh, guess I'm fine with it, as long as you don't mind. But if you agree, it's between you and my mother, okay? Leave me out of this. And remember, if you do this, it's still your showing, not hers. You don't have to go along with anything she proposes."

"Understood. I appreciate your concern."

"Darren Williams is here in the room with me. She stopped by with the painting I commissioned and witnessed Mom's latest brainstorm."

"Good to know, although I would have included Darren's things anyhow, even if you hadn't told me."

He hung up, still undecided how he felt about this latest development. Sure, it would be a great opportunity for Janice, and his mother seemed to be appeased with the idea. But the churning in his stomach suggested he'd set afoot something he was going to regret.

"That went well," Darren said. "Why are you scowling?"

"Am I? Didn't realize. I love my mom. Really. But she hasn't been back even a week and she's already making these big social plans. And dragging in Janice. I wish she'd slow down."

"Maybe she misses the life she left behind. Was she active socially in Michigan?"

He started to answer and drew a blank. "I guess. I haven't stayed current with her social life the last few years."

Darren appeared to consider his response. "Trust Janice. If things get out of control, I'm sure she'll handle them." She held up a seascape that bore no resemblance to the piece she'd shown him a few days earlier. This one was drenched in pale blues and purples. "I'm here with the changes you requested for your painting. What do you think?"

Her timing couldn't have been worse. The long list of the day's frustrations—his dad's comments, Jay's going out of his way to bug him, his mother's interference in his private life, and now her grandiose plans for a showing—reared up. Nothing was going his way. He'd lost control of his life. He didn't do vulnerable well.

Something inside him exploded, demanded satisfaction. "Geez, Darren. I know I told you I wanted a calmer piece, but you went overboard. I can't accept this."

Her eyes went wide, and her head jerked back. "What? I gave you exactly what you said you wanted."

"I know. You're right."

"I, I don't do business this way." Though she kept her tone flat, it carried an undercurrent of anger. "My clients either accept what I offer or pass. I redid this as a favor to Janice since you and her son are so close."

"I appreciate the gesture, but that doesn't change my mind."

She closed her eyes for a beat, then released a sigh. "Then I guess we have no further business. Thank you for teaching me a valuable lesson, not to rely on a handshake for a business commitment." She tore open the portfolio, rammed the picture in, and made for the door.

"Wait."

She pivoted, raised a brow. "Yes?"

"Nothing personal. I still admire your work. This just doesn't do it for me."

"Sorry." She resumed her trek to the front door.

He probably should accompany her. Not the best manners, but he'd already crossed that bridge by rejecting the painting a second time.

What was he thinking? He made a deal with her, as she'd said. She'd gone to a lot of trouble to finish a new piece so soon. He'd struck out at her because he'd been unable to contain his irritation with his family.

"Do you treat all your business associates that way?" His mother had returned, now wearing a jacket and carrying her purse.

"Thought you'd left."

"Would you have been as rude if I'd remained?"

"I've had a hellish day. Her arrival and what she brought hit at the wrong time."

She moved closer, appeared to study him. "That's your explanation?"

"As good as any. You have a better one?"

Her expression softened. "I liked her. More to the point, you like her, too. I saw the way you looked at her. And that scares you. So you've adopted the same approach with her as you have with your family by pushing her away."

He raked a hand through his hair. "That's crazy. You're so intent on marrying me off you're manufacturing feelings on my part that don't exist."

"Not from what I witnessed. Is this why you're not married yet? You chase away every woman who shows the slightest interest?"

He blew out a breath. He so didn't want to get into this discussion again. His mother really needed to find herself a hobby. Even if it was planning a gala art show. "I'm not married yet because I choose not to be. Why can't you accept that? Why do you keep bringing this up? Look at the track records of your other three children. Jay and Alicia have called it quits, Gardner lives in the shadow of Lilith, and Harper married the man you picked for her and gave up her ambitions to be part of the company so he could work for Dad instead."

"I just don't see why …"

"Mom, please drop this. I'm tired of trying to justify my life-style to you. We dance to different tunes. You're still doing the mambo or whatever you grew up with, and I'm hip to this century."

"The mambo's from the fifties," she said with a huff. "I grew up a generation later."

"Whatever. You get the idea. We're tuned into different issues."

"We're both talking about your life and what you're doing with it. Your sensitivity to the topic makes me think …"

"Stop!" He rarely shouted at his mother, but he couldn't help himself this time. He gulped. Enough of this constant bombardment. "This house is closing in on me. I'm leaving."

"You're moving out? We just got here."

He considered. He'd only meant to escape her harangue for the time being, but her mention of moving out got his attention. He charged from the room. Didn't have the slightest idea where he was going, but with Ned's words ringing in his brain, he knew he couldn't stick around any longer. Not when every encounter with Jay elicited an argument, when every time he saw his dad his career choices were questioned and when every discussion with his mother resulted in her harping about his single status.

CHAPTER 5

Mike tore out of the house, barely taking time to grab a jacket. He drove aimlessly for several minutes before he gave much thought to a destination. Sullivan's Creek? No, what would he do in an empty house? A bar? So not a good idea in this mood. Then it came to him. He may be furious with his home situation right now, but he had his own damage to repair. He pulled up contact information for Darren's studio on his phone.

Her studio and gallery occupied part of a converted barn. The gallery was about ten by twelve but large enough to display several of her landscapes. The studio must be located behind the gallery, judging from the back-to-back easels and half-done canvases stacked everywhere in that area. Both spaces were unoccupied. "Darren? You here?"

No one answered at first. She must've returned, or the gallery would be locked. He waited a bit longer, then called again.

After a few beats, she entered the room, her eyes red and swollen. Was he responsible for that? "Think of a few more insults?"

Anger. And hurt. Didn't blame her. "I came to apologize. I've been a real jerk where that picture is concerned."

She eyed him like one would a vicious dog that had suddenly backed away. "For being a jerk or for reneging on our deal?"

She wasn't going to make this easy for him. "You've managed to show up with your work in the midst of two very trying days. Not your fault. Just bad timing. I took out my mood on you, which was unforgiveable. I came to pay you for the painting. For both, actually." He caught the surprise in her eyes. "You wouldn't destroy that other masterpiece just to appease me."

"Thank you." Her voice emerged as a hoarse whisper.

"Are you okay? Have you been crying because of our run-in?"

She sniffed, brought out a tissue and swiped at her eyes. "You must think me so unprofessional. I've taken worse criticism with much less drama. I was just, uh, counting on the fee, and when you refused the painting again ..."

"The waterworks exploded. Has business been so bad you're living hand to mouth?"

She blinked, then turned her gaze away. "I've, uh, had some unexpected expenses recently."

Though he regretted her having financial problems, that gave him an idea. "Maybe I could help out there."

Her eyes sought his again. "Thank you. But I don't need a loan. Especially if you were serious about paying for the second painting."

"I'll pay for both, but I wasn't suggesting a loan. I still need an interior decorator for my new house. I know that's not your gig, but there's no denying you know your way around color and style. And I need my place done as soon as possible. Two weeks."

"Two weeks?"

"Yeah. You got a sample of my current home situation when you witnessed my mother in action. She as well as my father and brother are driving me crazy. I've got to get out of there."

"I thought you already had a decorator?"

"I did. But we had a parting of the ways over the design plan."

She narrowed her eyes. "They didn't want to follow your ideas?"

"Something like that."

"I can well imagine. Run out of names?"

She had him dead to rights. But he wasn't admitting as much. "No. I was offering you a viable means of augmenting your funds in the next few weeks. I'd be helping you, and you'd be helping me."

"Interesting solution to both our problems, but no, like I said, I'm an artist, not an interior decorator. On the other hand …"

"Yes?"

"Bottom line is to get away from your family, right? Why don't you find temporary quarters until your house is ready? A friend of mine manages a lofts complex downtown. I could see if he'd rent you a furnished one on a week-by-week basis."

There was a thought. One that had eluded him until she suggested it. "Uh, yeah. If you wouldn't mind after all the grief I've given you?"

"Grief forgotten, as long as you walk out of here with those two paintings."

He wrote her a check. "I added fifty dollars in return for your storing them for me until I'm either ready to move into the new place or need them for my new decorator to use in a design plan."

"Sounds good. Can you hold off moving out until tomorrow? I should have an answer by then. If my friend doesn't come through, there are always extended-stay motels."

"Another possibility." Without planning to do so, he pulled her into an embrace and hugged her. God, she felt good in his arms. So good, so natural. He kissed her again.

She backed away, surprise and delight written upon her face.

"This is getting to be a habit," he said. "One I'm fast coming to like."

"I, uh, I'm glad I could help. But what do I make of the kiss?"

"Make of it? I'm attracted to you. If I'm overstepping, let me know." Thanks to the family name and wealth, not many women rejected his advances, but he wasn't going to take her acquiescence for granted.

Though he'd hoped for an immediate yes, she took her time answering. "Overstepping? No. Overwhelming, yes. I haven't been involved with someone for some time. I'm a little rusty."

Oh-oh. Had she read too much into the kiss? "I'm not one for getting involved myself, but if I like someone, I show it."

Her lashes went to half-mast, apparently digesting his message. "Got you. I'm new to this game, but I'm willing to play, as long as you provide clues along the way."

He cocked a brow. "You're open to having fun with no strings?"

Her lips curved up. "Call it what it is, Mike. Casual sex."

He liked her candor. "Okay."

He left the studio feeling much better. Probably hadn't been such a great idea to hire her as his decorator. She seemed to realize that before he did. But she had also come up with the idea of temporary housing. She was practical as well as artistic. Nice combination.

THOUGH IT WAS late in the afternoon, Darren headed to the bank before she called her friend at the lofts apartments.

She called Colby and arranged to meet her in a parking lot on campus. This looked so sleazy. Almost like a meeting between a druggie and her dealer. Fortunately, student traffic was minimal this late in the day.

"Did you get it?" her sister asked as soon as she flopped into the passenger seat.

Darren retrieved the blank envelope containing the bills from her purse. "Before I hand this over, we need to talk."

Colby rolled her eyes. "Is this a lecture?"

"Up until an hour ago, I had no idea how we could pay your debt. What money I have isn't fluid. It's all invested in my business. Fortunately, a client came through and paid his bill. But you have to understand, Colby, this is it as far as my covering your debts is concerned. Gambling is not the way to make a quick buck. It's the way despicable people make slaves out of other people's greed and get-rich-quick dreams."

"I'm aware of that, Darren. I'm smarter than the average bear."

Darren let that comment slide. "Promise me your gambling days are behind you."

"Of course, they are. I appreciate your help, sis. You've really come through for me." She glanced out the window, as if checking for someone in the parking lot. "But I've got a class in ten minutes and have to get going. Hand me the money."

"If you find your will power slipping, there are organizations that help people get back on track."

"Yes, yes."

Though a sickening pain shot through Darren's gut, she gave her sister the envelope. Colby tucked it inside her backpack, slammed the door and took off.

Darren drove away immediately, unwilling to spend another minute in this place of shame.

TRUE TO HER WORD, Darren contacted her friend, who called Mike that same evening and offered him a deal on a one-bedroom furnished apartment on the third floor of a building near the river. With a little help from Tammy to pack some of his wardrobe, he was able to move in by ten that night.

"You really don't have to do this, Michael," his mother told him as he was on his way to his car with the last load of stuff he was taking with him for now.

"We'll all be happier this way. I'll get the rest of my things in a day or two."

He rented the place sight unseen. Fortunately, his haste didn't work against him. The bedroom was spacious and included a large flat-screen TV. The living room even included a desk, where he immediately went about setting up headquarters. Tammy had agreed to stop by the next day with groceries.

Had to hand it to Darren. So far, her suggestion had been a brilliant stroke. He even liked the austere stainless steel and acrylic glass decorating scheme. Not that he'd choose it for his house, but for now it gave him the unassuming, nonjudgmental backdrop he needed.

He slept well that night, despite being in a new bed in new surroundings. Maybe because of them.

As he was cleaning out the rest of his office at the mansion the next day, Jay arrived in his gym clothes. "So, it's true? You really have moved out?"

"No more having to share your gym with me. You should be delighted." He tried to say it without irritation. No point stirring things up further with his brother.

Jay held up mounting his machine long enough to return a confused expression. "Actually, I'm sorry it came to this. It's been a trip getting reacquainted after all these years."

Was Jay putting him on? Taking the high road in case their parents were listening? "No reason that can't continue," Mike said. He'd blurted out the statement without thinking. "There's a gym at the complex where I'm staying. Maybe we could get in a game of racquetball sometime."

Jay's lip curled. "I'd like that."

A little brotherly love could go a long way. Mike made for the door. "See ya."

He returned to his new digs just as Tammy arrived with his food. His mother had tagged along. Couldn't a guy break away from his mother's apron strings for even twenty-four hours?

While Tammy unloaded bags, stocked his fridge and put the dry goods away in the small pantry, his mother toured the apartment. What should have taken no more than five minutes in the small space lasted twice as long. The sounds of doors and drawers opening told him she was going through the place more thoroughly than she'd inspected his room at summer camp years before.

He gave the appearance of settling down at his laptop and studying the screen, but he couldn't concentrate as long as his new digs were under scrutiny.

At last, she came up to him. "This is what you meant by privacy?"

"Once it's just me alone here, yeah."

"Don't you find it somewhat austere?"

"Haven't had time to decorate and don't plan to." He deliberately avoided mentioning the decorating focus being directed at his new house. She was aware he had one under construction, but so far, he hadn't introduced the subject, and he had no intention of doing so now.

She settled a hip on the edge of the desk. Was this his mother? Her hips never settled anywhere other than chairs, lounges, and, he supposed, her bed. The woman wanted his attention and apparently didn't plan to leave until she'd had her say.

He took a long breath. "Yes?"

"Is this place a commentary on your new lifestyle, Michael? What you referred to as your own 'dance'? Monochromatic, sterile, secluded? What has happened to you? You've always been more the life-of-the-party type."

He took a moment to consider. Really didn't want to step on her toes. Just wanted her to leave so he could get some work done. "Guess I got spoiled living in that big mausoleum by myself and haven't been able to adjust to having you all around again. No offense. I jumped at the first place that sounded like it would meet my needs. Signed for it without even viewing it, even online.

Had no idea what the décor was, didn't care. So, no, this isn't my lifestyle."

She rose, examined a paperweight he'd set on the desk, his one bow to ornamentation. "I can't tell you how much it warms a mother's heart to hear her son say he would go anywhere else to escape being around her."

He released a frustrated sigh. No winning this discussion. The best he could hope for was that she'd soon tire of her harassment and leave. "This is just temporary, okay? Once the interior of my house in Sullivan's Creek is finished, I'm moving in there."

She blinked, out of character for his cool-as-ice mother. "You actually intend to live out there? In the country?"

"It's not that far, and yes, since Ned's making Iowa his headquarters, I figured I might as well stick around also."

"But we'll never see you. We relocated here in large part to be more involved in your life."

"I'll still be around. In fact, I should be moved in by late December. Why don't you all join me there for Christmas dinner?"

She backed up a step. "Really? Your father and I have talked about going to the Caribbean for the holidays, but we haven't finalized anything. Christmas on the farm is a lovely idea." She beamed.

He let the farm comment slide because he was too busy wondering what on earth had possessed him to make such an offer. No matter who wasn't speaking to whom or who was embroiled in either a business or personal imbroglio, the Woodleys celebrated Christmas together. The getting-together part of his offer wasn't that out of the ordinary. It was the getting together at his place that was. His place that currently boasted all of one card table and two chairs.

"Tammy?" his mother called. "We need to be on our way. We have plans to make." As swiftly as she'd invaded his space, his mother, with Tammy in tow, was gone.

Too late to rescind his invitation.

What had he done? He was an experienced businessman, entrepreneur, for God's sake. He could wangle his way through takeovers, mergers, stock options and a multitude of negotiations without breaking a sweat, but the minute his mother started questioning his lifestyle, he caved. Why? Just to prove he wasn't the cold, methodical automaton she was making him out to be? He'd had, what, all of twenty minutes today to believe he had his old life back, and now here he was at square one: he needed a decorator.

Christmas was how far off? A little less than two months away? Better time frame than the two weeks he'd mentioned to Lillian Cavanaugh, Jason B, and the others. Maybe they'd reconsider with more time. No, until he had a better idea what he wanted, no one was going to touch this project. Maybe he could ask Darren again.

He owed her a call to thank her for finding this place for him. Perhaps dinner? Couldn't hurt to run the idea by her one more time. Couldn't hurt at all.

CHAPTER 6

"You really didn't have to treat me to dinner just because I made a phone call, but I couldn't say no to restaurant food." Darren savored the creamy taste of Alfredo sauce on her tongue. The pasta was just the right texture, not quite *al dente*, which was too stiff for her, but not squishy overcooked either.

Mike glanced up from his steak. "Surely, you're not dieting?"

She chuckled. "Of sorts. I paint as the inspiration hits and keep going until it fizzles. I miss a lot of meal times that way, but it keeps me productive."

"Did I interrupt something tonight?"

"Just preliminary sketching. I've been off my routine today." No need to mention her earlier exchange with Colby. Although it would be nice to talk to someone else about this gambling thing. The only knowledge she had of the problem came from what she'd seen on TV.

Stop thinking about that. Focus on something else. She liked the way he cut his steak. With authority. He also ate with gusto, though he was no slob.

"I'd barely moved in before my mother stopped by to check on me."

"Good thing? She seems to really care about you."

"Would have been nice to have had a full day to unpack and make the place a little more my own. She took one look around and pronounced it cold and sterile."

"Is it? I've never been in one of those apartments."

"I'll have to show you. But in the meantime, I have a confession to make. I didn't invite you to dinner just to thank you, although that was part of it."

Oh, no. He didn't want his money back, did he? Too late. "Oh?"

"Now that you've bought me some time to get the interior of the house finished, you've also bought yourself some time to bone up on what it is a decorator does so you can agree to help me." His smile was a cross between a small boy asking for an extra cookie and a sales rep at the state fair enticing her to sign on the dotted line.

She put down her fork. Straightened her plate. "Uh, I'm flattered by your interest, even though I suspect it's based primarily on desperation. But like I told you already, I'm not a decorator. You're an important, wealthy man. You deserve someone who knows what they're doing."

"New one. Reject me with a compliment. Please, Darren. I don't care what it looks like so much as it's done by Christmas. My mother's comments about my present quarters forced me to make a stupid move. I invited the whole family for dinner that day to show that I'm not all that cold."

"But …"

He held up a hand. "Give it some thought overnight. I told you I'd pay big bucks to get this done. Surely, you could use that money to pay down your mortgage? And no, I didn't check. Just guessed."

She really wanted to finish her meal. And dessert would be

good, too. But she had to get him off this topic. Placate him. And get past the slight disappointment that the dinner invitation hadn't been simply his wanting to see her again. The last time they'd been together, they'd talked about pursuing a more intimate relationship. "Okay. I'll think about it. But only if you promise you'll also look for some other names. Deal?"

He returned a semiscowl but then stuck his hand across the table to shake on it. Yet again, the mere contact had the effect of flipping an interior switch in her body, making her all the more aware of his presence.

He must have experienced a similar sensation, because his eyes sought hers, went smoky. "Mind if we skip dessert? I need to get out of here. Want to see my new digs?"

Yes. No. Decision time. She'd already told him she was up for going to bed with him, but now that he was ready to follow through, was she ready? "Yes. I'd like that."

He paid the bill, then ushered her out to his car. Neither spoke during the ride to his new place, but each time she'd sneak a peek at him across the front seat, she'd catch him doing the same. Her body heat rose, and she found herself squirming in her seat, anticipating what was to come.

When they got to his door, he held her forearms. "Sure this is what you want?"

Her mouth had gone so dry she could only nod.

He opened the door, slammed it behind them, then pushed her up against it, his body hard against hers. His hands went around her, located the zipper in the back of her dress and pulled it down, leaving her only in her bra and thong. His lips smashed into hers as his hands went for the clasp on her bra.

Nerve endings long dormant in her core awoke with a rush and threw her sensory system into overdrive. Her knees nearly buckled as her heartbeat went ballistic with a rhythm of its own. The electric storm of desire returned with a vengeance even after lying dormant all this time.

Her cell rang.

"Don't answer."

She placed a hand over his. "Sorry, but I never know if something's up with my mom or sister."

He released a deep sigh and moved away to retrieve her purse from where it had dropped on the floor.

"Darren? Where are you?" It was Colby. Her voice sounded strained.

"I'm out having dinner. Can I call you later?"

"I really need to see you. Now. I'm already at the studio." Her volume increased.

Her sister's timing stunk. Typical. She grimaced. "Okay. I'll be there in twenty minutes."

She stuck the cell back in her purse and pulled up her dress. "This can't be helped. Can you zip me up?"

He blew out a breath. "Yeah, I can. Question is, will I?" But despite the abrupt end of their evening, he helped her put herself back together.

"My sister's been having a few problems of late. I really need to see what's up."

"Go. Take care of her."

"Raincheck?"

"Sure. Yeah." He bent down and kissed her forehead. "Next time."

Darren flipped a light switch as she entered the studio's living quarters.

"Turn off that light," Colby called from across the room.

She did as asked, then made her way to a nearby end table that held a table lamp. "Better?" she asked after turning it on.

"I guess."

"What's going on?"

"Got a bit of a problem. "

Only then did Darren notice her sibling's face and arms. Dark blue smudges covered all of one eye and part of the other, plus three-fourths of her face. Several mean-looking patches spread over her arms and wrists.

A jolt of fear ripped through Darren's chest. She shot to her sister to examine her closer. "Oh my God! What happened?" Although Colby's athletic activities had left her bruised and scraped over the years, Darren had never seen her look this bad.

"I debated whether to call first, but I thought seeing me in person would explain things better." Colby's speech was slow and somewhat slurred. Was her mouth hurt as well?

"Have you seen a doctor, been to the ER?" Darren asked on her way to her fridge for a bag of frozen veggies.

When she returned with the package, Colby had reclined and placed a pillow under her head. "Thanks. I didn't know where else to go. Mom's still at work. She'd freak anyhow."

No, she wouldn't freak, but she'd probably coddle her younger daughter just like she always had. Just like Darren had been doing the last few days. "Have you taken any painkillers?"

"Yes. It's been a few hours now. I went back to my place and wallowed first, but …"

A second bolt of fear seized Darren's heart. "Wasn't the five hundred enough for your creditors? Did they do this?"

Colby hung her head. "At first they seemed so accepting. Even let me use a hundred of it for another stake. Told me I could win back what I'd lost recently and be able to pay you back."

Darren could barely hear the response. "They know I gave you the money?"

"I, uh, guess it slipped out when I was handing over the envelope you gave me. They, uh, wanted to know who you were, what you did."

With horrible clarity, Darren realized Colby's supposedly friendly poker games were part of a much larger, much more dangerous web. How could Colby be so naïve?

Her sister reached for the afghan draped across the back of the sofa and pulled the top almost to her nose. "They let me win the first game, enough for me think my luck had turned. Then I'd lose, although every so often, I'd win just enough to convince myself fortune would smile on me if I could hang in there a little longer. But my debt kept mounting, and when it was time to pay up, I was amazed how much I'd lost. They wanted it right then, and I told them there was no way I could come up with the money."

"But your sister can," they said.

Damn! The girl was studying to be an attorney. They were supposed to be bold, have nerves of steel. See through others' lies. The little girl hiding under the blanket was so unlike that stereotype. "So why beat you up, if they knew you had to come to me for the money?" She was afraid to hear the answer, but everything needed to be out on the table before this situation got any worse. If that was possible.

"Since you'd paid off my other two debts. You might refuse to help me a third time unless ..."

"I received an incentive, like protecting your carcass from further attack."

Colby nodded.

Darren gulped, astonished she'd correctly read the situation without passing out from the shock and horror. This was her little sister. Not quite twenty-three. Things like this didn't happen to people like her. And in this city. Sure, there was crime here, like any other place. But loan sharks and their—what were they called?—enforcers?—weren't in her orbit.

Neither she nor Colby spoke for several seconds. Darren attempted to process the dead bird her sister had laid at her feet. Colby waited for Darren to come to her rescue.

Although she knew where this was headed, Darren took her time getting there. The prospect was so terrifying and so life changing, she needed more time to remain in her current, comfy world. Too late. The coziness faded the minute she'd eyed her beat-up sister.

She took a deep breath, probably the last of its kind for a while. "How much?"

Colby rolled toward the back of the couch.

"Colby! By coming here you knew telling me all the ugly details was inevitable. How much do you owe and how much time do you have to pay it back?"

"Ten thousand." It emerged a muffled sob, but Darren still got the picture.

Darren gripped her hands to stop them from trembling. "By when?"

"Two days. Said you should have enough in the bank from all your recent sales to cover it, or you could get a loan."

They knew all about her. Or at least thought they did, since her bank account was nowhere near as healthy as they presumed. That's how it worked. They picked their marks carefully. In fact, she wouldn't be surprised if those helpful friends who first put Colby on to the game weren't getting their own tuition paid by recruiting new blood. Listen to her. She'd definitely been watching too many TV crime shows.

She needed to do something before she lost it. "Want some tea?"

Colby turned toward her. "I could really use a drink."

Sure. Let alcohol insulate your humiliation. For now, though, she'd take the high road. "Tea's better for your injuries."

While she heated water and located her tea ball, she planned. It wasn't a question of whether she'd help. Of course, she would. She'd always cleaned up Colby's messes and held their mother's hand when life got too real. But ten thousand dollars? She could barely get her mind around the sum. She'd never had that much money in her life, despite her recent successes.

The only place she could get that amount was from the bank, and bank loans took time to process. Time she didn't have. Wait. She also knew Mike Woodley. Not well enough to ask for a personal loan, but... He wanted her to decorate his house and had told her to take tonight to rethink her refusal. It was a crazy idea; she didn't know a thing about interior decoration. Whatever personal feelings she might be experiencing about the man would have to be put on hold if she were to work for him. Maybe forever. She bit down on her disappointment. Desperate times. Worth the try.

She returned to her small living room with two mugs of herbal tea and found Colby sitting up on the couch, still swathed in the afghan but now examining her face in a small hand mirror. "Will you help me?" Her tone reminded Darren of the time when Colby had wrecked the bike their mother had worked overtime for two months to buy. Colby had been so distraught about their mother finding out, Darren had finally relented and used the babysitting money she'd been saving for a new easel to get the bike repaired. Their mother never knew.

"It's late. In the morning, I'll see what funds I can scrape together."

Now the tears poured forth as her sister thanked her repeatedly.

"You shouldn't go back to your place tonight. They'll probably leave you alone for the two days they've given you, but why borrow trouble?" Had she really said that? Her sister was already so far past that point. "Stay here. I'll take the couch. You take my bed."

Colby promptly rose and moved her laptop, study bag and purse into Darren's tiny sleeping area. Within minutes, she was out for the night.

Darren, however, slept little. The beginnings of a plan took shape in her addled brain, but she'd have to wait until morning to see if it would fly. Whether it did or not, their lives had changed forever. Even if she got the money, how was she going to stop Colby's gambling?

Up by dawn, she called Mike. "I know it's early, but could you meet me in half an hour at that coffee shop on the main floor of your building?" She tried not to sound too desperate or fearful. Not easy, considering the amount of money her sister owed and the "message" her "creditors" had already left on Colby's body.

After a groggy-sounding Mike agreed, Darren quickly dressed without waking her sister and drove into town.

She was already seated in a booth with two cups of coffee when he entered. She shoved one to him once he'd dropped into the place opposite her.

"Thanks. I can use this. How's your sister?"

She really didn't want to go into details, because she was humiliated and didn't want to involve anyone else in this disaster. But since Colby's call had interrupted their lovemaking, she owed him some sort of explanation. "It's not pretty. She got herself into some financial difficulty she can't get out of on her own, which I'd rather not discuss. Is your offer for me to be your interior decorator still on the table?"

He ran a hand through recently washed hair. "You've changed your mind?"

"Yes, provided we can come to terms."

He blinked. "Okay? What are we talking about?"

"I'll make your project my priority and will have it finished for you in time for your big Christmas dinner, but in order to put my other projects on the back burner, I need a retainer of ten thousand dollars."

"To cover her bills?"

She focused on her cup of coffee. "Yes."

He reached across the table and took her hand. Though the warmth comforted her, it didn't relieve her anxiety. "I'll take you up on your offer, because we both know how desperate I am. But why can't I just loan you the money?"

She wasn't expecting anything other than the check and the job from him. She shook her head. "Thanks. I appreciate the offer. Really. But this is something I have to do on my own."

He stared at her a bit. "I mean it, Darren. We haven't known each other long, but I can tell this is something big. Your eyes say it's something horrible. I'll respect your privacy. For now. But don't write off my offer to help."

She gulped. "Thanks."

He pulled out his cell. "I'll send this to your email."

"Uh, no. I need a cashier's check."

His eyes widened. "You have to turn this over to someone else without it being traced to you?"

"I really can't say."

"I'll have to get a certified check from the bank, and they won't be open for another hour. I'll bring it to your studio as soon as I get it. Okay?"

Moisture pooled in her eyes. She could only bob her head.

COLBY WAS JUST COMING out of the shower when Darren returned home. Normally, she would have respected her sister's privacy, but today she barged right into the bathroom to check out the bruises. The color was already changing to a less intense brown and mauve, and Colby seemed somewhat livelier. Why shouldn't she be? Big Sister was coming to her rescue. Again.

Colby gazed at her expectantly. "Were you successful?"

"Wouldn't exactly characterize what I just went through a success, but yes, I have a check."

Colby wrapped herself in a towel, then swept Darren into her arms. "That is such a relief! Thank you, thank you, Darren. You've saved my life."

"Perhaps. Physically. For now. But this is far from over. Get dressed. We need to talk."

She exited the bathroom and went to fix a light breakfast. Colby needed to eat. A little, anyhow.

"You made coffee," Colby said upon spying the fare Darren

had prepared. "Thanks. I could use something stronger than the tea you gave me last night."

"True. You're going to need your strength to get through this next period."

"All I have to do is give my creditors the money. Then I'm back to life as normal."

Was she that naïve or just attempting to downplay the incredible mess she'd made of both their lives? "You owe me ten thousand seven hundred dollars, Colby. For now, your life is in my hands and you're going to do as I dictate, starting first by setting up a meeting for me with your uh, *creditors*. The check is a cashier's check, which I'll hand over to them, not you. You've lost the right to handle your finances for a while."

Colby bounded out of her chair, spilling her orange juice. "You can't do that? They, they won't take the money from you. They don't want to expose themselves."

"I'm not letting you handle any more of my money. No more gambling."

Colby started to respond but on second thought clamped her mouth shut. Having drawn her line in the sand, Darren ate her toast while surreptitiously studying her sister. Had Colby gotten the message, or was she simply acting as if she was going along with the plan? Finished, Colby shoved out of her chair none too quietly, leaving Darren to clean up.

Several minutes later, Colby returned to the kitchen. "It's set up for eleven this morning." She mentioned a supermarket on the west side of town. "They weren't happy, but they finally agreed."

"Good. We can spend the time between now and then outlining what you're going to do to stop gambling."

"Huh?"

Darren was about to explain when the doorbell rang. Mike. She'd been so intent setting things up with Colby, she'd forgotten she didn't have the money yet. "That's one of my clients. He's stopping by to pay for a recent purchase. Stay in the kitchen so you don't alarm him with your appearance."

"Hi. Can I come in?" Mike called from the door separating her studio from her home.

No. "Sure." She opened the door wider for him to enter. Thank God she'd already put away the blankets and pillow on the couch. "My sister is visiting, but she's in the kitchen."

"No, she's not," Colby said, joining them and flopping on said couch.

Darren gritted her teeth. "I thought you were going to stay in the kitchen?"

"Got curious." Colby shot a glance at Mike. "I'm Colby, Darren's sister. Sorry about my looks. I overestimated how well my bike could take a corner and flew over the handlebar. I look worse than I feel."

Mike studied her briefly before replying. "I empathize. Haven't been out on my own bike in months due to a spill. Be sure to ice those bruises every so often."

"Good advice, except there are so many spots that ache, it'll take me all day to make the rounds."

Was Colby flirting with Mike while she lied her head off describing her make-believe accident? That was Colby. Drama queen all the way.

Mike turned his attention back to Darren. "Did you want to discuss our deal here or in your studio?"

Perceptive. Or else Colby had come on too strong. "I'll be right back, sis."

Once in the studio, Mike lowered his voice as he pulled an envelope from his jacket and handed it to her. "You didn't tell me she'd been beaten up. Have you involved the police?"

He called them like he saw them.

She shook her head. "Can't. Fear of retribution. She doesn't want anyone at school finding out about this for fear she'll be expelled."

He pursed his lips, like he wanted to say something but was holding back. "But …"

"No! I've never dealt with anything like this before, but I can still recognize a potential threat if we don't meet their demands. I told Colby to remain in the kitchen to keep you out of this, but as you can see, she has a mind of her own."

"Yeah. Did she really think I'd buy her story?"

"She's a budding attorney. Their egos know no bounds."

He took her hands in his. "Be careful. This is serious stuff."

He had no idea how much the physical contact reassured her. "I'm trying to."

"The payoff isn't going to take place here, I hope?"

"No. I insisted I go with her and be the one to turn over the money. I can't allow them to take advantage of her any longer."

If possible, his worried expression grew even more profound. "God, Darren. That's so dangerous. Please tell me it will be in a public place."

She nodded. Talking about this fiasco was proving more and more difficult, especially now that Mike had some idea of the scope of the problem.

"Okay. I get it. You're telling yourself the less said, the better. I'll go along with your wishes. But if you need help, call."

She couldn't keep from shaking. "Th-thanks."

"I'd like to get started later today on my house, if you feel you can leave your houseguest." It was like he sensed her need to return to some degree of normalcy.

"That shouldn't be a problem, although she's going to be staying here with me while she heals."

The hint of a frown crossed his face and then immediately disappeared. "You don't need to bring anything except something for notes. No architectural books or samples. Been that route with my first or second decorators—forget which—and it clogged my brain."

She set a time to meet him, and he headed for the door. "I meant what I said. If you need any other help, call."

As she watched him drive off, she steeled herself for the next act in the "Get Colby to Stop Gambling" show. Damn Colby. Mike had put two and two together already. He knew the need for the money concerned her sister. But he'd been kind enough, perhaps wise enough, to leave it alone other than to offer his aid if she needed it. That should make her feel better. But it didn't.

"Some client," Colby said once Darren returned to the living room. "I'd be willing to schlock a bunch of paint on canvas if all my clients looked like him."

"After all we're going through to keep you in law school, don't even joke about switching careers. Besides, we have more serious things to discuss."

"More? You've got the money, right? What else is there to talk about?"

"I've made an appointment for later today for us to visit a counselor who specializes in gambling addiction."

Colby's eyes went wide. "What? I'm not an addict."

"You apparently can't stop yourself from gambling. That's addiction." Darren spoke these words as dispassionately as she could. That's what the articles she'd found on the internet recommended. Get the addict help; force them to follow through; and don't let them cajole their way out of getting help, or threaten or play on your emotions. Stay cool. Right. Had that writer ever told a hotshot lawyer in the making she was an addict?

Darren struggled with her conscience. Her plan was full of flaws. She should turn this over to the police. Let them handle it. But she wanted to prevent any fallout to her sister's legal career. These people had picked their mark well. They knew she'd want to protect Colby at all costs. She should at least seek counsel from an attorney, someone who had a better grasp of all the implications of the tangled web in which they found themselves. But there wasn't time, and she couldn't afford anyone. Not with this new debt over her head.

They met their contact toward the back of the large grocery store in the dairy department. It turned out to be a woman in her early thirties dressed in a pair of black slacks and tan jacket. Down the aisle, a man in jeans and a heavy gray hoodie took an inordinately long time to select a carton of milk. In the other direction, an older man in khakis and dark windbreaker examined various types of yogurt. Who could tell these average-looking, nondescript people were part of a criminal ring that was destroying Colby's and her lives?

Darren swallowed hard. "Before I turn this over to you, I want to make it clear this is the last time my sister will be dealing with you."

"Of course, although my associates and I won't turn her away if she shows up again. You can't keep her under lock and key."

"She has no money with which to pay off her debts, nor do I. I had to take out a loan for this, as it is." Not quite the case, but she didn't want them to know about her deal with Mike.

The woman paused, glanced at her sister. "No one coerced you to play, Colby. In fact, you were offered several chances to opt out, and you refused. If you can't afford to play and your sister will no longer pay your debts, I'd suggest you keep your distance." She turned back to Darren. "Now if you'll hand over the money, we'll be on our way."

Hating that the situation had come to this but unable to think of any other way around it, Darren gave the woman the check.

The woman nodded to the other two men and all three took off separately.

"Whew!" Colby clapped her hands together and brought them to her lips. "Thank God, that's over."

Darren released the breath she'd been holding. "I guess."

CHAPTER 7

"You were great, sis."

Maybe. But who knew how long these reprobates would leave them alone?

Colby checked her phone. "Almost time for class. Can you give me a lift back to campus?"

"You don't have a class right now. I checked your schedule. What you do have is an appointment with a counselor."

"C'mon, Darren. Surely, you aren't going to hold me to that silly requirement. I got the message. No more poker."

"Silly or not, you agreed."

Colby asked who they were going to see and Darren told her.

"That's a public assistance agency. I'll be sitting in the waiting area with people who can't afford professional assistance otherwise," Colby said.

Darren let that pass. She couldn't afford a higher-priced counselor, but it was imperative Colby receive some kind of help. She couldn't even admit to being an addict. That being the case, the odds were against her staying away from the poker table. The progressively sharpening pain in Darren's stomach ever since learning of her sister's debts continued to grow worse. Several times she had to stop and catch her breath. This was serious business. Colby was putting her life in danger, and she was too proud or stupid to admit it.

"I can take it from here," Colby said as they parked.

"I'm coming along."

Colby arched a brow. "I'm perfectly capable of getting myself to the right office, Darren."

"Nonetheless, I'm going with you." Darren grabbed her purse and ran to catch up.

They rode up to the third floor in an elevator, and Darren followed Colby down the corridor. She stood by her sister's side as she checked in. Five minutes later, when Colby was called, they both rose.

"No," Colby ordered, "you wait here."

Darren looked to the receptionist.

"Our clients usually go in by themselves," the woman said. Would you like some coffee while you wait?"

"Thanks, no."

The receptionist escorted Colby from the room. When the woman returned, Darren asked, "Is there another exit back there?"

"Yes. It's a private entrance for the counselors."

Darren excused herself and went to find said door. She was barely there a minute before Colby popped out.

"Not so fast," Darren said.

Once again, Colby's chin protruded. "I said I'd go. I didn't say I'd stay."

"You're playing me, kid. That's pretty low treatment of someone who just rescued your booty."

"It's not that I don't appreciate your help. You've been a real trouper. But I got the message. No more friendly poker games. No gambling of any sort."

"Easier said than done, as you've already proven twice since the first time I bailed you out."

"Give me credit for a little sense."

Too easy to say. Too glib. As much as she loved her sister, Darren wasn't buying. "You've got two choices. Either go back in there, meet with the counselor, agree to a strenuous rehab plan, and come and live with me for a while, or you can admit yourself to a rehab institution with a gambling addiction program."

Colby returned a stunned look. "You can't be serious. Either way will affect my studies."

"You've already crossed that bridge. This is simply reality catching up with you."

"You don't have to worry further about me. Really."

Time to bring in the big guns. "There's a third choice. Not an action I'm particularly anxious to take, but I will if forced. I'll visit with your dean about these vultures swooping in on gullible law students and alert the school to the problem."

"No! You can't do that. I can't have anything that even hints at dabbling on the wrong side of the law on my record. They'll throw me out of law school before I've even completed the first semester."

Darren struggled to keep her tone even, but if she didn't put a stop to this now, she wasn't sure she could prevent Colby from proceeding down the scary path she'd begun to tread. "Don't you think I know that? I would have gone to see her already, had I not been concerned about your remaining in school. But if you refuse to pick one of the two options I've offered, I'll be forced to go that route."

Colby stuck her hands in her coat pockets and paced. Even faced with Darren's dire threat, she still wasn't ready to comply.

Darren gave her a few minutes to realize she had no other choices. Her patience eventually paid off.

"All right. I'll go back and meet with the counselor."

"And move in with me tonight?"

Colby sighed. "Only if the counselor thinks it's necessary."

Forty-five minutes later, they were back in the car. "She seems to know her stuff. Thanks for allowing me to stay. I got a much better idea how this all happened," Darren said.

Colby played with a tassel that hung on her purse strap, flipped it back and forth, ran her thumb through the fringe. "Where are we going? My car's back on campus."

"We're stopping by your apartment to get your things, whatever you'll need for the next several days. You agreed to move in with me. I have a call in to the student housing people to rent out your space for a few weeks. You might as well make a little money from the arrangement."

Colby didn't say anything until they were just a few blocks from her apartment. From the corner of her eye, Darren sensed her sister was about to explode. Not unexpected. It had to come eventually. This wasn't going to be fun for either of them for some time to come.

"I'll go in with you, so I can help carry things out to the car, not to supervise or make sure you don't run off," Darren said.

Her sister finally spoke. "What if I did run off? Would you send the police after me?"

"No. You're not my prisoner. You can leave, go off on your own whenever you want. But if you do, I'm not coming after you nor coming to your rescue any longer. Do you understand?"

Colby released a frustrated huff, but she nodded just the same.

CHAPTER 8

"Welcome back," Mike said as he opened the door of his new loft apartment to Darren later that afternoon. He lifted a brow. "Everything taken care of?"

"Yes, I think so."

The anxiety he'd seen in her eyes the previous times he'd seen her today seemed to have faded somewhat, although there was still an air of something off kilter about her.

He'd really like to know why she suddenly needed ten thousand dollars, not just out of curiosity, but also because he felt a sincere desire to help her. But she'd made it clear she didn't want to discuss her family crisis further, so he'd respect her wishes. Maybe as they worked further on this project, she'd feel comfortable enough to confide in him.

"How 'bout a tour?" he asked, sensing she needed to put that topic behind her. "Won't take long, but I'm quite impressed with the place."

"Sounds good."

"So, what do you think?" he asked, once the tour concluded.

"It's much smaller than what you're used to in the mansion,

but it seems to be providing you with the peace and tranquility you wanted."

"That it does. The location's okay for now, although I'm not crazy about it being so far from Sullivan's Creek, but I can work around that. Only need to sleep and shower here. The bed is adequate, mattress firm like I like them. Even the bonus of a walk-in shower." Both of which they could have checked out together the previous night had her sister's problems not taken precedence.

She didn't appear to pick up on his inference. The events of the last day seemed to have driven all thoughts of their hooking up from her mind. "You said your mother has already checked it out and called it sterile. Do you like that part?"

Ah, she'd moved on to interior decorator mode, trying to gain insight into his tastes for his own house. "I'm assuming she meant it reflected none of my own personality. Guess I'd agree with her on that. I want me in my new house."

She opened her tablet and made a notation. "Okay, that was the first clue. Good. So, what parts of you do you want the house to echo?"

"Beats me."

"You don't know who you are?"

"Sure, I do. But I don't know how that translates to decorating. That'll be your job."

She rolled her eyes. "I get that, but I need your help. Tell me about yourself."

He flopped in one of the two black leather easy chairs that faced the charcoal-gray tweed upholstered sofa where she planted herself. "Pull up my website. That pretty much summarizes who I am. I suffered through a long, boring interview with the PR person who put it together."

"Okay, this is a start. I'll read some statements out loud, and you tell me if they're still true or need to be updated."

He'd meant to put an end to the discussion, but she apparently wasn't to be deterred. "Is this really necessary? I don't like talking about myself."

"Hmm. No ego?"

"Didn't say that. Just exercise it other ways."

"Like how?"

"How? Now you're sounding like a shrink."

"No, I'm trying to pin you down with something we can use to get started on this project."

She was right. Quite serious about earning her ten thousand dollars. "Let me think." He stretched back in the chair, rested his neck on his hands. "Okay. I have money, both my own and access to the family assets. No secret there. I've grown up with it, so I'm not like others who've made their money on their own later in life and therefore feel they have to prove their worth all the time by flaunting it."

"I've noticed."

He lifted a brow. Not the response he expected. He'd meant he wasn't into displays of opulence. What was she getting at? "That's a good thing, right?"

"Let's not go there."

This had now gotten interesting. "Let's. You brought it up. Are you referring to when I refused the paintings? Did I intimidate you?"

"No, that angered and frustrated me." She paused, cocked her head as if a new thought had struck her. "You own another home already, out in California. How is it furnished?"

"Purchased as is. I'm there so infrequently these days it's more a like a hotel than a home."

Darren sat back, put down her tablet. "Did you hear what you just said?"

"What?"

"You said you view your place on the West Coast like a hotel rather than a home. That's telling, don't you think?"

"Never thought about it before. It's there for when I need it. It has the same things as here, comfortable bed, nice shower, fridge for storing beer and deli food."

"What color is the bedroom?"

"Hmm. Not dark, because I like the way the morning sun shines in when I raise the blackout shades. Uh, white, beige, light yellow. I guess."

"You guess. Okay, what kind of bed? Sleigh, four-poster, low post, upholstered?"

"Stop! I have no idea except the mattress is comfortable and there's plenty of room, so it must be king-sized."

She sighed, got up and paced. "Okay, forget that idea." A few beats later, she pivoted. "Quick, tell me your favorite color."

"Blue. But I don't want much of that in the house."

"Why not?"

"I hate this game. If you must know, it's my color. My go-to color when I want to be alone."

"Interesting. I'll keep that in mind."

"Ready to give up?"

The pacing stopped. She reclaimed her tablet and switched it off. "Not giving up. This was just my first pass. But it's clear these approaches aren't working as well as I'd hoped. Do you want to meet me at the house tomorrow so I can take measurements, or do you want to give me a key?"

He found a second key and handed it over. "I'd like to be there, at least for your first time in your new official capacity."

They made arrangements to meet the next morning at nine and she headed for the door. She jerked to a stop before she reached it. "You, uh, did take care of your unwanted visitors, right?"

He'd already forgotten about the raccoon family other than to regret their inopportune appearance. He chuckled. "That day. The crew searched the house for other sightseers and came up empty."

∼

Darren dropped Colby off at school the following morning. "Come back to the studio after classes. Don't go to your apartment alone. We'll pick up the rest of your things later."

Colby grunted and slammed the door.

At least the girl had gotten herself dressed and come along with her. Progress, of sorts.

Though Darren had spent the previous evening trying to gauge her sister's mood every few minutes without Colby noticing, she'd managed to get in a little research for herself. She'd gone on the internet and searched how-to information for wannabe interior designers. To her relief, many of the elements of art transferred to her new assignment. Problem was, even though she was thoroughly familiar with those elements, getting Mike to fill in the blanks was going to be one huge challenge. Still, she couldn't help believing deep down Mike knew what he wanted. It was just a matter of tapping that hidden well.

Mike had beaten her there. "Brought you coffee this time." He handed her a container. "You took it black yesterday, so I followed suit today. Okay?"

"Yes. Thanks." She tried not to recall the last time she'd been here. Now that she was Mike's decorator, the hanky-panky that might have happened then was a thing of the past. From here on, she needed to be at her professional best. She parked her tablet and purse near the card table and wandered around the first floor, getting a feel for the location of windows and other natural light sources. She'd always been a fan of Monet and the other Impressionists, but until her research the night before, she hadn't given much thought to lighting as a major element of interior design.

"What are you checking?"

"The light over here in the everyday dining area. Since your house faces east, this area in the back won't get much sun until later. Come over and tell me if this is enough natural light for you."

He flipped on an overhead light switch. "You're right. It is sorta dark. But it's okay with me."

"Additional fixtures will give you more light when you want it."

"If this is everyday dining, does that mean there's also a formal dining room?" he asked.

"Probably that spot over there on the other side of the kitchen. What do the plans indicate?"

He raised his shoulders. "Beats me. Never looked at them."

"You're kidding!"

"Should've, I know. But when I bought the place, I didn't plan to live here."

"Do you at least have them?"

"Not here. But I can locate them."

"And the specs." Once she had those, she wouldn't need to measure everything.

After a brief knock at the door, Ned Collier burst in. "Saw the cars outside. Thought I'd stop by and be neighborly." Then he noticed her. "Hi, Darren. Didn't expect to see you here."

Mike answered for her. "Darren took pity on me and agreed to do the interior decoration."

"Great idea! Leave it to my buddy to bring in a bona fide artist to do the job. I should've thought of that, although Shae's been having too much fun with our place."

That gave Darren an idea. "I'd love to see it. I'm sure Mike would, too."

"Hey, yeah. She's busy putting stuff in the kitchen cabinets, but she'd love to show off what we've accomplished. C'mon over."

"Now?" Mike asked.

"Sure. Mom has seen it, of course, but other than her, you'll be the first visitors. Only fitting."

Darren and Mike followed Ned in Mike's car. "Tell them whatever they want to hear about the place while we're there, but as soon as we leave, let's talk about what you liked and didn't like," Darren said as they drove

"You suggesting we copy Ned and Shae's place?"

"No, of course not. Besides your folks' place and your new apartment, it's the most tangible living lab available we have. Maybe this will work better than what we've tried so far." She certainly hoped so, because thus far she had pretty close to nothing in mind for his house.

Ned was waiting for them at the front door. "Welcome." He turned toward the inner part of the house. "Shae? We've got our first company."

A sound, presumably from the kitchen, where Ned had told them Shae was working, greeted them. In a few seconds, Shae—at least it looked like Shae under all that grime and dust—trudged around a corner. "Uh, hi, guys. Darren, isn't it? Haven't seen you since your showing." She turned to her housemate. "I didn't think we were quite ready yet for visitors, Ned." Her voice assumed that universally recognized, sickeningly sweet tone shared by couples who weren't quite in synch.

"Darren and Mike aren't exactly visitors. When I stopped by his house, I invited them to see how our place is coming together."

A smile broke through Shae's previously perturbed expression. "Yeah? We're pretty proud of what we've done. But we're not quite finished, so don't judge it yet. In fact, Darren, we could use your artist's eye a couple of places."

Darren had been prepared to make up some reason why they couldn't stay, but Shae's apparent change of heart kept her there, trying to take in the room without being too obvious and failing miserably. They'd stepped into a foyer about twelve-foot deep. What appeared to be closets lined one side, and the other wall boasted a small reception table. Nice place to hang a theme piece. Maybe something she could do for them.

At Ned's urging, they moved farther into a large room with a vaulted ceiling and exposed mahogany-stained beams. The walls were painted a nondescript neutral color. Depending on the light, it appeared to be gray, taupe, or green. Off to the left, a huge fireplace trimmed in light stone and topped with a mahogany mantel took the place of honor. Facing it was a long, tan sofa. Two honey-blonde leather club chairs framed one side, and a brown leather recliner held its own on the other side.

The floor was done in engineered walnut wood, although a large tan area rug filled the space in front of the fireplace.

All in all, charming.

While the two men went off to explore, Shae approached, wiping her face with a towel. "I thought construction was a dirty job. I had no idea prepping cabinets could also be so messy."

"You look fine. I'm sorry we surprised you. I had no idea Ned hadn't called you from his car."

"He may have. I left my phone in this room while I tackled the kitchen. Want to see? There's a lot more to be put away, but you can get a good idea from what's done so far."

The kitchen was large with cabinets on opposite walls and a large island down the middle. The same color from the great room was used on the noncabinet wall. White granite countertops with swirls of gold offset the mahogany cabinets.

"What do you think?" Shae asked, just a tad too anxious.

"It's beautiful. A real showroom, although I'm probably not the one to assess this particular room in the house. I don't cook much."

Shae indicated one of the barstools while she took the other. "Me, either. I'm more into ordering, opening fast-food bags or heating frozen food."

"Of which Ned is, of course, aware?"

Shae chuckled and nodded. "Oh, yes. He figures this fancy kitchen probably won't change my style, but he wanted it to look good in case some journalist comes calling to do a story about his home life, now that he's relocated to Iowa." She examined a platter before putting it away. "Are you and Mike a thing now? You didn't exactly seem to hit it off that night at the showing."

Now it was Darren's turn to chuckle. "Believe it or not, I'm his interior decorator."

"Really? I didn't know you'd branched out."

"I haven't, with this exception. Seems Mike goes through decorators like I go through paint rags and was desperate to get started. I took pity on him. No, that's not true. Well, maybe a little, but I also needed the money for a personal issue. To make matters worse, he wants this all done by Christmas. Maybe doable for a professional decorator, but I'll probably spend most of that time trying to pin down his tastes."

"Mike? Luxurious. High end. At least that's been my impression of him since we met several months ago."

"I would have thought that, too, except when I've mentioned those terms, he shies away from them. Almost like he's denying his background."

Shae gathered up several boxes that had formerly held dishes and glasses, then eyed Darren. "That's why you're here, isn't it? So Mike can check out our situation and say yeah or nay."

Foiled. She squeezed her eyes shut. "Saw right through that, huh? I hope you don't mind. This is just my first day on this project, and I'm already running out of ways to determine what he wants."

"I don't understand. As a big-time businessman, Mike makes decisions constantly. Decisions involving thousands, sometimes millions, of dollars. He can't tell you whether he wants tile or hardwood, dark or light kitchen cabinets?"

Darren made a face, the kind that said she'd run up against a brick wall and had no idea where to go from there. "That's about the size of it."

"That's so unlike Mike. He tends to have too many opinions. Same as me. Our whole relationship has been characterized by one negotiation after another. Why don't you just start putting together something you'd like and let him react to that?"

"I've already struck out twice attempting to outguess him." She related how Mike had rejected both seascapes until he took pity on her and bought them both.

"It was just a thought. I'm sure you'll come up with something." Shae's eyes strayed to a box of silverware that had yet to be opened.

"Would you like some help with all this?"

Shae pursed her lips. "Another pair of hands would get me through all this faster, but …"

"You really want to do this by yourself. I'm not offended. It's your first home, right? Far be it from me to keep you from that enjoyment."

Shae gave her a bright smile. "Thanks for understanding."

Darren went in search of the two men, who were just emerging from one of the rooms on the other side of the house.

"This guy has some layout," Mike said, "complete with music room."

"That was a given," Ned replied. "Especially since this is home from now on." He turned to Shae, who'd followed Darren from the kitchen. "How's the kitchen coming?"

"I need you to finish off the top shelves."

Ned faced their visitors, held up his hands surrender-style. "Duty calls."

Mike and Darren said their thanks and took off.

Darren pounced as soon as they were inside Mike's car. "So? What did you think?"

"Nice place. Suits Ned. As well as Shae."

"Suits them how?" She wasn't letting him off the hook that easy.

He scratched his head. "Geez, this is more of that psychological stuff, isn't it?" He released a drawn-out sigh for show. "Okay, it was formal and casual at the same time. What Ned needs for entertaining and to look filthy rich for the media and yet still comfortable enough for just the two of them to relax."

"Could you live there?"

"I suppose, if I had to. But ..."

"Yes?"

"Those beams didn't do it for me. Don't ask why. They just seemed imposing."

"Thought you said you liked wood in your decorating scheme?"

"Not overhead, I guess."

"We'll scratch that idea off the list."

"Obviously, I don't need a music room, but it might be nice to use that same amount of space for an office. Two separate rooms or one that blends into another, so I have my own private space but also a place for business meetings."

"You don't want to use your living room for that?"

He considered as they pulled into his driveway. "No, I want the living room for nonbusiness company and entertaining."

She opened her own door before he could make it around the car. "Business associates will have to go through the living room to get to your office. Or will you want a separate entrance, which means more construction."

He shrugged. "Don't mind their traipsing through the living room to get there. In fact, I kinda like the idea. Intimidating."

Interesting sidelight. "How about the colors?"

"Lighter than theirs. Cheerier. God, did I say that?"

"You did. And I'm holding you to it," she told him as they reentered the house. Time to get to her tablet and record these insights before she forgot any. It wasn't much to go on yet, but it was more than she'd had an hour ago.

She glanced around the great room and could picture it done in a cheery color. A cheery *light* color. Something between cream and yellow.

One more detail she needed to nail down before she set about ordering any furnishings. "You haven't given me a budget yet. How much do I have?"

He twisted around from gazing out the back windows and tilted his head. "Beats me, although I'm not going to give you carte blanche. How 'bout you put a list together before placing any orders and let me decide from there?"

"I'd prefer we decide on something now so I can get going. If it's not enough, I'll come back to the well and ask for more."

He closed his eyes in what appeared to be "give me strength" mode, but after a few beats, he opened them again and gave her a number. About three times more than she anticipated, but she wasn't going to quibble. Time to start figuring out how to spend it.

CHAPTER 9

Three days had passed since Darren grilled Mike about his decorating tastes. He slouched at the desk in his loft, staring yet again at his sales numbers. Right after he'd met with Darren, he'd been called back to the West Coast to attend to brush fires in a couple of his enterprises. Potentially serious but no sweat for him, once he located the source of the problems and removed the irritants, which resulted in firing a manager in one case and holding tight on a renegotiation in the other.

On his return trip, he'd stopped off in Houston and spent a few hours considering a new venture. He'd been tempted to sign off, but in the end, some sixth sense told him the outcome wasn't worth the risk.

This was what he did—moved from prospect to prospect, juggled his resources, tap-danced from one management crisis to another. The challenges, the change of pace, had been what he needed, a diversion from Sullivan's Creek, though every so often he wondered how Darren was doing, both with the design plan for his house but also with her sister's problems.

Back in town, it was time to face the facts. Sales continued to be slow, lagging behind his estimates. He'd been overly optimistic about what they could accomplish, especially this time of year, when most residential sales typically dropped off during winter. His overall financial resources were still sound, thanks to the solid gains he continued to realize in his other investments. But his ego hurt. It wasn't like him to be so far off the mark assessing sales potential.

The cold, hard truth was that he wasn't a real estate agent. He might understand real estate finance in the macro sense, but down at the micro lot by lot level, he was stumped.

Ned's tie to Sullivan's Creek should have been enough to bring buyers calling, but somewhere along the line interest had drifted away or never materialized. Plus, his voice now mended, Ned was more focused on performing. Whatever time not spent on his career went to setting up housekeeping with Shae.

The sound of knocking brought Mike out of his wallowing. He opened the door to his father, who immediately charged past him. His dad didn't settle, despite Mike's invitation of a seat on the sofa. Instead, his visitor flitted throughout the room, checking the view from the windows, swinging through the small kitchenette, opening and closing whatever door he met along the way.

"For this you walked out on all the conveniences and comfort of the mansion and broke your mother's heart?"

Mike had learned long ago to avoid replying to direct questions like that. They only served to provide additional fodder for his parents' arguments. "It's just temporary. Until my own house in Sullivan's Creek is finished."

Joseph Woodley stopped pacing long enough to face down his son. "You're really going through with that idea? I thought you'd only built a house to reinforce your commitment to prospective buyers."

"Perhaps. At first. But the place is growing on me. I plan to stick around town a while longer than I originally thought."

His dad still didn't sit. The guy seemed more agitated than

usual. Why? Surely, Mike's moving out hadn't triggered such tension? Foolish or not, he plunged ahead. "What brings you here, Dad? Mom already visited the day after I moved in. Surely, she's kept you apprised?"

His father jerked his head. "I'm not supposed to visit my son myself and check out his latest bad decision?"

Mike again sidestepped his dad's comments, attempted instead to put the old man on the spot. "Of course, you're welcome. Any time. But I've been here over two weeks. Why pick today to question my relocation?"

Finally, his dad did take a seat. Not the proffered sofa, but one of the two club chairs. "Would have been here sooner, but you apparently chose to leave town."

Ah. His dad had been keeping tabs on his whereabouts. Shouldn't be surprised. Still, it irritated him that his life wasn't his own. "Want a tour? You've already seen most of the place, but let me show you my room."

"I didn't come for a tour. I want to know what it will take to get you back in the family business."

The man couldn't take a no. Perhaps that quality had kept his dad in the forefront of his business dealings, but Mike was tired of the tactic. He mentally counted to ten. "I don't get it, Dad. You've got the whole clan except me tied up in Woodley Industries. Why do you need me? Is it an ego thing? You have to secure a hundred percent involvement of your offspring to show your competitors you've got your family in line?"

Joseph Woodley slammed a hand against his thigh. "That's ridiculous. My ego doesn't need stroking."

Mike begged to differ, but it wasn't worth the debate. "Okay. For the sake of argument, what would you have me do? Jay, Gardner and Dash cover all the major responsibilities you don't handle yourself. Are you planning to demote one of them just so I'll have something to do?"

His dad's gaze shifted abruptly from him to a corner wall and back to him. "Don't concern yourself with details. Things will work out."

Interesting. This was no idle promise. Clearly, his dad had already connected the dots on this one. For the moment, though, probably until Mike caved, the man had no intention of sharing. "Look, Dad, I wish you'd stop placing me in the position of having to disappoint you. I don't like letting you down, but I've told you more than once, I don't see myself being part of the company. Not now, probably not ever."

His dad pulled himself up, a pink tinge coloring his neck. "Why do you have to be so stubborn? You're not a selfish person, Michael. You've always been the most dependable of my children. Except for this."

"Dad, I …"

"You said 'probably not ever.' You left just enough wiggle room to make me wonder what it would take to get your interest."

Geesh! Why'd he imply there might be the slightest bit of hope? Deep down, was there a chance he'd change his mind? "Forget it. I meant no. Not now. Not ever."

"But …" Suddenly, his dad grabbed his chest and struggled for air.

"Dad? Are you okay?"

His dad attempted to speak, but all he could do was nod, as if dismissing the very clear evidence all was not well.

Mike guided his dad back to his seat and ripped at the top two buttons on the front of his dad's shirt. Call 911? Instead, he charged to the kitchen and filled a glass with water. He returned to the living room within twenty seconds. His dad seemed to have improved slightly but still took a couple of swigs of the liquid.

"Dad? What's going on? Is it your heart?"

Still clutching his chest, his father shook his head, attempted to speak. "Nah! I'm fine. Don't concern yourself."

"The hell you're fine! What's really going on?"

"Just a slight chest cold. Coughing spell."

Mike hadn't heard a single cough. Chest cold? Maybe. But his dad had definitely experienced pain in the chest region.

"Look, I'm going to take you to the emergency room. Get this checked out."

His dad's head shaking increased. "No, no. I'm fine. Don't want to scare your mother." The *threat* of a hospital visit seemed to revive his dad enough for him to get to his feet and head for the door. "Got to be going. Think over my proposal. Give it some serious consideration." At that, he was out the door before Mike could stop him.

What was that about? He'd never seen his dad that way, as if he was about to keel over any second. One minute he'd been fuming about Mike's reticence to join the family business and the next showing every indication of a heart attack. But his dad refused to admit to any signs of human infirmity.

Before Mike considered his actions, he called in reinforcements. "Look, Mom, I don't want to scare you, but I'm worried about Dad. He was just here, pressuring me again to join the business, and all of a sudden he was out of it, gripping his chest."

"How is he now?" she asked. Strange, her reaction was calm and collected. He would've thought she'd go ballistic.

"Told me it was a chest cold. He took a few minutes to collect himself, sipped some water I brought him, then said he was fine. Then he left before I could convince him to go the emergency room."

"He, uh, has been complaining about a cough. I'll track him down and get him to rest. Don't worry. I'm sure he's fine."

She didn't sound like his mother. She was usually the first to go into hysterics at the least sign of physical ailment.

She even changed the subject. "I stopped by to visit with Janice Collier the other day. Sprung my idea about holding a showing at our house. I think she went for it, although we didn't sign anything."

He'd just told her he thought his dad might be suffering from heart problems, and she wanted to talk about a showing? What was going on?

Why did they do this to him? He'd deliberately moved out of their vortex so he could keep his distance from family matters, yet here he was, inserting himself into their business once again. If his mother wasn't concerned about his dad's health, maybe he'd overreacted to the scene he'd just witnessed. Right. He knew better. Resist though he might, he had to check this out further.

DARREN SPENT the same three days developing the design plan, when she wasn't either keeping an eye on her sister or helping her move into the studio.

"This really isn't necessary," Colby said as she unpacked the last of her underthings. Her mood ranged between petulant child and arrogant attorney-to-be. "If they want to find me, all they have to do is show up on campus."

"Probably so. But if they do, hopefully you'll be smart enough to stay in public places."

"You think that would discourage this group?"

"Group? How many people are involved in this setup?" There'd been three people at the supermarket when they'd turned over the money, but the two guys who'd served as lookouts for the woman who grabbed the check seemed more like flunkies than actual gang members.

"I don't know exact numbers, except that each time I've dealt with someone else. Yet I've never felt like any of them were the head honcho." For the first time in days, Colby's tone turned confidential. "This is a bigger deal than I ever imagined, Darren. At first, I thought only one or two grad students were calling the shots. But they're just the lackeys, the ones who pull in unsuspecting fools like me. The real brains may not even be in town. They could be part of a larger network."

Darren glanced up from her notebook. This was the most information Colby had revealed yet about the gambling ring. Until now, her comments had been denials or suggestions Darren mind her own business. Perhaps getting professional help really was helping. "How's your counseling coming along?" They'd agreed she wouldn't probe, but she couldn't stop herself.

Colby cocked a brow and stared her down. "I went yesterday, if that's what you're getting at. I'm not supposed to discuss my sessions. Plus, you agreed not to push. But if you want proof that I'm going, I'll ask for signed notes."

Damn! This was like feeling her way in the dark. She kept tripping over things. "I'm sorry. You're right. I promised not to push."

Colby continued to eye her. "You're concerned I'll backslide, since I've already done that. More than once. I can't promise I won't slip again, but I'm trying. Each day is a new day. That's one thing my counselor has instilled in me."

Darren gave her a quick hug, then backed away. "Good to hear."

"I know you're worried. You've always been there to carry my water when I've needed it. But this time, I have to step up. Late as it is. Those bruises were real. Convinced me what I'd gotten myself into was real."

Colby's words sounded good. Reassuring. But the girl was training to be an attorney. These could just be words to prevent Darren from worrying further, or worse, from questioning Colby's moves. Darren couldn't relax and feel confident the storm had passed.

Colby settled next to her on the davenport. "Enough about me. What have you been up to with all these design books? You haven't gone near your easel in days."

Darren had been so focused on observing Colby without asking questions whenever they'd been together, she hadn't bothered to mention her new job. "I've agreed to do the interior design for the new home of one of my clients."

Colby inclined her head. "A bit outside your bailiwick, isn't it?"

"Quite a bit. But he was desperate, and the money was good." She didn't say how much or for what she was using it.

Colby shifted position to once again stare her down, but when Darren didn't add details, Colby relaxed.

"This wasn't by any chance the *client* who bought those two seascapes that first night I was here?"

No point in hiding his identity. "As a matter of fact, yes. His name is Michael Woodley. He's partnered up with the entertainer, Jake Bonneville, to develop farmland west of town into a residential community called Sullivan's Creek. His own new home is located there."

"Wow. That's quite a score. Is he one of the town's famous Woodleys?"

Darren nodded. "But unlike the rest of the family, he's an independent entrepreneur and not part of the family business."

"But still wealthy, right?"

Where was Colby headed with this line of questions? Darren's palms itched, warning her to skate carefully. "I guess, but most of his money is tied up in his investments."

"He's just your client? Nothing more?"

She'd almost had sex with the man because he was available and interested. But she wasn't about to reveal any of this to Colby. "Nothing more."

Unable to gain more information, Colby rose, reclaimed the law book she'd been studying earlier. "Too bad. He'd be a great catch."

She was out of the room before Darren could reply, although she had no idea what she would have said.

Whatever. She had a design plan to finish. She'd already

landed on a tentative color scheme. Now it was time to select basic furniture pieces. After several false starts, she'd found software where all she had to do was enter dimensions, and the program would let her move the object wherever she wanted. The trick was to find items that didn't require special ordering, or if they did, special orders that could be turned around in a matter of weeks.

First, she had to select the big items. From there, she'd add the side pieces. And finally, she'd get around to decorations and auxiliary items. Easy enough, right?

She started with the living room. A sectional. Yes, that would take up the better part of the room and seat several people for entertainment purposes. But when she pulled up screen after screen of possibilities, nothing captured her attention. Okay, scratch the sectional. She'd do two sofas facing each other with a classy table in the center and some serious chairs filling in the third side. It only took a few tries before she found a medium-brown tweed she liked. These would look great with the pale yellow, almost-ivory paint color she'd selected for the walls.

Those details settled, she moved on to the master bedroom. She remembered the question she'd asked Mike about the style of bed he preferred. Too bad he hadn't given her a clue. What would she want if she had unlimited funds? Big. She knew that much. With night tables on both sides.

But the more she pictured such a bed, the more she squirmed in her seat, heat fanning its way from her privates down her legs and up through her belly. No, this couldn't be. Just envisioning herself in the bed meant for Mike was turning her on? Had Colby's insinuations about their relationship triggered this reaction?

Okay, enough fantasizing. Put the bedroom on hold and work on the dining room and kitchen. But the idea burrowed into her head and only got worse. She couldn't see the dining-room table without herself seated at one end and Mike at the other, enjoying a dinner she'd cooked for him. She'd cooked? This really was a fantasy.

The kitchen was worse. Once she pondered countertops, she was unable to conjure up thoughts of food prep. Instead, she imagined the two of them doing it on one surface after another. Not that she needed an excuse, but she doubted she'd be fixing meals for some time.

CHAPTER 10

ike thought he was opening his apartment door to Darren, a fifteen-minute-early Darren, and instead found Jay.

"Mornin', bro." Jay swept past him. "Brought you a moving-out present." He held up what appeared to be a coffee grinder. "Don't thank me, other than for delivering it. Mom sent it over."

"Uh, thanks."

"She's convinced you're living in absolute squalor," Jay said, nosing around the condo. "Like fresh-ground coffee is going to raise your standard of living."

"She meant well. I'll call and thank her later. How come she didn't bring it herself? If only to check on me again."

"She caught me sneaking out, and I couldn't come up with a plausible excuse fast enough, so I told her the truth. She grabbed this from the kitchen, so she'll probably be sending Tammy shopping for a new one later today."

"Wanted to make sure I remembered her." Back up. Jay had actually gotten their housekeeper's name right. Progress, whatever that meant.

That line of conversation ended, both were silent for a few

beats. "Since everyone else at the old homestead has been here to check out the place, including Tammy, thought I'd better make an appearance. The way Mom described it, your loft sounded like you'd moved into a monastery. But this place is far from it." Like their mother, he checked closets and the other rooms first. "Nice. Too bad there's not a second bedroom, or I'd consider moving in with you."

Mike thanked his stars he'd only asked for a one-bedroom. "What? With Ned and I both moved out of the mansion, you should have all kinds of space there."

"Space, yes. Privacy, no. Didn't realize how much I prized it since my divorce until moving in with Mom and Dad."

"Then why did you?" Blunt, but so far, their parents and Jay had remained silent about his accompanying them to town.

Jay studied his nails. "Cheaper. Alimony and child support were bleeding me dry."

While Mike didn't doubt that his brother's financial resources had taken quite a beating the last few years, he suspected his dad also wanted Jay in the same town for more direct supervision. But why push the point?

Mike changed the subject. "Got a question for you about Dad's health. What's going on there?"

Jay returned a blank expression. "Whaddaya mean? Dad's strong as an ox."

"Don't doubt you there, but how healthy is he? As he was blowing up at me yet again for turning down his offer to join the corporation, he was suddenly fighting for breath."

"Wonder if that's why he and Mom stopped talking when I entered the room a couple of times."

"Recently?"

"Yeah, since we've been in town. But if something's wrong, they haven't told me."

"Well, keep your eyes and ears open and let me know if you find out anything."

"Okay, sure." Jay appeared to turn inward, as if processing Mike's question. "The real reason I'm here …"

A gentle rapping at the door cut off the rest of his sentence. Darren. Right on time.

Mike opened the door to find her holding two containers of coffee, her purse and computer bag hanging off one shoulder and a portfolio clutched under the other arm.

"Wasn't sure if you'd had your morning java yet," she told him, dashing by him to set the brew on his kitchen counter. Then she noticed Jay. "Oh, sorry. I thought we were supposed to meet at nine. I hope I'm not breaking up a meeting."

"You're not," he replied. "This is my brother, Joseph Woodley Jr. Jay. He dropped by to check my new place."

Jay rose and approached Darren to shake her hand. "And you're?"

"Darren Williams, your brother's interior decorator."

Jay turned inquiring eyes toward Mike, a knowing smile playing across his face. "Interior decorator, huh? You just moved into this place and you're already redoing it?"

Damn. Why did Darren have to be so prompt? And open. Five more minutes and he could've gotten rid of Jay to avoid this scene. "Apparently Mom hasn't yet shared my invitation for the family to enjoy Christmas dinner with me at my new home in Sullivan's Creek. Darren is helping me get the house ready in time."

"Got ya." Jay switched his attention back to Darren, his eyes taking her in like a cat gazing at an unsuspecting bird. "Darren Williams? That name sounds familiar. We couldn't have met, because I just moved back to town. I know! Our mother mentioned having met you recently at the house. You're a local artist, right?"

"That's right. Mike commissioned a painting from me a few months back, and I was at the mansion delivering it."

"Then you're also an interior decorator?" In a flash, Jay's

interest level appeared to far outweigh his need for such information. "I'll keep that in mind when I get my own house."

"What's this?" Mike asked. "Thought you'd set up camp permanently at the mansion?"

"Like I just told you, you're not the only one who could use some privacy. Actually, that's why I'm here. Besides a friendly brotherly visit, I wanted to know if you've found someone to handle your sales at Sullivan's Creek yet."

Though he'd not had any bites to the subtle feelers he'd put out for a real estate specialist, Mike still didn't want to involve his brother in his business dealings. "Uh, nothing's changed there since we last talked. I'm handling sales."

"How's that going?" his brother asked.

Mike shot a glance at Darren, who, though sorting through some notes, was taking in this whole conversation. "Now that Darren's here, we need to get started with our meeting. How 'bout I call you later?"

"Why not finish your talk while I wait in the bedroom? I've got some quotes I want to check anyhow," Darren said.

"No, we can …"

"I'd really like a few more minutes, bro. I want to share some research I did on housing sales in the area."

Darren disappeared into the bedroom.

"Jay, you're forcing me to turn you down. I hoped we could avoid a confrontation."

"Just take a minute or two to read through this before you say anything more." He shoved a folder in Mike's chest.

Humor the guy. Read through his findings. He couldn't have unearthed anything Mike didn't already know. But to his surprise, the report was a summary of follow-ups from people who had shown interest in the development but later dropped out. Mike had called some of them, asked why they'd passed but failed to garner much more information from them than "the place just didn't meet their expectations." They hadn't gone into detail what those expectations were.

"Is this credible?"

"Of course, it is. Had to wine and dine three different agents to get them to spill."

"How did you get them to talk? I contacted them, too, after their clients walked, but they said they couldn't shed any light on the reasons."

"Took some finesse, several glasses of wine and a few well-placed hints that I might be in the market for a place of my own before they opened up. You, dear brother, for all your far-flung enterprises and entrepreneurial creds intimidate the locals. Plus, it's no secret around town that you got involved with Sullivan's Creek when your pal's finances tanked, and there's still a small cloud shadowing people's perceptions."

"Can I keep this?" To his surprise, his brothers' work could be a gold mine, but he needed more time to absorb and analyze the conclusions. If this stuff was true, it provided a whole new approach to marketing the vacant lots.

Jay returned a pleased smile. "Sure. This is just a sample of how I can help you, if you take me on. Plus, I've now established an in with three of the town's top realty firms."

"Look, Jay, you've definitely done your homework and demonstrated your ability, but what would Dad say if I hired you away from the family business? He's already furious with me for not signing on."

"I haven't exactly been Dad's star employee of late. A break might be good for both him and me. Plus, who's to say I'd have to join you for more than a year or so? Just long enough to reduce your inventory." He started for the door. "Give it some thought."

Mike stared at the folder Jay had given him for several beats after the door closed. Finally, he went to his desk and flung the analysis on top. Though anxious to review Jay's findings in more depth, he needed to meet with Darren first.

He found her in the bedroom, on her stomach on the bed, sorting through various pieces of paper. Her off-the-shoulder tan sweater had slipped to one side, revealing a red bra strap. The fact that she'd made herself so comfortable in his private quarters sent all thoughts of Jay's report and whatever Darren had come to talk about from his mind. All he saw was Darren, and all he could think of was joining her there.

"I knew there was something missing from this place. A woman warming my bed." His voice had gone low and hoarse.

She blinked, then seemed to realize the scene she'd set. "It's quite comfy."

"Yeah? Mind if I join you?" He didn't wait for her answer as he yanked his black pullover over his head, then unzipped his jeans.

"Suppose I say no?"

"Too late," he said. "I move fast when I want something. Besides discussing my house, we have other uncompleted business."

"Let me at least put my things aside."

Now in tight black briefs, an erection quite apparent, he grabbed her tablet, the stack of notes she'd been perusing, her purse and jacket and set them aside on a corner chair. "Let me do the honors," he said as she started to remove her sweater. "My first red brassiere. I like."

She leaned back on her palms and allowed him to make short work of stripping her down to her undies.

"Thought you'd be wearing matching panties." He feigned disappointment, although there was no disillusionment about the body he'd revealed. Taut muscles, long, slender legs and a chest that begged him to sample the wares.

"Sorry. Paying off my mortgage takes precedence over wardrobe. She grinned. "Plus, I didn't know I'd be showing off my lingerie when I dressed this morning. What happened to our meeting?"

"Later," he said, then attacked her neck column with his lips. She smelled so good, as he took in a citrus combined with floral scent. He nibbled her ear and just behind the lobe and felt her tremble. "You enjoy?" he asked, taking his lips away long enough to ask.

"Didn't know I was so sensitive there."

"Lay back. Let's locate your other sensitive areas."

She complied, and he climbed over her, his erection jutting into her stomach. He didn't want to kiss her just yet. Save that for once he had her begging for more. Instead, he ran a hand down one arm and around her waist to cup her butt, moving her even closer to him.

He whispered into her hair. "I like the feel of you. Firm and curvy at the same time."

In response, she skimmed a hand down his back and rubbed up against him. "The feeling's mutual."

Encouraged and aroused, he quickly relieved her of her bra, despite his interest in the color. Two full, perky, rose-tipped breasts waited his inspection. Inspect them he did. Inspect, touch, squeeze, taste. All the favorite things he'd been doing since he had sex in one of the mansion closets at age fifteen. This time was different. He couldn't get his fill despite his profound efforts to fill his mouth. Darren acted as if it was her first time sharing her pulchritude with a man, giving of herself while at the same time demanding his full attention. Who was he not to assuage the lady?

He sensed his need building. Time to get serious before he totally lost himself in the moment. In an instant, her panties joined her bra on the floor. His hands, then his mouth took over, savoring her reaction as he focused on her private parts. Almost blinded by his passion, he reached over to the nightstand, retrieved a condom and sheathed himself.

Before he entered her, he sought her lips and crushed his own over them. "You have no idea how much I've wanted this," he said as he moved his lips away.

"I hope it was worth the wait." Her own voice had grown dusky and breathless.

"God, yes!" He couldn't hold back any longer and plunged into her. After that, he lost focus while his body took over for his brain.

DARREN LAY BENEATH HIM, enjoying the feel of a man on her body. It had been so long, this was almost but not quite like the first time. Though she'd messed around with boys in high school and college, Gordy had been her first serious intimate relationship. That first time had been almost as much a free-for-all as this experience. They'd dated for over a month before they went to bed, and by then the tension had piqued to such a point they'd actually ripped off each other's clothes.

That was six years ago. They were in their early-twenties and thought they owned the earth. Maybe they did. For a few brief years. Then it all ended with his death.

She felt like a bear emerging into springtime after a long winter's hibernation. Her body had missed this, but with time, memories had faded—or perhaps her brain had stored them elsewhere to ease the pain. Sex with Mike threw her back into the world of taste and touch with a jolting reality she hadn't expected. She relished the sensations, delighted in his ministrations and started to feel whole again. She'd needed this, to be thrust into the male-female world again without having a chance to debate the sanity of it.

She was attracted to Mike, no doubt about that, but she'd agreed to join him in his bed as a way to heal. He didn't disappoint. He was older than Gordy had been before his death and definitely more experienced. Where Gordy had been tender and enthusiastic, Mike was proving to be knowledgeable and appreciative. He seemed to know every trick for leveraging a woman's sensuality, starting with the way he'd caressed her hair while savoring her neck and ending with his endurance during intercourse.

Her body felt hammered yet satiated as she waited for Mike to return to the land of the living. A tear slid unbidden from her eye. Then another. Before she could help herself, she was sobbing.

She rolled away from him, hoping he wouldn't hear. She sucked in deep breaths, swiped at her eyes. *Stop it. Get yourself under control.* Why was this happening? She'd just experienced the best sex in her life, and here she was weeping.

"That was great," Mike said on the other side of her.

"Uh-huh," was all she could utter.

He pulled her toward him and narrowed his eyes when he saw her. "Hey, what's going on? Why the tears?"

She couldn't talk. Just as well. What would she say?

"Are you okay? I, uh, didn't hurt you, did I?"

She shook her head, sniffed.

He left the bed briefly, returned with several tissues, which she gratefully accepted. He gave her a couple of minutes to get herself together. "Want to talk about it?"

No. Her loss still ran so deep she didn't want to discuss it with anyone. But since she'd been a ready participant a few minutes ago, she owed him some explanation. "I, uh, thought I was ready for this. It's been over two years since my fiancé was killed. But after a bit, memories kept sneaking into my brain to the point where finally I was overcome with emotions I couldn't put aside."

He propped himself up on one palm. "You lost a fiancé?"

"He was an engineering consultant in the Sudan and got caught in a surprise attack. I was told he was killed instantly, so at least he didn't suffer."

"I'm sorry. I didn't realize."

"I intentionally didn't tell you. I don't say much about him to anyone."

"This was the first time since …"

She nodded. "My body was ready. I've missed being with a man."

"Did I remind you of him? Is that what triggered this reaction?"

"No, it wasn't that. It was different with him. You're more, uh, masterful. But I was in love with him, so whatever he did, whatever we did, was our way of communicating."

He sat back. "Oh." He paused. "I get that."

She hadn't meant for him to feel rejected. "I'm sorry I went so weepy on you."

He took her hand. "Now that I know why, I understand. If I'd known about your fiancé, I would have respected your mourning."

"That's just it. It's been over two years. It's time to move on. Maybe the tears were my heart's way of closing the door."

He stared at her like he thought she was kidding herself. Couldn't blame him. He'd clearly indicated his aversion to commitments. That included playing counselor or comforter to an emotional partner.

He rose from the bed and grabbed for his briefs. "Why don't we just chalk this up to bad timing and get on with our meeting? Unless you want to shower first?"

She'd welcome a shower, but she sensed he wanted to get this meeting over with, including any more time with her, as soon as possible. She passed.

Dressed and back in the living room, she attempted to normalize conversation before launching into her big reveal of the sketches she'd prepared. "Are you going to take your brother up on his offer?"

Mike snapped his head in her direction. "What offer?"

"Maybe I misunderstood. I thought he said he'd like to take over selling your vacant lots."

"Oh. That. No. You just met Jay. You don't know him. I'd be taking a huge chance to hire him."

Better sense told her to drop the topic, but she couldn't believe the super businessman she believed Mike to be would turn his back on what seemed to her to be the solution to one of his major problems. "What about the report he brought you? Did it give you new information?"

"Some, yeah."

She continued to push. "Could you have come by it yourself eventually?"

"Maybe. But it was just one shot."

"A lucky shot, perhaps?"

"No. I'll give him that much. He does have some background in real estate. He used that knowledge to make this happen."

"In other words, he not only took the initiative, he succeeded?"

Mike had been pacing the room while they talked, coming closer to his desk with each pass. "Ready to talk about what you brought me?"

One more try. "Will you at least think about bringing him on board? You appear to be good at about anything you try, Mike, but why waste your energy on something at which you're not an expert when you could be investing in other ventures that will bring you a higher return?"

He faced her. She couldn't discern from his expression whether she'd gone too far. "Why are you pushing this? You barely met the guy, and yet you've become his advocate."

"Because I think he could relieve you of the unnecessary pressure under which you've been putting yourself. And he's your brother. We may not always appreciate our siblings, but we should take care of them."

He started to say something, but she cut him off. "That's it.

End of spiel. Now find some place comfortable to sit while I show you what I brought."

Why had she continued to bug him about his brother when she had her own project needs to satisfy? She had to break the tension somehow before she pulled out her drawings. "I could use some water."

He headed to the kitchenette. "I think our housekeeper stocked me up when she was here last week." He returned a minute later with a bottle for her.

"Thanks." She opened the liquid and took several sips, killing time and settling her nerves more than addressing her thirst.

Finally, she could put off the big reveal no longer. She flipped open her case and withdrew the drawings she'd carefully placed in sequential, and she hoped increasingly dramatic, order. "Thought we should do this like you're entering the house. Here's the great room." She lifted the cover page to show said area. "There's a few more to follow featuring specific parts of the room, but I wanted you to get the full picture first."

"Let me see it up close."

Reluctantly, she handed him the page. She'd hoped to go through everything before giving him the entire package, but maybe this was a sign of his interest. "Next, I've highlighted the entryway."

"Wait. What's this color on the walls?"

"It's somewhere between cream and yellow. That's what I created with my acrylic pens after I found a paint color called *Gosling Down.*"

"Why didn't you use the real paint on these?"

"I wanted to make sure you were okay with the color before I spent any money on supplies."

"From now on, spend the money. I want to see exactly what I'm getting. Make sure this isn't too yellow. I don't like yellow."

"But ..." Never mind. He may have indicated such a preference a few days ago, but if he didn't like it now, at least she had some definitive reaction to go by.

"Moving on to the entryway …"

"Will someone at the front door actually be able to see part of the kitchen?"

"Just the counter, stools and the everyday dining area at the back of the house."

"Is that the way it's built? I hadn't noticed."

She pulled out the photos she'd taken when she visited the house on her own and showed him. "Yes. I have the blueprints, too, if you want to see them."

He scowled at the photos. "When did you take these?"

"You were out of town, and I wanted to do another walk-through once I'd fleshed out a few of the ideas you see here. You gave me a key."

"Yeah. Okay. But this won't work. I don't want visitors to see the everyday dining area or this end of the kitchen unless they're invited back there."

This was news. Why hadn't he realized the openness of the layout before now? Or was that going to be her job, making him more aware of the house? "Uh, okay, but that's going to require additional construction, which will mean more time."

"How much time? And how much will it cost?"

"Aren't you the one who'd have that information?"

"No. The technical stuff I leave to Shae. You'll have to check with her."

She'd have to check with Shae? Why wouldn't he? Whatever. She'd give Shae a call as soon as they finished. Meanwhile, they hadn't moved beyond the sketch of the entryway. There were a lot more to get through.

The rest of their discussion proceeded along the same lines, with Mike questioning items she'd assumed were set, like the flooring—at least that hadn't been installed and she could switch without having to rip something up—and her lighting choices—

he wanted sleek and modern instead of the more traditional fixtures she'd selected. He was okay with her furniture choices in the great room, but he didn't like the colors, which at least gave her more to go on than his complete dismissal of the headboard in the master bedroom. "Get rid of that tufted piece behind the bed. It looks like an old lady chair."

"What do you want there instead?"

"Something different."

"Do you at least like the style of bed? You're too tall for a sleigh bed, and I thought you'd hate a four-poster or canopied style, so I went with this extra-wide simple platform."

"The bed itself is okay, but sometimes I work on my laptop in bed. I need to be able to sit up and lean back comfortably."

Which was why she'd come up with the tufted headboard. "You want something stationary and kind to the back?"

"There you go. Keep the night stands but make them bigger so I can store more stuff in the drawers."

Like more condoms? Uh-oh. She was back to thinking about sex. She kept her head buried in the notes she was making on her tablet so he wouldn't see the knowing look which must have crossed her face.

By the time she packed up her portfolio, she was beat. Yes, she had a better idea what the man wanted in his new home, but the long list of changes and additions frazzled her brain.

"Darren?" he called as she made her way to the door.

No, no more changes. He'd just about exhausted her patience. "Yes?"

"You did good. You really helped me envision what I want. Things I never would have thought important or irritants came to me."

She attempted to keep him from seeing the huge sigh of relief she felt. *Take the high road. You needed that ten thousand.* "I'm glad we made some progress."

"How soon can you have a new set of sketches ready for me?"

They'd have to go through this again? *Give me strength.* "It will take at least a day to get the estimates on the new construction. How about two days from now?" She probably wouldn't sleep much in the interim, but if she could put a bow on all the details, it would be worth the yawns.

CHAPTER 11

That had been fun. Mike stretched out his six-one length on his sofa, folded his arms under his head and examined the ceiling. Darren might not agree, but the experience had been like a trip down a buffet line laid out for him by cordon bleu chefs, where he could pick and choose from the best of the best.

He liked what she'd done so far. Probably could've gotten by with her plan first time out of the shoot, but why settle when they still had a little time left before it had to be finished? The additional construction shouldn't be a problem, because Shae would go out of her way to appease him since he'd saved her boyfriend's bacon. He'd caught Darren making a few faces when she didn't think he was looking, but by her giving him specifics to evaluate, she'd made it so much easier to visualize his preferences.

He allowed himself the luxury of a five-minute power nap, then rose and resumed reading his brother's report. On closer examination, he realized how deftly Jay had maneuvered the realtors he'd quizzed into confiding their clients' private opinions. He hadn't simply asked them why the clients had passed on Sullivan's Creek. He'd pumped each realtor about their interactions with their clients—how they elicited their client's needs, desires and financial capacity, how they selected properties to show them, how much time they allotted for each property and finally, how they sequenced the properties they showed their clients. Successful seasoned realtors developed a strategy for each client, a strategy designed to net them the highest possible fee. Only newbies and mediocre realtors approached showings without a plan.

What emerged from Jay's schmoozing efforts were three reasons clients had passed. One, they'd only been able to view the model house, which didn't meet their needs, though they loved the area. Two, with no particular blueprint in mind, they didn't feel they'd received much help from Mike finding one. Finally, and the worst blow to his ego, they hadn't felt comfortable with him. Geez, he was likeable, wasn't he? How had he offended those people?

He pulled out his cell and called Jay. "Racquetball late this afternoon? We can try out the courts in my building."

"Sure. Had a chance yet to read what I brought you this morning, or are you still in your *meeting* with that Williams woman?"

He skipped over his brother's innuendo. "Meeting's over. Thought I'd grab a bite for lunch and read it then. We can talk later."

Jay agreed on a time, and Mike hung up. Forget about lunch, unless he could locate something Tammy left. He had some heavy thinking to do in the hours before he hit the court.

HE HADN'T BEEN on a racquetball court in some time, and his absence showed. Jay scored three times before Mike landed one.

"Probably should let you score a few more, if it means softening your mood about hiring me," Jay said, broaching the topic of the hour.

"Hey, it may have been a few months since I've played, but it's all coming back. I'm good to go."

"If that's the case, are you going to hire me or not?"

"Not so fast. I've got a few questions first."

Jay held up taking his serve. "Okay. Shoot."

"What gave you the idea to follow up with the realtors?"

"Something you said when we first talked about your marketing plan. You said you'd had several potential clients back out after showing initial interest. People who have no interest at all either never check you out in the first place or let you know almost immediately once they do visit that what you're offering isn't for them. If they're interested at the start and later pass, something happened to turn them off."

"But that something could be in the client's personal life, something between the client and realtor, or something to do with us, the seller. How did you know to focus on the last part, me?"

Jay launched a ball, and they played for another point before he answered. "I didn't, at first. But in the course of meeting with the first realtor, your name came up, and his body language told me he didn't want to go there. So naturally, that's where I went. Not directly, because it was obvious the guy didn't want to say anything about you. Whether the Woodley name intimidated him or something he knew about you personally, I couldn't tell."

Jay was purposely drawing out his explanation. But since the news he'd delivered was Grade A, Mike would allow his brother a certain amount of leeway. "So? How'd you get him to spill?"

"Put the subject of you on the sidelines. Instead, asked him what we should be doing differently. That's when the story came out about the couple who loved the area but had no idea what they'd build there. He'd offered to give them several builders' names as well as a couple of architectural firms. But they were Jake Bonneville fans and wanted his advice."

"Let me guess. Jake was nowhere in sight. Instead, they got me."

Jay took a short water break, then returned to the fray. "Not just you, but a you who, when he learned of their disappointment at not meeting Jake, did everything he could to avoid the subject of Jake rather than play it up. You could've offered to get his autograph or asked Jake to call them back personally, but you dropped the ball."

He remembered the couple. They'd shown up during the first few weeks Jake/Ned was back on the road. Mike hadn't wanted to bother his friend. Instead, he should've gotten him involved long distance. Couldn't have taken more than a few minutes, which might have resulted in a sale. "If you'd been in my position, what would you have done?"

"To tell the truth, it probably wouldn't have occurred to me to link them up with Jake, because I don't know the guy that well. But having heard the story now, if you put me in this position and a similar situation came up in the future, I'd do everything I could to leverage Jake's celebrity, although I'd talk it over with him first."

Jay's response surprised Mike. Here was his brother's chance to show him up, make himself look more empathetic, and he'd not taken it. "What about their needing help with a floor plan? Would you have suggested the kind of house they should build?"

Jay put down his racquet. "Look, guy, if this is a test of whether I can beat you at this game and still answer your questions to your satisfaction, I'll concede the game now. But I could use a shower before I go on."

Probably buying himself time to come up with a viable answer. Fine. Mike had more questions than that one to ask.

Showered, they made their way to the same coffee shop where Mike met with Darren just days ago. Jay took a sip of his latte and then set it aside. "Okay, advising that couple about a house plan? Yeah, I would've taken a stab. Not suggested a specific one, but I would've asked them questions about their preferences to the point where they could've identified at least a general style of house."

Shades of what Darren had been trying to do with him.

But Jay wasn't finished. "I would've used the model house as a jumping off point, found out what they liked about it and what they didn't like. Then I would've taken what I learned and showed them several examples in Sullivan's Creek. That's one area you really need to examine, bro, either adding another model, displaying additional floor plans in the model, or best of all, arranging with current owners to show their homes on occasion."

"We can't take advantage of our owners, or their houses will go on the market. We don't need any 'For Sale' signs in the development."

"Of course not. But you could consider a quarterly open house. Offer participants a discount on HOA dues. Or at least let them know you'll be driving potential new buyers past their homes on occasion to show off the best of the best."

Jay's knowledge and suggestions were no fluke. The guy really could handle the job, at least from a conceptual standpoint. How had Darren picked up on that before he did?

Jay clasped his hands and laid them on the table, his eyes fixed on them. Apparently he had something more to say and was debating how to broach it.

"I wasn't sure if I should stick in that point about you. Or if I did, whether I should downplay the language. In the end, I decided it would do you no good, nor my case, if I didn't address it full on." He gave Mike his direct attention. "You're not a realtor, Mike. You might be able to learn the people skills you need to convince people to buy your properties, but your time could be better spent on all the other moneymaking deals you've got going."

Hadn't Darren said something similar? Still, he was loathe to turn over control of sales to his brother. Or anyone, for that matter. "How would Dad react to your leaving the family business? Have you even told him you want to come work for me?"

"Hell no. I'll deal with him if, when, the time comes. Who knows, he might even wish me well. It's not like he depends on me that much anymore. Or ever did."

Jay almost admitted what Mike suspected, that Jay was struggling in his job, a major reason why Mike hesitated now to bring his brother on board. "Dad actually proposed I find someone to handle sales, although I doubt he ever suspected that might be you."

"Look, I know you're the family's golden boy. Everything you've touched seems to have come off a major success. I wasted precious time resenting you. My attitude probably ate into my work performance. Certainly hurt my marriage, although that was mainly Alicia's doing, because she kept throwing your wins in my face."

That was news. "Won't this *resentment* get in the way of your working for me?"

"No longer a problem. I never would've approached you if I still blamed you for my failures. The divorce was probably my salvation, though I miss my kids. It forced me to sit back and reevaluate my life. It wasn't Mom or Dad's idea for me to move back in with them here. When I heard about Sullivan's Creek, I decided I wanted to be part of it. Probably shouldn't have hassled you when I first arrived, but old habits, you know?"

Geesh, no pressure. "You've made a fairly compelling case for taking you on, but I need a little more time to think through all the ramifications."

"Are you hesitant because I'm your brother?"

Mike set down his cup. Hadn't expected that question. "Huh?"

"You keep your distance from the rest of the Woodleys. I know we all sided with Dad when you came to Ned's rescue years ago to buy him out of his contract, but I thought we'd gotten past those days."

"Maybe so, but none of us have ever been that close."

"Is that why you moved out as soon as Mom, Dad and I showed up in town?"

If he admitted his sales slump was what had him in such a funk, he'd be making Jay's case for hiring him. Instead, he introduced another topic. "Mom wouldn't let up asking about my marriage plans, Dad immediately criticized my coming to Ned's rescue again, and you, well, let's just say I wasn't ready for all the togetherness when you moved your exercise equipment into the den."

"Don't you get it? I was looking for any way I could to bond with you. And make my case."

For the first time since Jay had shown up, Mike got a clue about his brother's desperation. "You're serious, aren't you?"

"I need to start over, Mike. Get my life back on track. You're my best chance."

Mike held up a hand. "Okay, okay. I get it, since you've laid it on so thick. If we can work out salary and commission details, you've got the job."

He was caught off guard when his brother burst from his side of the booth and caught him up in a bear hug. His family wasn't demonstrative. But he'd definitely made Jay's day.

"You won't regret this, bro."

"We haven't settled the money part yet."

"I trust you to be fair. Write up a contract. Stick in a bonus clause if I sell all the lots within a year."

They shook hands.

"I'll start today. Is there an office somewhere? No, you were working at the mansion. I'll take over that space."

"Wait. We both need to talk to Dad about this first. Together. You up for it?"

Jay scowled. "No. But I want this. Let's go for it."

~

Having convinced Shae that Mike's changes to the house were necessary, Darren hustled from the acting general contractor's office before Shae changed her mind. As Darren opened her car door to head back to the studio and begin her all-nighter to redo the estimates and sketches, her phone rang.

"Darren, sweetie. Could you stop by the restaurant? I need to see you."

"Uh, gee, Mom, can this wait? I'm working on a high-profile project that needs to be finished by tomorrow."

"Could you spare me even a few minutes? I'm worried about your sister."

Oh, God, did their mom know about Colby's gambling? No, if she did, she'd sound a lot more distressed. "Okay. But just for a few minutes. I'll see you shortly."

Her mother was just finishing up with a couple of late-break-fast customers when Darren arrived. She turned down the pastry and cup of coffee her mother offered. "Sit. Tell me what's worrying you."

Elise Williams stuck her order pad in an apron pocket and settled next to her. "I stopped by your sister's place yesterday to see how she was doing. Hadn't heard from her for a while. I knew she was busy with classes and her part-time job, but I wanted her to know I was thinking of her."

Hadn't Colby had the foresight to let their mom know about temporarily relocating to the studio? Rather than jump ahead, she waited for her mother to proceed.

"She wasn't there. I mean, she'd apparently moved out and others had already taken up residence. So I called her. Had to leave a message, but she got back to me in a few hours. Said she was living with you now." She raised accusing eyes at Darren. "Why didn't you tell me?"

Darren kicked herself mentally. She should have realized Colby wouldn't follow through and take the initiative to tell their mom on her own. "I'm sorry, Mom. This project I told you about has been weighing heavily on my mind, but that's no excuse. Did Colby explain why we're now roomies?"

"Something about her expenses being higher than she anticipated. She's living rent free with you."

Darren released a breath. Colby hadn't mentioned anything about her gambling debts. Their mom didn't need anything more to worry about than the ongoing need to keep a roof over her head. "It's just temporary, while she gets her finances in order. We're working on her financial aid application."

"But your studio is so far out. That means a lot more driving for her. And gas isn't cheap, either. Maybe she should stay with me."

Their mom's tiny studio apartment couldn't accommodate another person, but of course, she'd want to come to the aid of her younger child. Coming to Colby's aid had become almost second nature to both her mom and Darren.

"I've been taking her back and forth to campus as I could," Darren said. The less time Colby spent on campus when she wasn't in class or at the library, the less chance her gambling cohorts would have to tempt her back to the fold. Of course, that still didn't include phone calls, emails and texts, but Darren hadn't figured out how to control those yet.

"Oh, good. I told her my place is always available to her, but if she's doing okay with you, I won't push."

Her mom was probably relieved her space wouldn't be invaded, but at least she'd made the offer.

Her mom's shoulders seemed to relax, and a hopeful smile appeared. "I haven't seen you since that day a week ago when you went off to visit that young man's housing development. Did you have a good time?"

"It wasn't a date, Mom. He was a client. It was his way of apologizing for turning down the painting he'd commissioned from me."

"What did you say his name was?"

"Michael, Mike, Woodley."

"Right. One of *the* Woodleys in town, isn't he?"

Her mother was just being coy, pumping for more information, information Darren didn't want to share. But her mom deserved to know at least a little. "Yes, he is, although he doesn't appear to be close with the rest of his family. He's hired me to decorate the home he's built in Sullivan's Creek."

Her mom leaned across the table. "You're decorating homes now?"

"This one. As a sort of favor to him. Actual decorators kept leaving him. He's a bit demanding. Well, not so much that as he doesn't really know how he wants this house to look until someone suggests something, which he rejects."

"You're willing to put up with that?"

"So far. The money was good. Not that I'm going on a spending spree, because I have a mortgage to pay down."

Her mother's expression seemed to harden, just a tad, most likely disappointed at Darren's decision how to spend her money but accepting of it. "He's very handsome."

Probing again. "Yes, he is. But don't get your hopes up about something happening between us. He comes from a far different world than I."

Her mother inclined her head, the stub of pencil tucked behind her ear bobbing. "Sometimes coming from different worlds can lead to amazing chemical reactions."

Time to end this discussion. "I need to get going. I'm to present some revised sketches to him tomorrow, and I've hardly started." She hopped up, kissed her mom on the cheek and fled.

First her sister and now her mother wanted to pair her up with Mike. She wondered how they'd react if they knew she'd already *paired up* with him in his bed and ended up an emotional wreck. She also wondered what would have happened if she'd somehow managed to stave off the tears. Would their relationship have gone a different direction? Whatever. No point speculating now.

CHAPTER 12

When his alarm sounded the next morning, Mike was tempted to remain beneath the covers the rest of the day. The task before him gave him no excitement, though it had to be done.

He arrived at the mansion a little after eight. His mother would still be in bed catching up on her beauty rest. Jay would hang back on breakfast until he got Mike's signal. Only his father was present at the breakfast table.

"Doesn't a steady diet of cereal and orange juice get boring?" he asked as he plopped into a chair across from Joseph Woodley.

His dad continued to sip his juice. "Not as boring as that gray and steel mausoleum where you're staying. Tired of it already?"

As usual, he avoided his dad's questions. "Came to give you advance notice of a hiring decision I've made."

His father glanced at him. "Why would you do that? You rarely consult me about anything."

"I've asked Jay to join me and take over property sales. He seemed to think you'd be okay with the idea, but I wanted to make sure."

Lukewarm blue eyes assessed him. "You took my suggestion

to get out of directly selling those lots by turning it against me and stealing one of my team?"

"Jay came to Des Moines for a new start. According to him, the one area in Woodley Industries he really enjoyed and at which he excelled was in the realty division."

"How come he didn't feel he could tell me himself?"

"I wanted to be the one to tell you. If you're going to explode, do it with me."

His father rose. His complexion was nondescript, neither pale nor ruddy, and Mike couldn't tell by the guy's eyes what he was going to do. "Is he close enough to hear us?"

"No, he's still in his room. I'm supposed to text him when it's safe."

"You've thrown him the lifeline I've been unable to cast. His performance has been suffering for months. But give him something he's really interested in, and he'll soar." He held out his hand to Mike. "You did right, son."

The incredible weight that had ridden on Mike's chest since deciding to bring Jay on board lifted, allowed him to exhale a deep breath. "Thanks, Dad. I'll just let Jay—"

His dad held out a hand. Mike stood and took it. "Not so fast. I may be okay with losing your brother to your organization, but that still leaves a hole in mine. One I'd prefer to fill with family."

"Not this again. I've told you more than once, Dad, I'm not interested in being part of Woodley Industries." Should've known he wouldn't get out of this discussion without his dad pulling out the old guilt trip.

"Time's wasting, boy, with your constant refusals to join me. I'm not getting any younger. I owe it to my stockholders to assure the enterprise continues into the future with strong leadership."

New tact. "This your way of telling me you're about to step down? Last week at my apartment you nearly passed out during that coughing jag. Are you okay?"

His dad shifted his gaze away from Mike to focus on the sugar bowl in the middle of the table. "I'm fine. I just have to … slow down. That's all."

An icy shiver sped up Mike's spine. Joseph Woodley had always been the epitome of strength, energy, good health. To suddenly envision him in any other state distressed Mike more than he ever dreamed possible. "Are you planning to step down? Retire?" The concepts seemed alien to his father.

Now it was his father's turn to avoid a direct response. "How soon is this transfer supposed to happen?"

Though Mike was loathe to leave the subject of his dad's health and continued participation in the family business, he took his cue. "I'd like him to start as soon as he can put the details of his current job in order."

"Works for me. Check with him. His assistant should be able to take over for him on short notice." His dad was so calm, so accepting, almost as if he'd been anticipating a move like this.

"What about Gardner or Dash? Don't you want one of them to step in for Jay?"

"Them? Hell, no. If I felt one of them could carry the family name into the future, I'd have turned over more responsibility to them already."

Mike collapsed in his seat. This was the first he'd heard his father disparage the other two members of the family, although he wasn't surprised to hear his dad put down Dash. His brother-in-law had always impressed him as a dilettante who got by on his affiliation with the family. Their sister, Harper, had once primed herself as their dad's successor, but with three brothers and a husband in line for the top position, shortly after her first child arrived, she resigned from her job and from then on had thrown her energies into raising their two children and participating in various charities and women's groups.

His dad's assessment of Gardner was a bigger surprise, though unlike most youngest sons, Gard seemed to feel no need to prove himself. He'd joined the company because he'd never been one to talk back to their dad. Come to think of it, Mike didn't recall hearing of any big coups or successful projects attributed to Gard.

"Rather than seeing me as your last hope, why haven't you thrown your energies into helping them?"

"Don't think I haven't tried, especially those first years after you blew the better part of your trust fund bailing out Ned."

"Then I started making a name for myself."

No response. Instead, an awkward silence ensued.

"I'll get Jay," Mike said at length.

His dad didn't protest.

Once Jay arrived, their dad took the high road and congratulated his oldest son on his new job. Apparently relieved not to have encountered a war zone, Jay waxed poetic, thanking their dad for the opportunity to have worked together all these years. On a humorous note, he even suggested his dad and mother consider building their own house in Sullivan's Creek.

Their dad spluttered at that one.

"You never know," Jay said. I'd like to build there myself, when I can afford it. If you lived there already, you'd be closer to my kids when they visited."

Not the most effective sales pitch from someone whose ex rarely allowed their offspring near him for more than a day, but Mike couldn't blame his brother for his optimism. He filed away the part about Jay building his own home there. Probably not in the cards for now, given what he'd heard about Jay's finances, unless he helped. Would he want his brother living so near him? Hadn't he just escaped all the "family closeness"?

"Your mother and I are perfectly fine in this house. Don't know what we'd do with another one so close by, but feel free to include a nice guest room when you do build your home. We can always stay the night, if we get caught in bad weather."

Jay joined them for breakfast, and conversation shifted to less personal matters, like the current pro football season. Jay and their dad favored the Packers, reflecting their years residing in Michigan. Mike was a Rams fan, although he rarely attended their games anymore. "If we're all going to be living in Iowa from now on, perhaps we should check into the Vikings or Chiefs, since they're closer," Jay said.

Mike remained long enough so it didn't appear he was cutting out as soon as the topic of Jay's future had been settled. He felt pretty good about the discussion of Jay's leaving the corporation, but the niggling worry about his father's health and the future of Woodley Industries prevented him from totally enjoying the moment.

Once he got Jay involved in selling off the Sullivan's Creek lots, he'd focus on a succession plan for Woodley Industries minus him that his father would still accept. Hell, he'd rescued more than his share of ailing companies and breathed life into other fledgling concerns. Surely, he could come up with something for his own family?

Darren had texted him an hour ago, requesting they meet at her studio instead of his apartment, because she was still finishing the revised plan. Would her sister be there again? On his last visit, he wasn't sure if he was some kind of specimen her sister had placed under a microscope for closer examination or if she was attempting to lure him into her bed. She'd flirted at the same time she'd tried to give him the third degree. Not that he was interested. Too young. Besides, his eye was already on her sister.

After he'd called to her twice, Darren finally ran into her studio, breathless. "You're right on time. I hoped you'd be late. I worked up to the last minute on your plan and barely got in a shower." Her tight navy jeans molded to her long, shapely legs beneath, and the loose light blue chambray shirt failed to conceal her ample chest. She was also an adorable mess. His blood immediately heated. Not a good omen for a business meeting, but he couldn't deny the attraction.

"I see. You, uh, might want to rebutton that shirt, although being an artist, this might be your style."

She glanced down and released a frustrated sigh. "Never fails when I'm in a hurry." She turned around, redid the buttons, and then swiveled back to him. "There. Better?"

"The shirt is." He came closer and tapped on a single curler still entwined in her hair. "But you might want to remove this." She smelled of shower soap. Delicious.

"You're kidding?" She reached up and frowned as soon as she verified his comment. "I'll be right back. C'mon into my quarters. I managed to make a pot of coffee, if you're interested. Help yourself. There are mugs on the counter in the kitchen, if you can find them amongst the clutter that seems to surround my sister."

He followed her into what appeared to be a combination living room and office while she continued on to what must have been the bedroom. The kitchen, basically a few cabinets and appliances plus a small table for two, sat off to the side of the main living room. Part of the room was in good shape. Her tablet was neatly lined up next to a stack of books and magazines, even though it was clear she'd been working until the last minute. But the kitchen was a jumble, as she'd said. There was no other description for all the empty food containers, water bottles and condiment packets stacked on the small counter, although to his relief, there were several inches of space separating them from the coffeemaker.

"You want some coffee, too?" he asked as he poured some of the beverage into his own mug.

"Thanks, no," she called from the other room.

He rearranged what he could of the various items littering the counter.

He'd taken a few sips and settled onto the sofa by the time she returned, her hair pulled back in a ponytail. "Sorry about that. It's been great to have my sister around, but this small space wasn't built for two people. Especially two people with totally different personalities."

"I can see how you might get in each other's way."

"It seems to work out best if I sleep out here and she takes my bed. We've set up a small office space for her in the bedroom, so all her books and things can be isolated there and I can have what's left of the place to myself."

"Except for the kitchen." He shot her a smile so she'd know he was commiserating with her rather than chastising.

She rolled her eyes. "Right. Except for that. But I see you managed to find coffee."

"You sure you don't want a cup yourself? Might help you relax."

"Thanks, no. I'm fine. Don't let my distraction with my wardrobe sway you when you review the revised plan. My mind was crystal clear while I worked on it."

"Distraction? Is that your word for it? I thought you were just clumsy when it comes to dressing." He meant to be humorous, but she gave him a look that said she found his observation anything but. "Hey, I was joking. Trying to lighten the mood, because you've been a basket of nerves ever since I arrived." He jerked. "That it? I make you nervous?"

She waved a hand in dismissal. "Of course not. I'm just anxious for you to see what I've worked up and get your approval, so I can move on. I've only ordered the few items you already approved, and I can't even get the flooring in until after the construction changes you wanted are finished."

He touched her hand. "Hey, I'm not an ogre. I'm sure I'll be happy with whatever changes you've come up with."

"That being said, let's get to it then." She dug inside an accordion file, withdrew two folders and handed him one. "The first page summarizes the construction changes you wanted, estimated cost and time to complete. As you can see, at a minimum, it will take two weeks from the day you sign the change orders."

"Whoa. I had no idea it would take so long. I thought as part owner my items would take priority over other projects." Her eyes grew large, but she didn't say anything. "What? Don't you think I deserve a few perks, considering my investment in the project?"

She sat back and studied him. "Well, yes. No. Maybe. Isn't your first responsibility to your clients? I can see why you'd think that way. I just wasn't expecting to hear you voice those thoughts out loud."

Damn. She had him. "Guess I sounded like the arrogant, rich bastard I usually try to keep under wraps. You're right. I made my own deadline. Now I have to live with it."

"Would it be so bad if the house isn't finished in time for your Christmas dinner with your family? You could always host a dinner at a local hotel. Or even have it in a half-finished house. In either case, would they disown you?"

Her question was a punch in the stomach. Been there, done that. Survived that. Did she even know about those days when his family had kept him at arm's length after he helped Ned? More to the point, was there a tiny ounce of truth in what she'd said? No, of course not. He'd lived through those days and found success on his own, much to his family's surprise. "They wouldn't disown me. But I've gone out on a limb, inviting them to my new home, and I'd prefer not to renege."

She tilted her head as she eyed him. "Could I ask a personal question?"

Hadn't stopped her so far. "As the one who pointed out your dishabille a few minutes ago, I think I owe you. Ask away."

"That day you first took me to see Sullivan's Creek, over dinner afterward you told me you weren't close to the rest of your family. If that's the case, why are you worried about backing out on your invitation?"

He ran a hand through his hair. "You cut right to the chase.

Make me see and then admit things I haven't wanted to admit, even to myself."

"So?"

"I feel I have to prove myself to them. Stupid, right? I've proved my business ability several times over. But when my mother complained my living out in the country would prevent me from being more involved with the family, I offered the Christmas invite to placate her. I actually congratulated myself for putting her off for several weeks."

"Now those weeks are fast disappearing, and soon you'll have to deal."

"Stupid, huh? Afraid of disappointing my mother."

She came over to him, placed a hand on his shoulder. "Not stupid. Sons have been trying to please their mothers for time immemorial."

Her touch was subtle, yet so comforting he folded into her, clutched her to him.

They cuddled for several seconds. He didn't want to pull away, and she allowed him to stay.

Gradually, the safe harbor of her arms changed, morphed into something else as he took in the intoxicating fragrance of her hair, felt the soft curves of her body beneath her shirt. The smoldering fire in the pit of his stomach he'd attempted to contain since he'd arrived ignited. He held her tighter as his hands roamed up and down her back. Her intake of breath was all he needed to shift his lips from the side of her head to her face. He kissed her like a man fighting for air, unable to get enough of her sweet taste.

His hands moved beyond her back, cradled her butt, slipped under her shirt on their own accord. Some part of his brain told him to stop, but his brain seemed disconnected from the rest of his body and what it wanted.

Her breathing increased, but she didn't push away. A gentle moan escaped her as his hand tugged at her bra. Her breast emerged, warm, smooth, and oh so welcoming as his hand closed around it. "Oh, lady."

As good, great, as this felt, he wanted more. Had to have more. He twisted, bringing her with him as he lay back on the sofa. He removed his hand long enough to seek the buttons on her shirt. "Guess you didn't need to redo these after all."

While he worked on the shirt, she grabbed his jacket, brought it down over his shoulders, then off.

Although she seemed to be in this as much as he was, he took a moment to gaze into her eyes for her consent before proceeding. Her eyes, now limpid and hazy, blinked her answer.

In seconds, they were both naked. Her body lay under him, inviting him to playland. Play he would. His mouth shot to a breast, tonguing the tip, then the aureole. Sweet agony. He took it all into his mouth, unable to get enough of her.

Darren squirmed, moved her hips into him, rubbed against his hardness. What could he do but appease the lady? His hand sought her sweet spot. Found her moist. Destination reached, he attended to her need. She almost came off the couch in her response. She was so ready.

Time to take precaution. Good thing he hadn't thrown his pants across the room, or he wouldn't have been able to reach down and pull the condom from his pocket. Not that he carried protection around in his pants pocket all the time. In fact, he didn't remember sticking this one in. Must have been fantasizing about how this "business meeting" would go.

"I'm glad you think ahead." Her voice was a murmur. "I doubt I could walk to my bathroom right now." On the other hand, she could spread her legs.

His body went on autopilot as a blanket of sensual tension wrapped around him. Ready, he mounted her and prepared to enter heaven.

Somehow, though, one tiny connection to his brain had remained intact and flashed him a warning. *Abort. Remember how this ended the last time.* He jerked away from her. "We can't do this."

Her eyes flew open. "What?"

Before he changed his mind, he sat up on his haunches and climbed off the couch, went for his pants.

"What's going on, Mike? It couldn't be something I said, because I've hardly spoken the last few minutes."

"I'm sorry, Darren. I can't believe I forgot about the last time until just now, but I did. Once you were in my arms, all I wanted to do was have you here on this couch. But as primed as I am"—he couldn't resist glancing down at his still very evident erection—"I don't want this to end with you breaking down again."

"Oh."

He scooped up her pile of clothes and dropped them on her. "Here. Get dressed before my horny side stifles the gentleman."

She didn't argue, although she kept watching him. "Don't blame yourself. I was a willing participant. I guess I forgot as well. Maybe after that last time, I'm past my grief."

"I think you'd know if you were. And apparently, you don't." Could he sound any more like a spoiled child who hadn't gotten his way?

She pursed her lips. "I, uh, guess so."

He was dressed before she was. "Mind if I use your bathroom? Doesn't matter what shape your sister has left it in."

"Uh, sure."

He sped from the living room to relieve himself. Couldn't conduct the rest of their discussion in this condition. When he returned, he found her drinking a bottle of water.

She offered him one as well. He turned it down, since he still had his coffee.

He took a seat opposite her to keep his distance. "Okay, we should get back to your list." He kept his voice neutral, as if the last several minutes had never happened.

"Back to the construction changes. Are you ready to sign the change orders? They're in a separate folder."

"Two weeks from today, right?"

"I can fax them to her from here."

Maybe he could do an alternate dinner for his family, as Darren had suggested. Or maybe if he agreed to the rest of the changes on her list, he could still pull off this dinner in his own home. He preferred the last option. All he had to do was agree.

Change orders signed and sent, he began to read through the rest of what she proposed. It took exactly two minutes before he came to his first objection: the color of the wingback chair in the living room. She had listed hunter green. He wanted burgundy.

"But burgundy's so passé. It smacks of men's clubs and cigars and whiskey."

"No, it doesn't. My parents have a pair of them in their formal living room." God, had he really justified his taste with his parents' situation?

"That's in a mansion."

"Humor me."

"If I do, we'll need to change the color of the other chairs and the davenport."

"Okay. What do you suggest?"

"I need to think about it. Black and gray won't work. Maybe gold or some shade of brown."

"Gold. Yeah, I like that idea." He had no idea why, but it seemed right somehow.

"All right, we'll go with gold. I'll need to check whether the style I've picked comes in that color. If it doesn't, do I have your permission to find a close substitute, or do we do this again?" Her voice carried more than a tinge of irritation. Was she still smarting from their aborted lovemaking?

He was ready to agree, but he hesitated long enough so she wouldn't think he was caving. "Fax me a copy of whatever you decide," he said in afterthought.

The rest of their discussion followed the same path. He'd agree to a few items, and then something would catch his attention. He'd object, she'd ask why, and for the life of him, he had no idea, although he'd come up with some excuse.

When they finished, she still had twelve items to replace, but he'd agreed to everything else. Surely, she'd consider that a victory of sorts?

"I'll get these orders in today," she said, as he headed to the door. "And I should have the replacements selected in a day or two. Promise you won't change your mind."

"Me? I've been the picture of agreement today."

"Then I sure don't want to be around the day you disagree."

CHAPTER 13

Three days later, Mike informed Ned of their new hire. Ned had been out of town the day Mike and Jay had come to terms and now, at Mike's invitation, they met at Mike's apartment.

"Interesting new pad," Ned said as he wandered around.

"Serves its purpose."

"Which is what, to generate excruciating boredom?" Ned chuckled. He'd just checked out the bedroom. "What's with that closet? There's no way you got your extensive wardrobe in there."

"Room enough for what I need for now. Left my summer stuff at the mansion."

Ned shook his head. "I know I advised you to move out, but I thought you'd set up camp at your new house."

"Talk about boring. There's nothing there yet. Darren's the one who suggested I find temporary quarters. I booked this place sight unseen. It makes bland look overdone, but it got me away from the crazies. Plus, it gives me peace and quiet."

Ned flopped into one of the two armchairs. "You could probably be living there now if you'd simply gone online and ordered a bunch of stuff and used our subs to paint, put in flooring, and do the finish carpentry. But you had to have an interior decorator."

"I don't know anything about decorating. Didn't realize having and keeping one would be so difficult." Something about this conversation kept Mike on his feet, roaming the room.

"Have you fired Darren yet? What is she, now, number five?"

"Three," Mike replied too fast. "And we're doing fine. She's come up with some great ideas."

"Yeah? Like a major rebuild?"

Mike pulled up. "You know about that?"

"Shae does talk to me, even when I'm out of town. She wasn't too thrilled at having to shift the crews around to accommodate you."

"I was the one who wanted to make a few tweaks here and there. Not Darren. But I'm glad Shae could work things out."

Ned studied him. "Sit. Tell me why I'm here."

Mike would have preferred to stay on his feet, retain his position of power, but he took a seat on the davenport and told him about hiring Jay.

Ned raised a brow. "Thought you considered Jay a bit of a lightweight?"

"That opinion was based on seeing him flounder working for my dad." He told Ned about Jay's sales analysis. "That's what convinced me the guy knows what he's talking about when it comes to real estate. I made the decision on my own without consulting you because I feel responsible for the decline in sales, and essentially, I'll be the one paying his salary."

"Does he realize that?"

"Deep down, he probably does, but he wants a fresh start so much he's willing to overlook that detail for now. Plus, the salary is only enough to keep his head above water financially. His commissions will bring him the real money."

"How soon can he start?" Ned asked.

"He's been at it two days already. He's up to speed on the

unsold lots, at least the basic details like asking price, dimensions and location. I was hoping you'd do the actual walkabout with him, share your knowledge of the property. I want him to feel the same excitement you do about the land, as well as assume the same commitment to a green community."

"I'm only back for a few days before my next concert, so we'll have to do this fast. We can start today."

"That'd be great. He's already made a few suggestions for improving sales, setting up an on-site office being one of them. He couldn't believe we didn't have one."

"Not a bad idea. I take it that would be his office?"

"Or ours as well, if we want to put the money into it."

"You still have your folks' RV, don't you?" Ned asked. "It worked pretty well for me when I was project manager. Or is it off limits now they're back in town?"

"We want to put our best foot forward, impress potential buyers. There are several parcels around the development that were set aside for community applications. Thought we could stick a sales office in the one we designated for a community center until most of the lots have sold. We could use the RV on a temporary basis, while the new building is under construction."

Ned sank further into his chair, crossed his legs. "We already have the architectural plans for those buildings. Do we have the financial resources?"

"I can swing it. But the investment has to net us more sales. What I need you to do is run it by Shae. She's not too fond of me right now, and you have more pull anyhow."

Ned smirked. "Wouldn't exactly characterize it as pull, but you're right about her feelings for you. Okay to give her the green light on the project?"

"Sure. I'll call my banker and let him know this is coming."

After Ned left, Mike breathed easier. Ned was okay with bringing Jay on board and building an on-site sales office. Good. These days, Ned was content to sit back and let Mike take charge of the project. Other than his not-so-subtle hints to stop dumping additional work on Shae.

Since Jay had already jumped into his new job feet first, the pressure on Mike had already lessened. Didn't even have the completion of his own home to worry about now that he'd more or less signed off on Darren's plans. Things were running fairly well in his other ventures. What would he do with himself?

For half a second, he considered his dad's offer. No. Dumb thought. He didn't want to join Woodley Industries. He'd fought against the idea for years. But if his dad truly didn't put much faith in either Gard or Dash to lead the organization in the future, who else was there? Did he really owe the family business the rest of his life?

Forget about Woodley Industries. Maybe Darren needed help. Right. Like he'd *helped* her already, by second-guessing her expertise. Still didn't know where his opinions had come from. Hell, he didn't know what he wanted until she gave him her vision. Then, like a gut reaction, he was pointing out what had to go.

Did he just like hassling her? Like he had with the paintings? Was there something about their personal relationship that spilled over into their professional dealings? Whoa. What prompted that idea? What exactly was their personal relationship? He was attracted to her, no doubt. And she was a great sex partner, at least as far as getting his engine going. But after two crash-and-burn episodes with the lady, he'd decided to keep things platonic from now on.

Like that was going to happen. He couldn't stop thinking about her. Not that he wanted anything long term, except maybe friendship. Maybe he should call her. Or stop by the studio. It'd been a few days. He could see how successful she'd been finding the items he'd greenlighted.

Midday. Her sister should still be in class. Yet again he wondered how Darren could stand to live with such a slob. Why, if her sister was saving rent thanks to Darren's generosity, wouldn't the younger woman curtail her slovenly habits out of gratitude?

Another thing. It seemed mighty coincidental that Darren's bruised and obviously beaten sister moved in right about the same time Darren's financial problems forced her to take his job. Darren hadn't wanted to explain her sudden need for ten thousand dollars, but he was pretty sure the two situations were connected.

One of his fraternity brothers, Jamison Carey, was now an assistant professor at the law school. Hadn't seen the guy in a few years. Couldn't hurt to renew old acquaintances now that he was planning to stick around town.

Before giving himself a chance to reconsider, he contacted his friend, who happened to have a few hours free between classes and agreed to meet him for lunch at a place near campus. Only after he hung up was Mike hit by second thoughts. What did he want to learn about Colby Williams? What would he do if he found out?

Carey was already seated at a table near the back of the restaurant by the time Mike arrived. His pal rose and shook hands. "Well, Mr. Moneybags, the years have been good to you. Still have all your hair, I see."

"I could say the same for you, pal," Mike said. "Though I can see a little more forehead than the last time we were together." At six feet, Carey didn't appear to have put on any weight, although he now wore dark-framed eyeglasses.

They quickly ordered, then each sank back in his seat to eye the other. Carey broke the silence. "You've done well for yourself, Mike. Even after you struck out on your own."

"I've been in the right place at the right time when some great opportunities came my way. But what about you? Last I heard, you planned to be a litigator, and here you are, an assistant professor in the law school."

The corner of Carey's mouth curled up. "Fell in love with the dean's daughter, and my father-in-law talked me into applying my courtroom skills here. Fortunately, my wife has grown up in this environment and is quite comfortable living on my university pay. Plus, I'm working on a textbook that, if it makes it to print, should augment our income nicely."

Their drinks arrived, water for Mike and hot tea for Carey. Carey swished his tea bag a few times. "So, to what do I owe the privilege of this get-together? From what I hear, you've been around town for months."

"Yeah, well, first off, my mind and time have been preoccupied with this residential development I'm working on with Jake Bonneville, Sullivan's Creek. But to be frank, I'm here for a friend. A friend's sister is in her first year at the law school and may not be doing very well. I don't expect favors, just information, if you have any."

Carey stiffened, went into professional mode. "Can't help you there, I'm afraid. Everything about our students is confidential."

"Figured. Not asking for anything like that. Just want to see your reaction when I say her name. Fair enough?"

"I'm not ..."

"Colby Williams."

One of Carey's eyebrows shot up. But he took his time answering. "It's not that big a school. I know all the students, so yes, I'm familiar with Ms. Williams. In fact, she's eating lunch here right now. Didn't you see her when you walked in?"

"No. I've only met her once, and I was intent on spotting you, since I was a little late."

"Don't look behind you, because she's seated our direction, but she's up front with one of the second-year students."

Colby had probably made him already. *Made him.* That's what they said in spy novels, wasn't it? One feeble attempt to learn more about her situation and she'd already seen him.

"Based on that guilty expression on your face, I'd say you didn't expect her to be here," his friend observed.

Mike sipped his water, attempted to calm his nerves. "Some investigator I am. Probably shows I've never done anything like this before. I'm doing it for my friend."

"Is this *friend* of yours someone special?"

Mike jumped in his seat. Shook his head vigorously. "No, no. Nothing like that."

"But it's a woman, isn't it?"

"Yes. Why?"

Carey chuckled. "I may not have seen you in years, pal, but I know you well enough from before to realize you wouldn't put yourself in a situation like this unless you were somehow involved in it yourself."

"Like I said, she's a friend. In fact, she's the interior decorator for my new home. I've just observed some strange behavior on her part and her sister's and thought maybe I could help. Don't read anything more into it than that."

Carey glanced at the table up front, then immediately back at him. "Your instincts may be correct. Doesn't look like Ms. Williams' lunch is social."

A commotion of some sort emanating from the area where Colby was seated interrupted them. Without thinking, Mike slid out of his chair and made his way that direction. "Problem here, folks?"

Colby didn't notice him until he reached their table. Though she blinked in recognition, the other person held up a hand, as if cautioning her not to answer. "No, man. No problem here."

"Really? I could hear you from way in the back." He turned directly to Colby. "You okay, miss?"

Colby pursed her lips, apparently torn between asking him for help and not irritating her tablemate. "Uh, we're law students arguing different sides of a case. Sorry if we got too loud."

She wasn't going to admit she knew him. If she'd been with a friend, she would have introduced him. Better sense told him to let it be. For now. But if anything further happened, he wasn't waiting for pleasantries. He was getting her out of here and away from this guy.

He returned to Carey, making no effort to disguise his concern. "I may regret doing that, but I was worried about her."

"Understood. Apparently all is well?"

"She didn't acknowledge me to the guy she was with, so I took that as my cue not to intercede any more than I had. Told me they were arguing different sides of a case."

"You didn't believe her?"

"Don't know what to think."

"She's leaving," Carey said. "Correction, she just ran out. You want to follow? I'll catch the tab here."

"What about the guy she was with?"

"Still there. No, he just threw some money on the table and bolted also."

Mike shoved a twenty on the table. "Sorry. I need to make sure she's okay. I'll be in touch."

"Do that. Be careful."

The other student threw himself into a car and burned rubber getting away as Mike emerged. No sign of Colby.

Now what? No point returning to the eatery. Call Darren? And tell her what? He and Carey could've just witnessed a lovers' quarrel rather than something more serious.

Time to stop poking around. At its best, he'd looked like a fool to Carey. At its worst, he'd probably alienated himself from Colby, and if she did need help, erased himself from her list of people to whom she could turn.

THAT EVENING, Colby returned to the studio later than anticipated. She should've shown up around five. Instead, it was almost seven when she arrived.

Her usual routine was to slam into the living quarters, drop her backpack, books, and whatever else she was carrying on the first open spot she spied and head for the refrigerator. Tonight, she quietly placed her things on the coffee table where earlier Darren had stuck her folders for Mike. She settled onto the couch, where she remained, silent.

Darren debated whether to leave her alone or intervene. In the end, she backed away and busied herself in her small kitchen, heating up the chicken soup remaining from her own dinner an hour ago, then fixing a green salad. After ten minutes, she carried a tray into the living area and set it on the coffee table. "Brought you some dinner. You look like you could use some sustenance."

Colby raised her eyes as if just realizing she wasn't alone. "Thanks." She dutifully picked up the soup spoon and took a few sips before setting the utensil aside.

"Not hungry?" Darren asked.

"Rough day. Trying to decide what to do next."

"Need to bounce your thoughts off someone else?"

Colby found the fork and stabbed at a piece of tomato. "Actually, I already did, with Katrina, my counselor. But I'm not sure what to do about her advice."

"Oh." At least Colby was checking in with her counselor. Darren had suspected her sister was missing some of her sessions. Still, it was a bit of a letdown that Colby didn't feel she could confide in her. "I won't press, but I'm here, if you want to talk." To illustrate her point, she wandered out to her studio. She'd been working on her prelim sketches and paintings whenever she wasn't buried in details concerning Mike's house.

One of her new projects was actually for Mike, a view of the woods behind his house with Sullivan's Creek in the background. One would think she could find something that wasn't connected to Mike Woodley in her off-hours, but she'd had this great idea he could take this with him to hang at one of his other properties so he'd never be too far from Iowa.

"Got a minute?" Colby asked from the doorway separating the studio from the residence.

Darren put down her pencil. "Sure. What's up?"

"I saw your boss today. On campus. At the restaurant where I ate lunch."

They returned to the living room. "Okay?" Darren prodded.

"I must've missed him when he entered. Probably because one of my classmates had just joined me, uninvited, and I was trying to get rid of him."

Darren struggled to keep up. Mike on campus. Colby and an unwanted guest. "Go on."

Her sister paused, clasped her hands. "This guy and I argued. I'll get to that in a minute. Anyway, our voices must've risen, because the next thing I knew, this Mike guy was at our table attempting to calm us. When I told him we were arguing a case, he backed off."

Sounded like Mike had attempted to play mediator. She liked that he'd come to her sister's aid, even though it didn't appear to be needed. "Is that all you talked about?"

"Yes. It was over in less than a minute. Then he returned to a table where he joined, of all people, Professor Carey, my court prep prof."

"Is that so unusual?"

Colby seemed to think through Darren's question. "No, I guess not. It was just a surprise to find myself in the same place as your boss."

"Go back to the part about your lunch partner. Who was he, and why were you arguing?"

Colby examined her nails, then rose and went to the fridge. When she returned with a bottle of water a minute later, she made a production of opening the cap without spilling water on the couch, placing a napkin Darren had stuck on the tray to cover the cap as she turned it. "He was one of the guys who got me into the poker tournaments. I won't give you his name for fear you'll do something heroic like going to the police. Honestly, Darren, he just showed up. I haven't had anything to do with those people since you had to fork over all that money."

This discussion had taken a much more serious turn than Darren was expecting. Her stomach clenched at the mention of poker. "What did he want?"

"They're not done with me. They think they can lure me back to the fold with this special game they're running this weekend."

These people were monsters, the way they preyed upon college students who always seemed to need money. "What did you tell him?" She could barely breathe.

"I turned him down flat, of course." Tears formed in Colby's eyes. "You think I'm a pushover for these guys, but I've put both of us in jeopardy three times already because of my greed. If it hadn't been for this Woodley guy trying to come to my defense, I could've ended things right there."

Darren was both relieved and scared at the same time. "How did his showing up change things?"

"All my energy was going into saying no to this poker game. I wasn't paying enough attention to the guy's interest in your boss after he returned to his table, so when he asked if I knew him, I let it slip that you were working for him."

Though her insides were already queasy, this admission made things worse. Something terrible was coming. "Why did he want to know about Mike?" She desperately hoped she was wrong.

"I'd been making the case for having tapped out all my resources as well as yours as my reason for refusing to join the game. This guy apparently recognized your boss. All of a sudden, my story about being broke lost credibility, because now there was a whole new source of revenue for this group to tap."

Bingo. Just as Darren had feared. "This guy actually thought you could get money from my boss?"

"I was so angry with myself for giving away his identity I got all haughty. God, I should never practice law in court. My emotions get away from me too easily. Anyway, I told him something like 'forget it,' and got out of there as fast as I could."

"Did he follow you?"

"Tried to. I slipped into the store next door and hid behind a display until he took off in his car. But with a new fish to fry, these guys aren't going to leave me alone."

One part of her was proud of her sister for both refusing to play anymore and for realizing she wasn't off the hook. But the other part was tied up in knots, unable to see a way out of this horror. "Is that it?" God, she hoped so. She couldn't take any more.

"That's when I went to see Katrina. Had to talk my way in between two appointments, but she'd told me from the start, if I ever needed immediate help, she'd be there for me. Which was amazing because I've, uh, sorta missed a few sessions."

Darren held her response in check. "Okay, we'll put that issue aside for now, while these poker monsters are still on the loose."

"We need to warn your boss, but I'm afraid, like you, he'll insist we bring in the authorities. Plus, he already seems to know people at the law school. My days there are doomed if he does."

No wonder her usually verbose sister had been so quiet earlier and so reticent to discuss the situation. "You and I both know there's only one answer when it comes down to it. But it's not going to be easy," Darren told her.

Colby didn't reply. Instead, she picked up her spoon and went back to her soup, but not for long. "You're saying we have to tell your boss?"

"That, and it's time for you to let the authorities at the law school know what's been happening."

The spoon went flying as Colby jumped to her feet. "I can't do that! It will ruin my chance of becoming an attorney."

Her sister's words stabbed her heart. Colby had come a long way by refusing to participate in the poker game and running out of the restaurant. Then she'd gone to her counselor for advice.

Plus, she'd been willing to share the story with Darren. But that was as far as Colby's growth went. Colby was still letting her career take precedence over doing the right thing.

For now, she'd celebrate her sister's progress. Sleep on this. Tomorrow, they'd talk to Mike. If Mike reacted as she thought he would, he'd also urge telling the school's administrators. She could only hope.

"WANT A DRINK? I've got beer, too." Mike headed for the bar part of his kitchenette while his guest, Jamison Carey, made himself comfortable on the sofa.

"No. God knows I could use one, but I want to keep a clear head for this." He'd called about forty-five minutes earlier and asked to meet Mike somewhere private. Mike had invited him to his loft.

With Carey refusing, Mike followed suit and joined his friend in the living room. "Okay. Apparently this isn't a social visit. What couldn't you tell me over the phone?"

"Those two students who were arguing at noon? You tried to mediate whatever was transpiring between them."

"Right. Colby Williams and some guy I didn't recognize."

"Well, I did. Not at first, or I would have said something. Only figured out his identity after the two of them had run out and you'd followed close behind. His name is Trey Hardy, or at least that's what he goes by. We've been watching him and a few of his pals for weeks. We think they're connected to a gambling ring that seems to be preying on our students."

"Gambling? The ponies?"

"No, something much closer to the lifestyle of college students, cards. Poker, to be exact. They suck these kids into what appear to be casual poker nights. Let them win a few bucks to get them hooked, then raise the stakes. These poor kids get taken for hundreds of dollars. Many apparently have had the means to pay. Some haven't. They're the ones who finally came to us, embarrassed but desperate, hoping we could get them out of their debts."

Darren's sudden need for ten thousand dollars and her sister moving in with her fit the scenario Carey described. "Surely, you don't think Colby Williams is one of these sharks? She's more likely a victim."

Carey got up and drifted over to the window, took a quick glance outside, as if he expected to see something down below. "I got to wondering about her after we saw her today. She fits the victim pattern. She doesn't come from money. Her mother's a waitress, and her sister is a fledgling artist. Colby applied for student aid, but her application was received after the scholarship money had already been awarded for the semester, although we were able to grant her a small loan."

If Carey knew all that, he also knew that Darren was the friend he'd mentioned earlier.

"College, especially law school, is expensive," Carey said. "The Williams girl could have been a prime target, except we don't know where she would have gotten the money once she started losing. That may have been what we witnessed today. Her telling Hardy she couldn't pay her tab."

"You're telling me all this because you want me to alert my friend, Colby's sister. You can't do anything about this because you've received no official complaint from her."

Carey stared at his shoes a few beats before facing Mike. "Technically, I can't even admit that much. This ring of sharks is wider and more dangerous than we first imagined. They've got to be stopped before more students are taken in. For all I know, Hardy saw me with you and assumed we were on to him. That's why I didn't want to call. I took a chance coming here, the way it is."

This was more serious than Mike imagined. The idea that

Darren had been pulled into this messy vortex chilled him to the core. The sister, though probably unaware what she was getting herself into, had still made a conscious decision to play. But he was sure Darren had been totally out of the loop. Until the ten thousand. God, these creeps were taking college students for that much money? Reprehensible.

"Time is of the essence?" he asked Carey.

His friend nodded. "Now that Hardy may have assumed I'm on to him, there's no telling what they'll do. They could go to ground, even relocate their operations to another town."

"I like that option, although I hate to see them get away with no consequences."

Carey hesitated, released a heavy sigh. "There's another option. Hardy got a good look at you when you tried to break up the argument. Since you're a bit of a media darling, he may have recognized you. If that's the case, he saw his next big score."

Mike processed Carey's speculation. As the idea sank in, the chill he'd felt earlier went ice age. Hardy and his cronies had no reason to believe Colby knew him. Thank God they'd both kept their cool and not acknowledged each other. But if Hardy did discover who he was, the creep might continue to hassle Colby until she broke down and revealed their relationship. If that happened, these jerks would consider it open season on his bank account.

CHAPTER 14

"How long has this been here?" Darren asked Mike the next morning as he let her into the RV. "I don't remember seeing it before."

"Arrived yesterday. This is our temporary on-site sales office while the permanent one, eventually to be used as the community center, is under construction."

She'd never been inside one of these contraptions. Not bad, if one could get past the immediate sense of claustrophobia. "Good idea. I've wondered why you didn't have a place out here for meeting clients."

"Should've said something. As it was, the suggestion came from my brother, Jay, our news sales manager."

She twisted around to face him. "You did hire him."

"Not only was the sales analysis he prepared for me right on, the glowing endorsement you gave him went a long way. This rig belongs to my parents, who haven't used it in years. Ned borrowed it last year for his office while he served as project manager, but it's been in storage since we became partners."

"Are you okay?" she asked, noting the dark shadows under

his eyes, not unlike her own countenance. Two hours of sleep could do that to one's looks.

"Actually, no, although I could say the same for you."

"Sleepless night. I was about to call you to explain when I received your text asking me to come here right away. What's up?" she asked.

He gestured for her to take a seat in one of the two leather club chairs, while he settled onto the couch facing her. "I'd offer you coffee, but I just got here myself, and I'd rather get into this immediately."

"Does this have something to do with your seeing my sister yesterday?"

"Yeah. How much did she tell you?"

She shouldn't have interrupted him. She'd rather he tell her how much he knew first. She repeated Colby's story.

"Pretty much matches what I know, up to that point. I was having lunch with a college friend who now works at the university."

His tone was different than usual. Somber, serious. He must know more.

"The rest of this I've learned since about her lunchmate. I felt you needed to hear it. I have to warn you, though, this is sobering stuff."

"I'm already aware of some of this from Colby. What do you know?"

Mike described the gambling operation. "Colby got caught up in it, didn't she? To the tune of at least ten thousand, the money you suddenly needed?"

She lowered her head. She hated admitting her knowledge and Colby's part in the deal, but he was being up front with her. She should return the same. "Yes. I was able to cover the first two times they got her with your check for the paintings, but all my commissions go into paying off the studio. I didn't have anything close to ten thousand liquid when they hit her up a third time."

"I'm glad you finally felt you could share this with me."

"Not much choice."

"There's more. Are you ready?"

She'd suspected as much from his tone. "Not really, but go ahead."

"My friend shared this with me in confidence, although he's okay with my telling you. The university administrators, campus security and the local police have been working together to nip this operation, but their hands are tied unless more students come forward with information."

"Meaning Colby."

"She's one of them."

Time for Colby to come clean. Darren had warned her of as much, but she wasn't ready to admit this to Mike. "She would be jeopardizing her law school career, not to mention the danger she'd be facing."

"She may no longer have a choice."

His words gripped her heart. "Why do you say that?" Her voice was no more than a whisper.

"My family and I are no strangers to the media. Nor is our wealth a secret. If the guy—he goes by Trey Hardy—gets an inkling of any connection to me, they're not going to leave her alone until she agrees to come back to the game. Then she's going to lose. Big time. Because they'll want me to bankroll her debts."

"Hardy already knows, thanks to Colby. That's what I came to tell you. I'm so sorry we got you involved."

He sprang from the couch to kneel before her and take her hand. "I involved myself by playing mediator. I don't know that I'd have gone to the rescue of anyone else, but I knew she was sitting there. When I heard their voices rise, I couldn't stop myself."

"You're one of the good guys."

"No. I'm not. I was on campus having lunch with my friend to pump him for information about Colby. It really ticked me off to see how she was messing up your place when she was supposed to be a guest. I couldn't stop wondering why you needed all that money so fast. If I'd left well enough alone, the whole incident could've been avoided."

He'd been investigating Colby? She tried to pull her hand away from his, but he gripped it tighter. "Why?"

"I've come to care for you. A lot. I was worried about you. You're so proud about standing on your own and handling your own problems. I just wanted to help."

No one had ever said that to her before. Emotions she didn't understand made her heart race. "I don't know what to say, Mike."

"How about 'thank you'?"

"Definitely, thank you. But see where your *helping* has got you? Now you're a target, too." His hand holding hers was so comforting, but she couldn't expect him to stick his neck out farther. With his wealth, there was no telling how much those crooks would want.

"About that?" He stood, drawing her up with him. "Let's sit over there on the couch. There's more."

More? She wasn't sure if she could take more. But she followed him to the couch and waited for the ax to fall.

"As it turns out, my friend, Professor Jamison Carey, is one of the university's people investigating this gambling ring. He thinks this operation is more widespread than anyone knows. More sophisticated, too. They're anxious to stop it before it gets even worse. They want Colby and me to play along, and in return, they're willing to look past whatever school rules she may have broken, if that's even the case."

Darren gulped. "Oh no! She's finally taken a stand and refused to play anymore. This would mean going backward."

"I get that. Wouldn't blame the two of you for running as far the other direction as you can. But I've been assured there'll be police protection around us both every step of the way. There'll be nothing on her school record except perhaps a commendation. Something like that could go a long way when it comes time for her to apply for law jobs."

As scary as the proposition was, he had a point. Actually, she'd already advised Colby to go the authorities. But working with them to bring down the crooks?

"Where's your sister now? I'll go with you to talk to her, if you want?"

From the way Mike had described this group, they would continue to harass Colby anyhow until she succumbed. Why not use that to bring them down? But the reality of it all was so scary, were Colby and her up to it?

Scary or not, they could no longer run away from it.

"Okay. You're right. She needs to do this."

TWO NIGHTS LATER, Darren sat with Mike in his car several houses down the street from the poker tournament. It hadn't been easy convincing Colby to go to the university authorities and to agree to be part of the sting. But in the end, Colby had listened to Mike's arguments. Darren was blown away with the way he'd taken over and reassured her sister they could do this. After all these years, it was like having their very own champion.

"Don't look so worried. This will be no different than her past experiences, except they'll jack up the stakes. If she's serious about being a courtroom attorney, she'll need the acting skills there she'll be called upon to use tonight."

Darren couldn't help but laugh. "That's actually what sold her on participating."

"It's my own acting skills I'm not so sure of when they come to me for the money. Although the negotiations I go through for my businesses aren't too far off."

"You really think they'll come straight to you rather than go through Colby?" That was the most critical point in the plan, to get Colby out of the action and let Mike take over.

"According to the police, who've now brought the feds into this, that's how these crooks operate. I'm the big payoff they've been waiting for. They'll come to me with a whopping number in return for leaving her alone afterward."

This whole conversation seemed surreal. Police, feds, sting, high-stakes blackmail. None of them part of her life. Until now. She tightened her neck scarf and adjusted her gloves. Neither action stopped the small tremors that had plagued her the past several minutes. "How will the police catch them?"

"They'll be recording any contact I have with these folks. As soon as I turn over the money, law enforcement will step in and arrest them."

He made it sound so cut and dried. But it wasn't. Bile tasting like tin rose in her throat. She attempted to swallow, but it wouldn't recede. "How can the police be so sure they'll be able to nab the top dogs? They appear to function from the sidelines, in the shadows. How will you get them to dirty their own hands?"

Mike didn't reply immediately. His silence scared her all the more. "As usual, you've cut to the chase," he said finally. "Wish I could swear with a hundred percent certainty we've got that part sewn up. I have to insist the exchange take place with the head guy at a location I determine. The only leverage I have is my dominant personality and the amount of money they want."

She closed her eyes, attempting to block the image of a bunch of thugs attacking Mike, beating him to the point where his face resembled raw meat, no longer recognizable. He talked tough, and she was sure he'd do everything in his power to maintain that stance, but he was only one man up against an unknown group of crooks.

She forced herself to take a deep breath, expel it slowly. "That's a pretty big *if*. Are you sure you want to put yourself on the line like that?"

"I'll have police backup the entire time."

"Don't take any chances." She tried to make herself sound brave, not to choke on her words for his sake.

His cell rang. "Hmm. Sooner than I expected. It's Colby. Yes? Uh-huh. How much?" His voice rose on the question. "Let me speak to them. Yes? Who is this? What's going on?" He listened as if this was all news to him. Though it would have been natural for him to question them further, he went with inflexibility. "How soon? No, that's not possible. I can't get a check until morning. No. I don't write checks for that amount on my personal account. No. Let her go. Now. I assume you know where to find me. Call me tomorrow morning. I should have it by then."

When he hung up, he took a huge breath. Rested his head on the steering wheel.

Darren grasped his forearm. "Have they taken her hostage?" Her heartbeat had increased to the point where she could barely hear. What would they do to Colby if they suspected she was working with the authorities? *Don't go there, Darren.* But she couldn't stop her brain from conjuring up pictures of Colby being slapped around, gagged and bound. Did the gang have guns? Would they use them?

As if in response to her question, Colby emerged from the house within seconds. She hustled down the front steps, ran for her car, gunned the engine and raced down the street.

Darren collapsed into the seat, her breathing slightly more normal than before. Her sister was out. Colby's part in this was almost over. Relief battled with her fear of what was to come. Mike's part.

After a few beats, Mike lifted his head. "I'll drive around the block so they can't see us when we switch seats. You drive while I contact the police."

How could she drive when she couldn't stop shaking? Because that was the least she could do, considering what Colby had just endured and what Mike still faced. She hoisted her butt over the console and slid into the driver's seat. Gripping the steering wheel actually helped stifle some of the quivering.

She listened while Mike explained to the authorities how the timeline had been moved up. "Yeah, they let her go. Good, let me know when she gets home safely." He turned to Darren. "A police officer will stay with Colby and you tonight. As soon as I drop you off, another's going to join me. I'll stay at a motel overnight, just in case these yahoos send someone to my loft. They're working out an exchange point for some time tomorrow morning."

"What about your family?"

"A police car will be stationed near the mansion all night. No need to alarm my family."

"I, I don't like the way this is going." Her teeth chattered so much she could barely get out the words.

"I don't either, Darren, but we're still in control. At least they let Colby go. They were threatening to keep her there 'til I showed up with the money tonight."

A police car was parked in front of her studio when they arrived. "Do you want me to go in with you?" Mike asked as she parked.

"I should be okay with the police here. Go on to wherever you're meeting your police guard." She leaned over and hugged him, clung to him a few minutes.

His arms immediately folded her into him, his lips seeking her hair, and then her own lips. Their kiss was one of comfort and shared courage.

"I'll let you know what happens as soon as I can," he said. "Don't leave here until you get the all clear. Don't let your guards leave unless they're replaced by a new shift. And if they are, make sure the new guys are legit. Okay?"

She nodded. "Take care."

"You, too." He kissed her forehead, and then she left.

She stopped by the police car to introduce herself and offer coffee before she called it a night. They held up thermoses and politely refused and gave her a number to call them directly if she got the least bit worried.

She entered the residence with trepidation, not sure she had it in her to console Colby if her sister was freaking out. To her surprise, Colby greeted her with a hug, a bounce in her step.

"I did it, Darren! I played along with those creeps, like the police told me. Actually won a bit before I started losing. That game is so fixed. I couldn't have won if I was a poker genius."

"You did good, kid. I'm not sure I could've played along with them as well as you. I just hope Mike is as lucky with his part."

"Oh, right. Mike. I've been so focused on the game and getting out of there safely, I almost forgot about his role in this."

No surprise there. Still, Colby was free of them as well as back in the good graces of the university. A huge relief. "We're to stay put until we get word from the police it's all over. I'm sure the school will understand your missing classes."

With both of them still so hyped, Darren offered to make chamomile tea. They settled on the sofa to drink it. As the minutes passed, her body relaxed for the first time in hours. She even yawned. But by no means had she forgotten about Mike and what he was facing.

Colby flipped off her shoes and stuck her feet on the coffee table. Darren was too tired to say anything. "I am so sorry for involving you in all my problems. You've been great."

"Counting the lectures?"

"I deserved them. But once this all settles down, we need to talk. Katrina thinks part of the reason I got sucked into gambling was because of my dependence on you and Mom."

"Oh? Are you suggesting Mom and I are to blame for all this?"

"Oh no! That's not what I meant. It's just that the two of you have always, well, at least since Dad's death, babied me, let me shirk responsibility for my own actions."

Katrina was one smart lady. "You took Dad's death the hardest. You were always his baby. I guess Mom and I tried to make up for his loss."

Colby blinked several times. "My nerves and lack of sleep are catching up with me. We'll talk more soon." She dragged herself from the sofa but stopped after a couple steps. "This sofa can't be easy to sleep on every night. Come to bed with me. I could use your company."

They hadn't slept in the same bed since they were living with their mom in her tiny apartment. "Good idea." Darren rather liked the idea of keeping her baby sister close this night.

MIKE STAYED in the kind of hotel suite intended for business travelers. He got the bedroom, and his police guards took turns at their watch in the living room. One slept on the couch while the other propped himself near the door.

Before collapsing on the king-sized bed, which looked so inviting, Mike took a hot shower. He wanted to rid himself of the stench of this whole operation, although this would only provide a temporary cleansing. Tomorrow's action would sling even more dirt over his usually calm life.

Sometime around three thirty, he dozed off until his alarm woke him at six. Time to get going.

The call came shortly after eight. They wanted cash. Left in a duffel bag near a particular bench in a downtown park. The police had briefed him on how to deal with this contingency. "I can't get that amount of cash together so fast. My banks are bound to ask questions."

"You're a very powerful man in this town, Woodley. I'm sure your financial people will do whatever they have to do to keep your business."

"Even if I can get the money, how do I know you won't approach Colby again?"

"You don't."

"Unacceptable. I'm only going to do this once."

"Then she'll have to find someone else to pay her debts."

"Not if she doesn't play again."

The voice became more threatening. "Oh, she'll play."

Forewarned they might resort to this tactic, he raised his voice as planned. "What do you mean?"

"Greed and ego aren't the only ways to lead her to the table. Fear can be even more powerful."

"You dirtbag!" He screamed the words with even more vehemence than he'd planned. "Leave her alone! You've nearly wrecked her college career the way it is, if the cops ever find out."

Pause on the other end. "There might be a way to end this for her."

Mike let his response reflect a glimmer of hope. "How?"

"Surely, as a successful entrepreneur, you know the answer to your own question?"

"More money. You want more money?"

"Very good, Woodley."

Mike called him a few choice names.

"Do you want to explore this avenue or continue to rant?"

Mike counted to ten. Let the voice on the other end think he was considering his options. "What's the price tag?"

The voice spelled out the terms of their demand. The amount was four times the number mentioned earlier. "Surely, you're good for it. How much is the girl's freedom worth?"

Mike didn't say anything for a bit. "If I do this, I want to do it face to face."

"I don't think so."

"I do. You want that amount from me in the short period of time you've given me to get it together, you can face me to receive it. You or whoever is in charge of this operation, if it's not you. I want to see what kind of monster would do this to college kids."

"Don't be so fast to judge, Woodley. You take advantage of others' vulnerabilities and greed every day."

"One big difference. My business deals are legal, and more often than not, mutually beneficial."

"Whatever. No face-to-face meeting."

"Then my checkbook is closed."

"You do that, the kid will suffer."

"Yeah, well, maybe it's time she cuts her losses and goes to the police." He let it stop there for effect and held his breath until the voice on the other end responded.

The voice didn't respond at once. "All right. Face-to-face, but not the park. Somewhere less *public*. How long will it take you to get the money together?"

They dickered a bit more about where and when, but in the end, they agreed on a time and place. The place was the third Mike suggested, the one he and the police wanted all along. They knew the crooks would never go for the first and even the second suggestions.

Once he hung up, his part was done, at least until evening. He'd brought his laptop with him so he could work throughout the day. When he could concentrate, that is. The authorities allowed him to call Darren and reassure her things were moving along, but they warned him not to share any details.

A little after midnight, he called her again. "It's over. They got the head guy and several others they'd been surveilling since the poker game."

"Are you okay?" she asked, her voice tense.

"Nothing several tranquilizers and two days' continuous sleep can't cure," he said, attempting to minimize the hell he'd gone through so recently. He still couldn't believe it was over and he'd survived. "Tell Colby she can go back to school tomorrow." The other end of the line went silent for several beats. "Darren? You still there?"

"Uh, yeah. I'm just so relieved I can hardly speak. I still can't believe the nightmare's over."

"Me, too. But the police had me talk to their psychologist afterward to help me come down. That plus the paperwork I had to complete kept me at headquarters until now."

"We can't thank you enough."

"Hey, I got myself involved in this. Just glad I was able to help."

"Colby and I will put our heads together to figure out some way to repay you."

He hung up and wandered off to his waiting bed, anticipating Darren's repayment.

CHAPTER 15

Darren updated Colby with Mike's news as soon as she hung up. Colby, not the most demonstrative of people, swooped in and hugged her for several seconds. As they broke apart, they both swiped at tears and laughed at the same time.

"It's over. I can finally breathe again," Colby said.

"And go back to class."

"Sure. That, too." Colby lowered her voice so the police officer couldn't hear. "I promise you, I'm done with gambling. For good."

She sounded sincere. But Colby being Colby, time would tell. For now, though, Darren chose to reinforce her sister. "Those are the words I've been waiting to hear."

Darren turned to the police officer. "I trust you've already heard? Your colleagues have rounded up the gang. Guess you can leave any time now. We've appreciated your being here with us."

The police officer appeared to be in his forties and was slightly overweight with a bit of a paunch. "You're stuck with us a few more hours, Ms. Williams. They want us to hang around through the night while they assure they've got the entire ring in lockup."

"Oh. I guess that makes sense." She glanced at her sister. "Hope you don't mind me sharing the bed with you one more night?"

"After all you've done for me? How could I refuse?"

"Mike really went to bat for us. For me," Colby said.

Good. For once Colby realized how much she owed someone else. "That he did."

Colby paused in the process of pulling down the blankets on her side of the bed. "Why did he do it? Is there more going on between the two of you than you've told me?"

"He's becoming a good friend. That's all." If she divulged any details about having sex with the man, Colby would never let this drop. Still, Colby's question ricocheted around her brain. She wasn't feeling something more, was she? The man had been quite clear about avoiding commitments. But what about her?

"Too bad. I wish there was more. Not just because he's gorgeous and rich. He's a decent guy. They're not easy to come by."

No, they weren't. But she'd already found hers in Gordy, and now he was gone. Could lightning strike twice in a lifetime? Gordy would be the first to tell her she had to move on, but did grieving ever come to an end?

Unlike the night before, Darren slept well this night. Mike had done more than save her sister from prosecution and ejection from law school as well as help end the gambling ring. He'd given Darren back her peace of mind. Why had he risked so much to help them? Had Colby detected something she'd been too afraid to recognize?

Colby took off early for classes, leaving Darren to herself, since the police also pulled up stakes at daybreak. Time to check progress on Mike's house. With all the focus on felling the gambling ring, she hadn't visited Sullivan's Creek in days.

But as her car drew up to the intersection where she would turn west, something made her turn east instead and head toward downtown. She'd already talked to Mike the night before, and he'd reassured her he was fine. But she had to find out for herself.

Throughout the twenty-minute trip, a part of her brain kept asking her why she was doing this. It wasn't necessary. She resisted answering. She had to do this.

He buzzed her up and met her at the door, a robe thrown over his briefs. "Didn't expect to see you so soon."

In response, she grabbed his face and drew it to her lips. She kissed him so ferociously even she was surprised.

Mike uttered something. A question or a moan? She wouldn't let him talk. Not yet. Not until she'd kissed him silly, releasing the pent-up worry and fear she'd carried for days.

He didn't fight her. In fact, his arms went around her in a steely grip that signaled his appreciation. They stumbled around a bit, each trying to get closer to the other. He bumped into a chair, then picked her up and carried her to the sofa, where he placed her on his lap.

She finally came up for air and stared into his eyes. "I was so worried about you getting hurt. Or worse."

"I'm fine. But I like how you show concern."

"I would've come to check on you last night, but our police watchdogs stayed until this morning." She kissed him again. She'd be lying to herself if she saw it as simply a show of grati-tude. She wanted him. Couldn't get enough of him and didn't plan to stop any time soon.

He was the one who next pulled away. "Hey, babe, this is great. More than. But are you sure you want to continue? A guy can only take so much *appreciation* before his body interprets it as something else."

"I stopped *appreciating* a while back. This is me wanting you. Last night made me realize how easily I could lose you."

"Thought that was what's been in our way. You already having lost one man."

She placed a hand around his neck, loving the feel of the short hairs at the nape on her fingers. "I needed a push to emerge from my grieving period. Last night was a kick in the pants."

"Then I'm doubly happy it turned out all right." He nibbled at her neck, sending heat all the way to her core.

"I still don't understand why you stepped up."

"You don't? I could see the pressure you were under and wanted to make it go away. I've become very fond of you."

"And I, you. Now you're my hero as well."

He lifted a brow. "Really? I've never had that honor before."

"Besides taking care of the fire in my stomach, I must also take care of my hero."

He drew away slightly, offered a lascivious grin. "The hero part isn't necessary, but I like the part about fulfilling your needs."

"Thought you might, although let's keep this mutual."

No further invitation necessary, he lifted her and carried her to his bedroom.

But she'd meant what she said. She wanted to take care of him. Rolling onto her knees, she pushed him onto his back and removed the robe. She removed his briefs and nearly caught her breath.

Mike got the hint and simply lay there, gazing up at her with eyes growing cloudier by the second.

Remaining on her knees, she pulled her sweater over her head and tossed it aside. "Stay." She climbed off the bed so she could unzip and remove her slacks. His eyes never wavered as she stood before him in only her bra and panties. She'd never felt such intense power over a man, not even with Gordy. Everything with Mike seemed so much more grown-up than the college lust she'd shared with her dead fiancé.

She was tempted to linger, draw this out like a striptease. But she was too anxious to get to the next part. To show him how much she cared. And wanted his body. Wanted him inside her.

She deftly slipped out of the bra, let her breasts swing free.

Shook her hair. Her panties came next. And then she was completely naked, standing before him for his approval.

He licked his lower lip. "Come here."

She complied and crawled over him from the bottom of the bed. She caught his hand when it came up to enfold her. "No. Just lie there. Let me do this."

"I'll try." His voice croaked.

Her actions were improvised. She'd never taken the lead before. If possible, the prospect added even more excitement to the moment. Palms planted on each side of him, she leaned down, dangled her breasts, and let her nipples barely touch his chest hairs. Shock waves exploded within her. Her private parts went wild.

A moan escaped him, but he continued to lie flat below her, let her do the work.

As he had done to her minutes before, she nuzzled his neck, inhaling the scent of recently awakened man and nearly going faint. She soldiered on, moving her mouth down over his clavicle and tonguing her way south over his abdomen. Darker hairs sprinkled his chest, though by now she barely noticed the color because she'd shut her eyes as her tongue flicked downward.

Never had she been so stimulated, so aroused. She was ready for him to take her right then, but age-old womanly intuition told her she wasn't finished.

For the next several minutes, she explored his body with her mouth, her other senses alive and motivated.

Beneath her, Mike continued to squirm and groan in pleasure. But he could apparently only take so much, because at length he pulled her up to him over a very hard and ready erection. "So good … but enough … want you now."

He took over, climbing over her and spreading her legs with a knee. She was so ready, he entered her with little difficulty and began to thrust. Just in time, he remembered to sheath himself; in her enthusiasm, she'd lost track of such details.

Their coupling assumed a dreamlike mood as she let her mind drift through mists of pleasure. As he plunged deeper and faster, her hands tore at the bedclothes beneath her until finally they both came together and lay spent.

She didn't move for several seconds. Instead, she savored the incredible satisfaction of afterglow. Completeness.

Mike stirred beside her. "Darren?"

"Hmm?"

"Are you okay?"

"More than."

"No tears? No regrets?"

"No. Only unbridled pleasure. Thank you for waiting."

He swiped a loose tendril of hair from her face, his tenderness palpable. "You were worth it."

Only staggering forbearance kept her from saying what was on her mind, "I love you." Where the thought had come from, how long it had laid low under her mind's radar, she didn't know. Given Mike's feelings about commitment, she held back. Her feelings were so new she needed time to absorb them herself. Perhaps it was just the thrill of the moment, gratitude for helping her break away from her grief.

As much as they were tempted to shower together, Darren begged off. "Time to check the progress on your house. I've put it off the last few days as I dealt with Colby's problems."

"Good idea. I'd like to see the changes myself," he replied.

"Uh, why not let me act as the first wave, in case things aren't quite where they should be."

"You gonna whip the crews into line for me if they're behind?" His tone was teasing.

"Something like that. No need for you to intervene unless it's necessary."

Once they were both dressed, he walked her to the door. Before she left, he kissed the top of her head. "Best wake-up call ever, lady."

Darren adjusted the rearview mirror before setting off for Mike's new home. The reflection wore a goofy smile. The kind of smile resulting from incredible morning sex. That was her! And she was one happy woman. Better pay extra attention to the road. If she let her mind wander back to Mike's bed, no telling what kind of accident she'd encounter along the way.

She arrived at the house to find Shae just leaving. The other woman was shaking her head. "I hope Michael likes it, after all the rush and extra staff we've brought in."

"Does that mean you're done? Ahead of schedule?"

"Getting there. Most of the construction is finished, awaiting paint, when the rest of the place is painted. Can't do the floor 'til that's done."

"Can I go in?"

The temporary head of Two Rivers Construction zipped her jacket. "Sure, just keep out of the crew's way. I have to admit it does look better, but I'll deny ever saying that if you tell Mike."

Darren had to smile. Shae really did like her boyfriend's partner. "Your secret's safe with me. I've experienced the same revolting discovery when he's rejected furnishings I thought were perfect picks only for him to come up with something much better. Where he got those ideas is beyond me."

"Mike's a complicated guy. Ned seemed that way at first, too. But once I learned how he was working through his guilt at not being there for his dad before his death by overcompensating with his mother, he got easier to read."

Shae was sending her some kind of message. Darren wished she had more time to pursue this conversation, but she was anxious to see the progress on the house, and with each passing minute, the weather was getting another degree colder. "Are you suggesting something similar is going on with Mike?"

Shae offered a benign smile. "Could be. Up to you whether you want to dig deeper."

Darren remembered all too well the scene she'd just left as well as Mike's recent heroism and help to her family. "Yeah. All I have to do is decide whether or not I want to let the archaeologist in me come forward."

"Sometimes you just have to listen to your heart." Shae let those be her parting words and headed off to her SUV.

Darren scuttled to the front door. Listen to her heart. That sounded so easy. But it wasn't. Especially when said heart was only now beginning to emerge from cold storage after two years.

As soon as she came through the threshold, the change in the great room's appearance caught her attention. "Wow," she told no one in particular. One of the workmen sent her to the crew leader, Marty, who was working upstairs in one of the bedrooms.

"You the one who ordered all these changes post construction?" Marty asked after she'd introduced herself.

"Ordered them, yes, but they came directly from the owner, Mike Woodley, one of the developers here at Sullivan's Creek."

"Good thing you waited until now to show up. Earlier? You might've been chased away. Today? You can bask in your own wisdom. Every one of the revisions we've made improved the place."

"Wish I could take the credit, then."

"If you're the one who's been ordering all the furnishings, you need to rethink your delivery instructions. Three packages have already arrived. We didn't know what to do with them, since they'll be in the way of painting and flooring, so we stuck them in the garage. But we'll be gone after tomorrow."

Did anything ever go the way interior decorators planned? "Nothing was supposed to show up until next week at the earliest. Thanks for taking delivery. I'm, uh, new at this and doing this job mainly as a favor to Mr. Woodley."

"Suspected something like that. But since what you've done so far seems to be pretty good, I'll let you in on a trade secret. Most interior decorators I know spend the better part of their time on the phone checking and double-checking delivery times. Furniture dealers and the like pay little attention to the customers' delivery dates. Something about production runs and availability of materials from overseas."

"In other words, I have to be on them constantly."

Marty made a pistol out of his right index finger. "Bingo. These days, some text when they're on their way, but not all. If you're not around, you can't depend on whatever crew is here at the time to take delivery."

Her job as Mike's decorator had just become ten times more difficult. "Thanks, Marty. You've just added more hours to my day, but you've saved me from likely disaster."

He saluted and returned to his work.

She dashed downstairs and out to the garage to check the first deliveries. Two small boxes from the same accessories concern were stacked on top of a larger carton from a lighting supplier. She borrowed a box cutter from one of the crew.

Thank God Marty had mentioned these arrivals. Two out of three had to be returned. A ceramic garden stool in the small package was broken, and the floor light in the carton was the wrong item. Was this typical? She hoped not, or her life for the next few weeks was going to be that of inventory clerk. As well as shipping clerk, since it would be up to her to return them.

Before she left, she checked in again with Marty to find out when the painting would be done. She needed to stop by before then to assure the painters had the right colors.

She considered stopping at the RV on her way back to the studio but decided not to alarm Mike. They'd parted on such a positive note, why ruin things too soon? He might not even have arrived yet, if he still had to work with the police.

As she was approaching town, her phone rang. But it wasn't Mike. Instead, it was Janice Collier. "I haven't heard from you for several days. Had to learn from Frances Woodley that you were decorating my house—can't seem to call it Mike's house yet."

"Sorry. My life has gotten out of control the last few weeks.

Mike and I worked things out on the paintings and then, out of the blue, he asked me to furnish the house. Long story, I'll fill you in over coffee sometime."

"How about in the next hour? While you were teaming up with Mike, I agreed to partner with his mother on a gala holiday showing at her home. Since, of course, it will include some of your work, I was hoping you could meet me there for backup?"

Backup? Janice was one savvy businesswoman. She didn't need reinforcements. "What kind of help do you need from me?"

Her friend didn't reply at once. "As important as this event could be for the gallery, working with Mrs. Woodley is proving to be a bit of a … challenge. She's mentioned more than once, repeatedly, actually, that she knows you. I was hoping you could, uh, serve as a sort of buffer."

"Run interference?" Darren kept her tone light so her friend would know she was gently joshing her.

"Okay, you got me. I'll take you to coffee or lunch afterward if you'll come help."

"I don't know how I can help, but I'm on my way. I should be there in thirty-five minutes. Where should I meet you?"

Later, Darren parked her car at a coffee shop not far from the Woodley mansion and joined Janice in her vehicle. "Tell me how Frances Woodley is getting on your nerves."

"I didn't say that. At least not in those words."

She'd never seen her friend this tense. "Okay, talk to me. Tell me what's been going on."

"She wants to use my client list for invites, instead of providing me with the names of her friends. I don't want to overuse my list, or they stop showing up. I had hoped to gain new names from her."

Darren vaguely remembered walking in on a discussion between Mike and his mother about gaining new social contacts when she'd delivered the second seascape. Intimidated by the very thought of being in the presence of not only Mike but also his mother, she hadn't taken in much of that exchange. All she'd wanted to do was give him the new painting, receive her fee and get out of there. "What reason did she give you for not providing her list?"

"She's hasn't actually refused to give me any names. She's much too smooth. That's part of what's getting to me, since I pretty much tell it like it is."

True, except when she was schmoozing a potential sale. Janice could talk a fine line then, too, but it wasn't worth reminding her at the moment. Janice needed to vent and hopefully get the anger out of her system by the time they arrived at the Woodley home.

Darren's loyalty to Mike had increased tenfold these days, and by extension, to his family. "Mr. and Mrs. Woodley have only recently returned to town. Maybe she feels out of touch with former social acquaintances."

"She implied something like that. But surely they still know a few people through their business or their church."

"You want me to encourage her to come through with a few names? Like how?" Although both times she'd seen her, Frances Woodley had treated her well, Darren hardly knew the woman. Mike had fled the house within days of the woman's arrival.

"Could you? If this showing is going to be the event of the social year she seems to envision, it needs to include more of the town's so-called elite."

"I'll see what I can do, but I can't promise anything. If I noted anything about the woman, she appears to be quite persistent."

Janice shot her a quick glance as she brought the car to a stop in front of the house. "We agree on that point, at least."

"I brought one of my top artists along with me," Janice said to Frances Woodley as she and Darren entered the house. "Thought we could benefit from her perspective as we plan this party. I understand you've already met Darren Williams?"

Mike's mother broadened the smile with which she greeted

Janice and extended her hand to Darren. "Ms. Williams, how nice to see you again."

Darren employed the smile she usually saved for actual showings and returned the handshake. "The feeling is mutual, Mrs. Woodley. Please call me Darren."

The corner of Mrs. Woodley's mouth curled up. Dressed today in a dove gray sweater—most likely cashmere—and a charcoal gray pencil skirt that showed off her slim body, she was the epitome, at least as far as Darren was concerned, of elegance. "Darren, then. I understand you not only did a painting for my son Michael, but you're also now decorating his new home. Joe Jr., my oldest son, told me."

Darren wondered if Mike knew his mother was on to their working relationship. "That's right. I had a little downtime today, so I was able to come along with Mrs. Collier."

"Then follow me, both of you. I thought we could walk through the rooms we'll be using and finalize plans as we go." She led them into the area where Darren had confronted Mike on past occasions. "Guests will enter here in the formal living room after handing over their wraps near the front door." She held out a slim hand trimmed with a narrow sliver of silver bracelet. "The first bar will be set up here. Get them drinking immediately to encourage their full participation in the event."

In other words, ply them with alcohol so they'd buy more. *Grow up. That's the business you're in.*

"I'd suggest serving only white wine," Janice said. "Or champagne. If guests spill, the stains will be less visible than red wine."

Darren noted how Janice had omitted *our* in her reference to guests.

"Oh. I hadn't thought of that. Of course. I'll let the caterer I've selected know."

"And who would that be?" Janice asked. Her hostess shared a name. From Janice's tight smile, it was apparent this wasn't one of her favorites. "Have you signed a contract yet? I haven't had the best experience with them in the past."

"Really? I had such a nice chat with the owner. I feel totally confident they can deliver great fare."

Janice didn't challenge her. Apparently, food and drink fell into Mrs. Woodley's list of tasks. "Okay. Your choice. If they fall through, I hope you'll keep my guys in mind."

The tour continued into the next room, which Woodley referred to as the casual living room. "I thought we'd set up some of the displays in here. Through those double doors over there is the drawing room, where we can place the rest. That should give us enough space, don't you think?" she asked Janice.

Janice wandered about the rooms, narrowing her eyes at times, as if optically measuring every bit of square footage. At other times, she'd open her arms to verify what her eyes had told her. "Is this it?"

Woodley took a step back. "Yes. These rooms are larger than your entire gallery. Surely, this space will be enough for what you plan to bring?"

"For a showing, you have to plan for extra space between items to accommodate the crowd," Janice said. "Also, since we're getting close to the holidays, I assume you'll be decorating these rooms?"

"Well, yes." Woodley now sounded less sure of herself.

Janice seemed to realize she'd assumed the upper hand with her questions about space. "This will do fine, Frances. Would it be possible to send me a floor plan of all the rooms we'll be using, including dimensions and your plans for decorations? I'll use those to make the final determination of items to show."

"Of course. I'm meeting with my holiday person tomorrow and will have them forward their plans to you. But I was under the impression as hostess I'd be contributing my thoughts to the selection of items?"

One of Janice's eyebrows rose imperceptibly. "I handle that part myself."

"Oh. I just thought in my role as patroness of the arts, I would be included."

Darren shot a meaningful look at her friend. Time to intervene. "I've got an idea. Why don't you each serve as the other's consultant? Mrs. Woodley, you could tour the gallery and offer your suggestions for pieces to be shown, based on your knowledge of your friends' tastes"—she deliberately referred to the guests as Mrs. Woodley's friends—"then you could share your list of food and beverage choices with Janice for her input." Neatly put, if she did think so herself.

"I, I suppose that might work," Mike's mother said.

"Uh, yes, Darren, good idea."

After a few more minutes of parting small talk, Janice and Darren escaped the mansion. Once they were sure they were out of eyeshot of their hostess, they ended the visit with much enjoyed fist bumps. Nonetheless, something about her tour of the mansion's public rooms kept nagging at Darren. It wasn't exactly an uneasy feeling, more like something she'd noted subconsciously that wouldn't go away until it made its way to the surface on its own.

CHAPTER 16

Though Mike resumed his normal activities, concentration took effort. His brain kept replaying the events of earlier in the morning with his surprise visitor. After both their previous attempts at sex had fizzled, he'd taken great pains to keep his hands off her, until last night, when he'd reassured her about the sting.

Thank God for that. He still couldn't believe the danger he'd put himself in to help Darren and her sister, though he wouldn't have had it any other way. She'd called him her hero. Him. He'd just wanted to make their problem go away. But hell, it felt damned good to have gained such respect.

At the RV, he spent the better part of the day on the phone reorganizing the divisions of a company he owned in Missouri. The previous president had retired a few months earlier, leaving a distant relative to take over. As a result, revenue had decreased by ten percent. Time to retread that one.

Around eleven, Jay made an appearance. "'Bout time you showed up," Mike said. "Just because you're in tight with one of the partners, doesn't mean you can clock in midday."

Jay plopped down on the couch next to him, unperturbed by Mike's comment. "I've been out selling Sullivan's Creek, dear brother. Took a breakfast meeting with Ned before he hit the road, and then I met with prospective customers."

"Did they sign on the dotted line?" Mike meant it as a way to deflate his brother's optimism, though he couldn't help hoping maybe the guy had been successful.

"On the first date? Be serious, man. This'll take at least two more rounds of my glowing personality and subliminal arm-twisting before they're begging us to let them buy. But I made progress."

"I'm sure you did. I'm just impatient."

Jay went over to the fancy new coffeemaker he'd insisted they acquire to impress clients and poured himself a cup. From the few potential buyers he'd seen in the RV, Mike suspected the new appliance was more for his brother's caffeine habit than anything else, but if the stuff kept the guy sharp, what did he care?

Jay lifted his mug. "Want some?"

Mike shook his head. He'd had enough of the brew while he waited for the gambling issue to be resolved. It would be a while before he drank more.

"This impatience about sales you mentioned? That wouldn't be a sign that, like Ned, you've overextended yourself with this project?"

"Hell no!" Why did he respond so vehemently? He blew out a breath. "Yes, I invested a bundle in Sullivan's Creek, and no, I have yet to see that decision pay off, but I'm in good shape financially. Learned a long time ago my best defense is a diverse portfolio. I'm actively overseeing my other ventures and still seeking new ones."

Jay settled across from him and took a few sips of his joe. "Just checking. Wondered how much pressure was on me to produce immediately."

"I may have established overly lofty sales goals for this place, which have now spilled onto your shoulders. Take the time necessary to develop these leads."

Jay stirred his coffee, even though it was black. "Good idea for Ned to give me that tour of the place. Did you know he spent his summers out here when it was his grandparents' farm? Everywhere we went, he shared some memory about a crop that had been planted there or learning to drive his grandfather's tractor over some field."

Over the years, Mike had heard all this from his friend, but Jay's hearing about Sullivan's Creek directly from Ned had apparently fired up his brother's enthusiasm, because he now leaned closer, his eyes glowing. "Ned is a walking, talking advertisement we need to tap. When he gets back from his next gig, we're working up a sales video for your nonexistent website. Another item I can't believe you haven't developed."

Who would've guessed Jay would take a shine to Mike's friend, the guy Jay had always resented for dipping into Mike's trust fund?

DARREN RETURNED to her studio on a sugar high from overindulging in doughnuts and coffee with Janice.

After lauding her for her diplomatic handling of Frances Woodley, Janice had returned to the earlier topic. "You not only sold Mike Woodley your paintings after he rejected both, but you agreed to be his interior decorator. How did I miss out on so much?"

"I didn't intentionally exclude you. I've been extremely busy. Had to learn interior decoration on the run. And my sister has moved in with me temporarily, which has also cut into my time."

"I thought your sister had an apartment in town?"

"Uh, yes, she does. She's subleased it for a month or so for the extra money." She considered telling her friend about Colby's gambling but withstood the urge. The less people knew about Colby's situation, the better. "The first year of law school is proving to be more expensive than we anticipated. Hopefully, she'll receive additional financial assistance next semester."

"What's it like having Mike as your client?" Janice asked.

Her friend was trolling for information, and they both knew it. Darren's feelings for Mike were so new she didn't want to allow the slightest hint she might be falling for the guy. Instead, she regaled Janice with tales of her trials at getting Mike to decide what he wanted.

"Mike sounds so different from his mother, who seems to have an opinion on everything."

"He's a good businessman, so he must have a pretty keen take on that area. But when it comes to furnishing his own place, he comes up blank. At least until I present him with something I've picked, then he's Johnny-on-the-spot with his preferences."

Janice finished her latte. "Interesting. Do you think he's trying to addle you?"

"I did, at first. But the more we've worked through selections for the house, the more I get the impression that some place inside his psyche, some place he barely knows exists, he does know what he wants. Why he seems to have so much trouble connecting with it, I don't know."

They rose to leave. "And I get the impression you are enjoying this assignment more than you let on."

Darren let Janice's speculation go unanswered. Maybe her friend had a point.

Nearing midday, Darren could finally set to work checking up on her orders, calling distributors and home-furnishing companies where she had a telephone number or emailing where she didn't. An hour later, she'd contacted four of over twenty companies. Of those, only one could give her a specific delivery date, although even they hedged, saying it could be a day or two before or after. For two, she'd had to leave a voice-mail message. The fourth couldn't find her order but promised a return call once they'd checked their records. Clearly, she would have to devise a smarter method of getting on top of deliveries.

Her original calendar had everything arriving two weeks before her absolute final deadline, December twenty-fourth. That deadline had been a fantasy. The question was, how much of that clearance would go down the tubes?

She stayed with her project the rest of the afternoon but only garnered a few more commitments. Commitments? More like predictions, best guesses, maybe even outright lies.

Her phone rang. Someone was actually returning a call? No, it was her mother. "Just wanted to check when you planned to arrive Thursday."

Thursday? Good grief, this Thursday was Thanksgiving, two days away. How had she missed that when she'd been studying the calendar all afternoon? For the last few years, she and Colby helped their mother serve Thanksgiving dinner at the Blue Iris to those down on their luck. The restaurant management provided the food, but they needed extra help getting diners through the line, finding seats for them and cleaning up afterward. "Uh, I'll check with Colby, but let's tentatively say ten thirty. Will that be soon enough?"

"We start serving at eleven thirty, like every year, but that should be enough time to set up the tables."

She hung up feeling anything but thankful. Now she wouldn't be able to work on Thursday, or at least part of the day. *Check the attitude, Williams. Surely, you can spend one day caring for others' needs?*

If she worked into the night today and did the same tomorrow, she could take Thursday off. She had to catch distributors today, because many might be taking off early for the holiday tomorrow and not returning until next Monday. Damn! How had she missed this detail in her planning?

The people she needed to call weren't the only ones who'd probably be off eating turkey and watching football games. Would any of the crews be at the house tomorrow and Friday? Better call Shae and find out.

But before she could ring up the general contractor, her phone rang again.

"Hi." Mike.

God, he sounded sexy. His voice surrounded her like a caress. "Hi, yourself. What's up?"

"How about dinner? Wherever you want to eat."

So tempting. But she had work to do. "Sorry. Much as I'd like to say yes, I've got this very *demanding* client who expects me to finish his project on time. It's nose-to-the-grindstone time from now until it's done."

"Oh." Deflated tone. "How about tomorrow night?"

"Uh-uh." She owed him an explanation, but she didn't want to admit she'd overestimated her suppliers' follow-through on her delivery dates.

"Didn't think my hero cred would have run out so soon." He sounded like a disappointed child. "Okay, how 'bout this? Spend the day with me Thursday. Surely, you're taking time off for Thanksgiving? I'll take you out or have a full turkey dinner catered at the mansion, since my parents will be in Florida a few days. We can watch the games on their big screen."

Three turndowns in a row? She couldn't do that to him. "Why don't you join me on Thursday instead?"

"You cooking?"

"Uh, no. I'll be at the Blue Iris along with my mom and sister, feeding an army. Want to help? We can always use another pair of hands." And strong shoulders.

"Like for the homeless?" Skeptical tone.

"Some are. Some are just barely getting by but still deserve a warm meal for the holiday. We're usually done by three, once cleanup is finished."

The other end of the line was silent a bit. She'd really disappointed him. "Yeah, sure, I'll join you. Never done anything like that, but I'll be happy to help. Got enough food? I can make some calls."

"Thanks, but I think we're fine. The restaurant has been doing this for several years."

He lingered. "Uh, could you use another pair of hands besides mine? My brother, Jay, is remaining in town. Thinks he might get some potential buyers after the holiday."

"Of course. I should've asked about him. We'd love to have him join us."

MIKE HUNG UP IN A FUNK. Ever since he'd decided he needed to see Darren again today—one time in bed wasn't enough—he'd let his imagination run wild conjuring up just how and where they'd do it. God, he was worse than a randy teenager wanting to cop his first feel.

As if that weren't enough to make him crazy, it finally sank in that he'd agreed to spend time with Darren's mother and sister. On a holiday, no less. Why hadn't his usual radar kicked in to help him avoid this familial encounter? He wanted to see her so badly he probably would have agreed to anything short of a wedding. Thank God that word still raised his hackles and sent him running.

He arrived at the Blue Iris promptly at eleven Thursday morning. Surprisingly, Jay was there waiting for him. As he approached, his brother rubbed his gloved hands together. "Nippy morning, huh? They're predicting a covering of snow by evening."

They being the weather forecasters, who every Iowan worth

his salt, not just the farmers, followed religiously, because the weather could change on a dime.

"This'll be my test. Haven't spent much time here in winter for years," Mike said. "Probably will have to augment my wardrobe soon with heavier sweaters and wool pants."

"Like you need more clothes." Jay nudged him as they walked toward the front door."

Mike chose to avoid the comment and instead attempted to bring his brother up to speed about the Williams family. "You've met Darren. Her sister, Colby, is a first-year law student, and their mother—think her name is Elise—works here at this eatery."

Armed with such information, Jay acquitted himself well when introduced to the Williams women a minute later. "You've saved me the bane of eating my Thanksgiving dinner alone, Mrs. Williams," he told Darren's mother. "For which I am quite grateful and eager to do my share helping with your event."

Elise Williams blinked a few times, apparently not accustomed to such manners.

"What do you want us to do?" Mike asked. "I see you've got the tables set up already.

"The owner allows most of the staff to spend this day with their families, as long as a few of us are here to do the serving. In return, whoever's here the prior day does setup before leaving," Mrs. Williams said.

Mike noted only the Williams women and an older couple were there this morning. He and Jay would actually be able to contribute. "And the food? Did you come in early to do that also?"

"The cook and her staff came in at four and left a little while ago. All we have to do is keep things warm and serve," Darren said.

Colby showed them where to stow their outer garments. Jay sported a navy-blue pullover and tan cords, but Mike had worn a gray suede jacket and navy dress slacks. "You may want to hang up your jacket, Mike. You'll get an apron, but that won't cover your sleeves."

Damn. He'd spent time this morning pondering how to dress. Didn't want to look like a snob to the folks they'd be serving, but on the other hand, it was a holiday. His mother had drilled a formal dress code for holidays into her children years ago. He'd guessed wrong.

"Don't you look festive," Darren said, coming up to him. She took his jacket and handed him an apron. Colby did the same for Jay.

"Guess I should've checked with you on the dress code today."

"Phooey. As long as you're comfortable. And warm. It's getting quite cold out there."

Mrs. Williams divvied up serving duties: Mike would stand first in line and offer slices of turkey. Next, Darren would provide dressing and cranberry sauce. Colby followed her, serving green bean casserole, and then Jay would do either mashed or sweet potatoes. Last, Mrs. Williams would oversee pie distribution. They had pumpkin, apple and minced.

"As much as we want our guests to enjoy the meal, we serve them rather than let them serve themselves, or there might not be enough food remaining by the time the last guests go through," she said.

Smart. Wouldn't have occurred to him until they were out of food too soon.

He and Jay were introduced to the owners, Ron and Carol Dortman. They would be the runners, they explained, and would keep the servers' food containers filled.

"They're lining up outside already," Colby said.

Darren glanced at her watch. "Five more minutes. We always start exactly on time."

Mr. and Mrs. Dortman went to the door. "Take your places, everybody."

Once Mike had examined his aluminum pan of light and dark meat and grabbed his tongs, he glanced at the crowd outside the doors. The line had grown in the time it took him to get settled. He had no idea there were so many who wouldn't have Thanksgiving dinner otherwise. He made a mental note to add to the festivities next year.

In orderly fashion, the crowd swarmed in. The Dortmans greeted almost everyone by name and then directed them to the serving line. It was his job to ask them to take a paper plate and packet of utensils rolled in a napkin.

Showtime. For the next half hour, it was all he could do to shovel turkey fast enough. Faces swam by, he didn't notice. All he cared about was hearing whether they wanted white, dark, or both and getting it on their plate fast enough to keep the line moving.

Around noon, there was a slight break in the queue, although guests continued to wander in. He was finally able to say something to Darren. "Wow. I wasn't prepared for these numbers. Is it like this every year?"

"Pretty much. Even when it snows, they're here."

At twelve forty-five, the Dortmans sent each of them through the line. They placed their plates on one of the several now-empty tables. They finally ran out of food around one, just a few minutes after the last person had come through. The Dortmans locked the door, placed a Closed sign on it and they all settled in to devour their own Thanksgiving dinners.

Turkey and dressing had never tasted so good. Not to mention the two pieces of pie Mrs. Dortman insisted he take.

They took their time enjoying their meal. "Thank you, boys, for your help," Darren's mother said. "It went so much smoother with you here this year."

"I'll say." Colby put down her fork for a moment. "Usually Darren and I are doing double duty, and Mom not only hands out slices of pie, she also makes sure the guests know where the beverages are."

"This food and the company have been great. I'm stuffed," Jay told his tablemates.

"Me, too," Mike said. "On this day, I usually eat at whatever hotel I'm visiting or grab a hotdog somewhere. This has been truly special."

"We still have to do clean up," Darren's mother said. "I hope you're up for that as well? It goes so much quicker with more of us to help."

The women took care of cleaning and putting away the few nondisposable pots and pans in the kitchen while Mike, Jay and Mr. Dortman handled the garbage and rearrangement of the tables. As Darren had predicted, they were done well before three. The Dortmans said their good-byes and thanked them one more time.

Colby waited until then to thank Mike for extricating her from the gambling scheme. "I'm just glad everything worked out okay for you and that it's over."

He gave her a direct gaze. "It is over, isn't it?"

"If you mean, am I still in trouble with the school, no. My record is clean, and I've been assigned a financial advisor who's helping me apply for scholarships and assistance next semester."

"That's great. But …"

"What about my—she stole a look over her shoulder to make sure no one else was listening—uh, problem? I've learned my lesson. I don't think Darren's convinced, so I'm continuing on with my counselor."

He shook her hand. "That's what I wanted to hear."

"What I want to hear is what's going on between you and my sister."

The attorney-to-be was attempting to put him on the stand. Not ready to testify. "What has she said?"

"Not much. But you wouldn't be here today if something wasn't going on."

They headed toward the others, who stood near their cars looking puzzled. "You won't believe it was the promise of a full Turkey Day meal?"

She shook her head.

He pulled up from joining the others. "I really like her. More each day. You'll have to be satisfied with that answer for now."

She twisted her head toward him and grinned. "For now."

CHAPTER 17

The next day, Mike went back to work at the RV. He'd only been there a half hour before he was seeking caffeine from the new coffeemaker. His entire body ached from standing for over ninety minutes in his dress shoes, especially his feet and shoulders—why he hadn't thought to wear more comfortable footwear, he didn't know.

Jay showed up a little later, appearing to be in much better shape. "That was some great day yesterday. Haven't enjoyed family stuff like that in years."

"Did our family ever serve others like that?" Even with his protesting body, Mike had been smiling to himself ever since he'd left the restaurant, though he'd been unable to persuade Darren to join him at his loft. It took his brother to put the feeling into words.

"Mom and Dad's idea of charity was writing a check, which they've done liberally. But hands-on stuff, no. I really felt good afterward."

"Me, too. I want to do something like that next year. Maybe augment the Dortmans' food supplies so they can serve more people."

Jay dropped into one of the club chairs. "I miss the things the kids and Alicia and I did together. You don't realize it while it's happening. You grouse about giving up naps so everyone can be together, and then when you no longer have it, it hits you how those were the golden times."

"Our mom does her share of *insisting* we all get together."

The comparison of Mrs. Williams' and their mother's actions and their kids' responses had already struck him. "Yeah, but Darren and Colby do it because they don't want to disappoint their mother. You and I and probably Harper and Gardner only agree to family activities out of guilt."

"Hope you didn't feel *guilted* into bringing me along."

Now he'd gone and insulted his brother. He'd considered them both on the same side, them against their parents, but Jay had taken his comments personally. "Look, I invited you yesterday because I didn't want you sitting around by yourself all day. And if you must know, I was feeling a little ill at ease at the thought of serving all those people."

"Misery loves company?"

Mike hung his head. "Well, yeah."

Jay's phone rang. He glanced at the readout. "Gotta take this. It's Ned." For the next several minutes, Jay's side of the conversation was mainly a series of "yeps" and "nahs." His eyes sought out Mike. "Yeah, I'll let him know. See you next week. Oh? I'll ask him. Wonder if he knows."

Now what?

"You want the bad news or the badder news first?"

Not what Mike wanted to hear. "Build up."

"Ned reminded me that our mothers have teamed up for a holiday showing at the mansion," Jay said.

"Yeah? I was there when Mom hatched this brilliant scheme. Even tried to warn Janice to no avail."

"It's next Wednesday. Ned's mother wants him to attend. He said if he has to suffer through it, so do we, since our mother started it."

"Are you kidding me? See, this is why I have no fond memories of family events. Mom gets some crazy scheme in her head, and then she expects the rest of us to just go along with her. It's no wonder Harper stays in Florida and Gard holes up in California."

"All you have to do is dress pretty, which we both know you can do, be nice to the people, let them think you're happy as a clam to be there, and talk up Mrs. Collier's artists, which include Darren Williams. See, there's the bright spot. I saw how you looked at her yesterday. She's getting under your skin. So go support Darren, if nothing else."

There was that. She'd warned him she was going to be super-busy finishing his house before Christmas. Wednesday night might be his only chance to see her for a while.

"Okay. Guess I can't get out of it. You should come, too. Who knows? You might unearth a prospective client."

"Speaking of which, my realtor contacts paid off. I've got two appointments today. One couple is in town for the holiday and may be relocating so one of them can be closer to their parents. The other finally has a day off."

Mike high-fived his brother. "Nice going."

"My realtor friends came through. That wining and dining is paying off, although I've really gotta watch my diet when I'm not on the job."

Late Wednesday afternoon, Darren pulled out the same cocktail dress she'd worn months before at her prior showing. The night she met Mike. Her life had changed so much since then, and he was largely responsible. Not just hiring her as his decorator nor saving Colby from her predators, but also for helping her emerge from two years of nothingness.

Per Shae, her crews finished most of their additions to the

house the previous Wednesday. A couple of guys had gone in Friday morning to complete the job. Darren had stopped by Monday to check in with the paint crew. Couldn't tell much until the next day. This morning, she'd found all the painting completed and the flooring crews there. The wood floors would go in today. Tomorrow, the tile. After that, the house was hers to finish.

Everything seemed to be converging at once, starting with tonight's showing. She didn't anticipate any commissions this time. Mike's order had been unusual. But with only a few more deliveries in the garage, tomorrow she'd be back on the phone threatening, cajoling, bribing and whatever she had to do to finish the house in two weeks.

The big pieces—the davenport, the dining-room table, a desk for Mike's office, and his bed—were among the items yet to be delivered along with most of the window treatments. It wouldn't mean much to have the bulk of the accessories on board if there was no place to put them.

Thus far, she'd kept her delivery problems from Mike. He hadn't asked, so she hadn't volunteered. No telling what he'd do if he found out, although if she was still missing things as she neared her deadline, she might have to set him loose to kick some ass.

She arrived at the Woodley mansion an hour ahead of time to give herself a chance to take in the layout and check her pieces and the promotional materials Janice had prepared. She was struck immediately with holiday splendor, no other way to describe all the gold and silver decorations that had taken over the room. Even unpopulated, the space made her feel as if she'd wandered into a high-end garage sale. How was Janice reacting to all this extra "stuff"?

She didn't have long to find out. Janice charged into the room, a glass of wine in hand. "Thank God the bar's already set up. I rarely imbibe during these things, but I needed this."

"I thought she sent you the layouts? Did this catch you off guard as much it did me?"

Janice gulped her wine before replying, apparently needing it before she could speak. "Yes, if you want to call them that. Whoever prepared them simply drew circles and squares around the rooms with such specific descriptions as 'gold bush,' 'silver tree,' and 'silver fountain' written in. They weren't even to scale. If they had been, I would have protested immediately. As it was, I still wanted to know if the fountain would have actual water. Last thing we need at a showing."

Darren was simultaneously interested and horrified. "How'd that go?"

Janice swept her hand toward the back of the room. "See for yourself. The word *compromise* is nowhere in the woman's vocabulary. The best I could do was get it placed as far from the artwork as possible."

"Where is she now? Have you told her how you feel about this bizarre bazaar?"

Janice shook her head. "Too late. What's done is done. Mike tried to warn me, but I was sure I could deal with her. As for her current location, she's off getting ready for her grand entrance. This wine is helping me arm myself for whatever that turns out to be."

To get her friend's mind off the antics of their hostess, Darren asked where her station was located. To her surprise, she'd been placed in the center of this first room. "Thanks, Janice, for putting me in the thick of things."

"Actually, you can thank Mrs. Woodley for that. I had you front and center in the next room, but she wanted you here."

Good sign or bad sign? Darren wasn't sure. "Think I'll take things in while I can still navigate my way through the room."

"Do that. The other artists will be arriving soon. I'll need time with each of them to convince them the venue will be good for sales."

In other words, lie. But Janice excelled at the care and feeding of her people, which was a major reason why Darren allowed Janice to show her work.

Starting in the middle of the room, where her paintings were displayed, she made a counterclockwise circuit of the area. Everything was so close together, this was a disaster in the making. When she came to the silver fountain, she stopped in her tracks. It was pretty, in its own overly gauche way, but totally out of place for this event. The closest display was of glass items, which should withstand any stray water.

Voices interrupted her thoughts as she completed her tour. The other artisans had arrived. Their reactions grew louder, and not just from proximity. They, too, were shocked at the sight of their surroundings. Should she help Janice reassure the troops? No, Janice was up to the task. Besides, just like her visit to the mansion the previous week, something she had yet to identify had worked its way into her subconscious and was trying to free itself. It couldn't be all the gold and silver finery, because it wasn't here then. The room? She narrowed her eyes and surveyed the rest of the area. *Oh. My. God.*

Why hadn't she picked up on this before? Because she'd only recently inspected the painted rooms at Mike's house. Rooms the same color as these.

Darren turned around to find Shae. "Hey, interior decorator, what do you think of this design job? How does all this fit with your showing?"

"So, it's not just me and Janice freaking out?"

"Ned stayed with his mother to help bring her down. He sent me to find you. How are you doing?"

"Been better. But I'm worried about Janice. She's already drinking."

"Not for long. Ned finessed the glass away from her before she emptied it. If you're okay, I'm also charged with finding food of some sort to get into her."

"I'm fine. Well, as fine as I can be under the circumstances. Go take care of Janice. I want to browse through tonight's brochure before the guests arrive."

Shae was barely gone before a member of the catering staff found Darren. "The lady up front said you'd show me the other two food areas."

"We're almost ready to start. Aren't you fellas sort of late?"

"Not my idea. The woman who hired us insisted we keep the cold appetizers on ice until the last minute. Boss wasn't able to talk her out of it."

Mrs. Woodley had struck again. She'd made such a big deal about being in charge of the food and alcohol, then was conveniently absent when they showed up at the last minute. Darren hoped Ned was still with Janice. The woman didn't need anything more to frazzle her.

After the catering guy took off to find the rest of the crew, she next ran into three bartenders, who'd apparently missed Janice up front. By the time she got them situated at their respective stations, it was almost time for the guests to arrive.

A few of the other artisans now drifted back to their pieces. One passed Darren. "Do you believe this place?"

"You mean the holiday decorations competing with us for space?"

"Oh, no. I've lived in this town all my life and have always wanted to see inside this house. It's incredible."

At least someone wasn't thrown by their surroundings. "Yes, incredible." Which reminded her of her recent discovery. But once again, her thoughts were interrupted.

"Darren? You all set?" Ned asked, coming up to her. He was dressed to impress. From past experience, she knew the Jake Bonneville persona would soon emerge. But for now, he seemed more like his mother's assistant.

"I'm fine, Ned. How's your mother?"

"Breathing normally, now that the food people and bar staff

have showed up. I suggested she post herself at the door to greet people as they arrive. As far away as possible from the stairs, where I presume Mrs. Woodley will make her grand entrance."

"Good thinking. This whole night is turning out much different than your mother anticipated."

"Where's Jay? He should've appeared by now."

"Haven't seen him yet. What about Mike?" She tried to keep her tone noncommittal. She hadn't talked to him in days, partly because she wanted to avoid having to tell him about the problems with deliveries, but mainly because she wanted to steer clear of temptation. As much as she looked forward to a repeat of last week's session in bed, better sense told her she wouldn't finish the house in time if she gave in to dallying with him.

Jay pulled up next to them. "Did I hear my name mentioned?"

"There you are," Ned replied. "I've been looking over the script for my sales video. Got a few changes. We'll talk later, once we've both done our schmoozing duty." He moved off, leaving Darren alone with Mike's brother.

He shrugged. "That's me. Always schmoozing potential customers these days. But, hey, I'm not complaining. Love this job. I understand I have you to thank for a great reference."

"I called it like I saw it, that's all."

"Thanks also for including me on Thanksgiving. That was a great experience."

"You were a big help."

They'd run their course of conversation topics. "I'd, uh, better make the rounds. See ya later." He sauntered off.

Arriving guests created a slight buzz in the room. The aisles between displays soon were filled. At length, chatter dropped off and an audible hush swept the room.

"Good evening, friends," a clipped female voice said over the PA system. Mrs. Woodley had finally arrived. "Welcome to Woodley Manor and a special holiday showing just for you of the top artists featured by the Serenity Gallery. Please enjoy the goodies we've scattered throughout these rooms, and when you need to wet your whistle, partake of the wine and champagne offerings."

Darren stepped away from her area to view their hostess. The woman stood on the fourth step of the massive stairway. Whereas most of the female guests were in black or holiday colors, Frances Woodley wore a long-sleeved winter-white gown trimmed at the wrists with very expensive-looking white faux fur. Her hair was a simple updo sprinkled with flecks of gold and silver.

An older man who must be her husband and Mike and Jay's father stood behind her in a black tux, staring straight ahead. Jay stood on one side of his mother and Mike occupied the other side. Both had pasted on smiles for the crowd, although even from where she stood, Darren detected a tick in Mike's jaw.

No doubt about it, the woman was in her element, even though her menfolk weren't.

"I'm joined this evening by my supportive husband, Joseph, and my two handsome sons, Joseph Jr. and Michael." All three men, appearing ill at ease, simply nodded. None of them added their own greetings. "Enjoy this kickoff to the holiday season, everyone, especially the extraordinary ambiance provided by the creative mind of Frank Poulet, my designer."

Her big entrance concluded, her two sons helped her descend the rest of the steps, and she began her grand tour of the room.

That was it? No mention of Janice, let alone offering her the "stage" as well. Reference had barely been made of the artisans.

Darren hoped Janice had continued her vigil at the entrance and hadn't heard the slight, but that was unlikely, since Mrs. Woodley had spoken with a mic. Was this what Mike meant when he'd told her he wasn't very close to his family? Mrs. Woodley was a real prima donna.

To her relief, Darren was spared having to deal with the woman right away, which was good, because Darren was drawing a bit of a crowd herself. For well over an hour, there was hardly any downtime between one prospective buyer and the next. One definite sale came out of it along with two other possibles. Darren's mouth ached from constantly smiling, and a headache drilled into her frontal lobe from being *on* so long.

"Hi," a very sexy male voice said from behind her during the next break. Mike. Perfect timing. "How's it going?"

She related the surprising interest in her pieces, ending with the sale. "Since there's such an eclectic group of artists here tonight, I wasn't sure if my paintings would have any draw."

"You're a standout no matter who you're competing with." His eyes took in their surroundings. "Even in the midst of all this overly enthusiastic splendor."

"Nice way of putting it. Is your mother always so …"

"Over the top? Actually, this is beyond even her usual standards."

Did he not recognize his mother's extravagance as a cry for help? The woman was overcompensating for something she felt lacking in her life. But now wasn't the time or place to share that thought with Mike. Instead, she was reminded of her earlier insight. "I stopped by your house today to inspect the work of the painters and flooring people."

"Yeah? I've stayed away, like you asked, but temptation is growing. How's it look?"

She almost told him about her earlier observation, but at that moment they were interrupted.

"There you are, Darren. I knew you had to be here somewhere." Then Mrs. Woodley noticed Mike. "And, Michael, don't tell me you've intruded on this young woman's exhibit to plague her with questions about your little house?"

How could someone sound so pleasant and still be so condescending? To her own son, no less. "Actually, I was prevailing upon your son to get me some water," Darren said in her own sugar-sweet tone. "My voice is parched from all the small talk I've been making with your guests."

Mike took his cue from her. "I'll get right on that, Ms. Williams. How about you, Mother? You could probably use some refreshment also."

His mother waved him off. "No, darling, I'm doing fine. But you go run your errand while I stay here and get my first view of Ms. Williams' paintings."

So much for catching up with Mike. "I'd be delighted to show you these, Mrs. Woodley. But before I do, let me congratulate you on this spectacular event. People will be talking for weeks about the way you've combined the fine arts with the decorative art of the holidays."

"Thank you, my dear. I'm so pleased with the way things came together. I wasn't sure I could pull it off, but in the end, voilà."

Voilà? The woman actually thought this was all her doing? Was she that needy or that self-involved?

Enough of the compliments. Showtime. "I brought both seascapes and landscapes with me tonight. Which do you prefer?"

"What about still life? Do you paint those also?"

"Not really. I've experimented with floral arrangements and fruit in the past, but mainly for practice. If that's what you're seeking, Marlys Remmers' pieces—she's in the other room—might be more to your liking."

"Oh, I, uh …"

Shouts of "Oh my God!" and "Look out!" bounced off the back wall. Guests sped past them toward the front, almost upending Darren's paintings in their haste.

"What the …" Darren said.

"Those, those people nearly knocked me down." Mrs. Woodley was near tears.

Jay suddenly appeared. "Problem back there. Fountain knocked over. Water going everywhere. You and Darren need to get out of here. Fast."

Mrs. Woodley blinked, not processing her son's words.

"I, I need to get my paintings together."

"No time for that," Jay said. He pushed his mother toward the front, just as Janice ran by toward the back.

"Where's Mike?" Darren asked.

"He and Dad … attempting to cut off the flow. Sent me … get you two out. Don't make me look bad. Go. Now."

Darren ran her index finger across her chin, contemplating how she could possibly leave her babies behind. They represented so many months of work. She grabbed two and steered Mrs. Woodley to the front door.

Her hostess floated trancelike as they made their way past other fleeing guests and the catering staff. They descended the front steps and stood clustered with the others in the front yard. "It's so cold. Thank God this gown has long sleeves."

Though Darren had worn a sleeveless gown, in her shock, she didn't notice her goose bumps for several minutes.

The other artists gathered nearby. Some had stopped long enough to bring their wraps or a few of their items. They stood huddled together, sharing their outer garments, speculating on what had happened. One who had been posted near the back of the front room offered, "It was that damn fountain. Someone backed into it, probably too much to drink, and the top part went crashing down."

Once they had some idea what had transpired, conversation turned to their artwork and whether it was in danger.

"If water gets to my textiles, they'll be ruined."

"I hope my glassworks weren't broken by the mob."

"Who puts so much water near art displays without proper protection?"

The last statement resonated with Mrs. Woodley. "I, I had no idea. I just wanted things to be pretty. For people to remember me." Only Darren seemed to hear her.

Oh, I'm sure they'll remember you after tonight. "We need to stay calm, Mrs. Woodley. And wait for someone to come out and tell us we can go back in."

But that didn't happen. Instead, two fire trucks and an EMT vehicle pulled into the yard. At least they'd not used the sirens, which would have pushed Mrs. Woodley over the brink. The occupants moved quickly into the house.

Despite her claim of the warmth her dress afforded her, Mrs. Woodley began to shake with the arrival of the emergency vehicles. Within a minute, her tremors were pronounced.

"Can anyone spare a coat or anything for this woman?" Darren called to the group around her.

At first, it seemed as if no one heard her. Or if anyone had, they didn't care or had nothing to offer. Finally, a man came forward with his overcoat. "I'm wearing a wool jacket and sweater. I can spare this."

Darren thanked him and spread the coat over Mrs. Woodley.

"What about you? You're wearing less than her," the man said. He yanked off his jacket and stuck it around her.

"Thanks again. You're very kind."

Noting a bench off to the side under the trees that miraculously no one else had yet found, she led Mrs. Woodley to the spot and got her seated. Darren placed her two paintings next to her. "Here, this is out of the way. You should be more comfortable. I'll watch for your family."

Her temporary ward didn't reply, but her shaking subsided.

Within minutes, several first responders emerged from the house, boarded one of the trucks, and took off. A good sign?

Mr. Woodley wasn't far behind. Darren called to him so he'd know the whereabouts of his wife. "There you are, Frances. Jay told me he made you come outside."

"Ms. Williams, Darren, has been seeing to my welfare." Mrs. Woodley finally found her voice.

Joseph Woodley turned to Darren. "Thank you. Everything got so crazy in there, I'm glad she was spared all the drama."

"How are things now?" Darren asked. "Was everything ruined?"

"No, only a few things near the fountain. The flooring is a disaster, along with some of the decorations. All rented. Hopefully the event insurance I told you to get will cover that damage, Frances."

If possible, the woman's face assumed even more pallor. "Uh, I decided to forego that option, Joe. I thought our home insurance would suffice."

"You didn't follow through?" His voice rose. "Even after you brought in all those fancy doodads and that fountain? That fountain … Don't get me started on what a poor decision that was. How you let that decorator talk you into it, I don't know. Maybe we can sue."

Mrs. Woodley wrung her hands, the faux fur covering her wrists. "The fountain seemed like such a good idea at the time, Joe. And it went so well with the gold and silver garlands and wreaths."

Mr. Woodley opened his mouth to respond, then eyed Darren. "We'll discuss this later. When you've had a chance to warm up and the damage has been assessed. The authorities want us to stay somewhere else tonight."

Mrs. Woodley rose, straightened her shoulders. "Thank you again, my dear, for helping me escape that bedlam. Please return this coat to that nice gentleman and thank him for me as well."

No longer needing to babysit Mike's mother, Darren wandered back to the crowd, which was considerably reduced from before. Several guests must have left, even without their wraps. She returned the coat and jacket to their owner and thanked him. "Have you heard any more about the damage?"

"You're one of the artists, aren't you?" he said. "Wish I could set your mind at rest about your things, but all we've heard, surmised, actually, is there's no risk of fire, or over half the firefighters wouldn't have left."

About that time, Janice appeared on the front steps. Although her long party skirt and silver over blouse looked none the worse for wear, her hair was tousled. Even from where she stood, Darren detected deeper wrinkles on her friend's face than she'd seen before. Mike, Jay and Ned stood behind her. Mike's tie was loose, Jay's had completely disappeared. Ned's shirt had been pulled out of the cummerbund.

"Gather round, everyone. I'm sure you'd like an update on the events of the evening." Janice waited long enough for the assembled group to come nearer.

"First, to our guests, I sincerely apologize for any inconvenience caused by the mishap with the fountain. For tonight, the authorities are requiring nothing be touched, so they can better determine the damage, to the artwork, to any guests' belongings and to the house. That process should be completed sometime tomorrow, at which time, we will transfer all the artwork and guests' belongings to my gallery. You can come by the day after to pick up your things, be they personal or artwork you may have purchased tonight. Please, if possible, bring your claim tickets with you."

A rumble of discontent rolled through the crowd. Poor Janice, not only having to pick up all the pieces left behind by Mrs. Woodley, but also dealing with these clearly disgruntled clients. She may have lost several patrons tonight.

"To all my wonderful artists who came here in good faith tonight to display your best pieces, I am so sorry. I will stay here until every last item has been identified, examined and then painstakingly prepared to be taken back to my gallery. I will be calling each of you personally tomorrow, as soon as I have news."

Janice opened her arms, indicating the whole assembled group. "If you need to pick up your wraps, purses, or any other checked items before leaving, please get in line here on the steps and have your claim check ready. Someone will get to you as soon as possible. As soon as you have retrieved your items, please leave. We need space and quiet to complete this process. Again, I apologize for any inconvenience you experienced here tonight and will do my best to make it up to you."

Although several audible groans met her announcement, people began to queue up. Still lugging her two paintings, Darren waited for the crowd to subside before joining the line to reclaim her wrap and purse. Couldn't very well leave without her car keys.

Mike, who'd been helping distribute wraps after each person signed for them, spotted her and came right over. "You okay? I worried about you being out in the cold with no coat."

She stepped out of line to pump him for information. "A very kind gentleman in the crowd loaned me his jacket. How's my stuff? Was it damaged by the water or the stampede?"

"Your stuff's fine. I checked it as soon as we took care of the water."

He filled her in on how the fountain had been tipped over. "I knew the minute I saw that thing it meant trouble. Mom was so intent on impressing her guests that she let better judgment slide."

"I think she realizes that now. She and your dad already left for a hotel."

"He's furious with her. And Janice? I've never seen her so angry and at the same time look so panicked."

"She's got a lot of cleanup on her hands. I can stay and help, if she needs me."

"Wish you could, but the fire chief would only allow those of us who remained inside to stay." He disappeared for a bit and came back carrying her coat and purse. "I'll let Janice know about your offer to help. Maybe she could use you at the gallery tomorrow."

Hopefully not, because Darren really had to get serious about her decorating duties. But if Janice needed her, that took priority. At least for a day. After that, she'd be working around the clock to finish the house.

As she drove home, she was unable to shut out the events of the past evening. Then it hit her. She still hadn't told Mike about her discovery nor briefed him on the challenge the deliveries were presenting. Oh well, tomorrow was another day.

CHAPTER 18

Miraculously, Janice was able to convince the fire chief to allow the temps she found available at that late hour to help with the massive job of matching every piece of artwork against her master list, assuring every piece had been located, and then preparing it for transit back to the gallery. With the senior Woodleys gone from the premises along with all the artists, Mike, Ned and Jay got the job of assisting Janice and company.

Within the first half hour, the men realized the temps could get a lot more done without them helping, so they essentially turned into gofers and provided strong shoulders for Janice.

At one point, she pulled up and bent over, her hands on her thighs. "What was I thinking, letting that crazy woman talk me into this shindig? Oh, sorry, Mike and Jay. I keep forgetting she's your mother."

"We try to accomplish that same trick, Janice, but with no success," Mike told her.

"No, I was out of line, especially since you two stayed around to help when you could've taken off."

Janice set the group to work on the items that had been

collected near the back of the room that were either obviously or potentially damaged. She wanted them inventoried and wrapped for transit first and set apart from the other items in a different area of the gallery for their owners to claim and review.

Mike personally oversaw their wrapping and placement in the van. To his relief, Ned and Shae rode along to take charge of the unloading. Janice remained behind to supervise the handling of the rest of the exhibit.

Before Ned left, he drew Mike aside. "Keep a discreet eye on Mom. She's resilient, but cleaning up this damage is a lot for anyone."

No thanks to my mother. "Will do. And make sure Darren's things are handled with care."

Ned lifted a brow. "Of course."

Janice began to drag within an hour. "You've been going all day, Janice. Why don't you sit back and catch your breath?" Mike said.

She flinched. She appeared offended as she shook her head. "So much to do. Inspecting and inventorying everything takes so much time. Only I can do that part."

Though Mike had told the catering staff they could have the remaining food, the caterer was sharp enough to leave several things behind for the temps. Mike grabbed a few appetizers and a bottle of water he retrieved from the kitchen and took them to Janice. "At least get some food into your system. You've gone for hours without eating anything."

"Okay. If you insist, but you're being far too …"

Before she took a bite of anything, her knees gave way. Mike caught her just in time. She was barely conscious, and she'd gone quite pale.

"Someone find a blanket. Anyone know a doctor close by?" he asked the others.

Jay took off up the stairs. "I'll get the blanket."

One of the temps joined him. "My mom's a nurse. I'll call her for a name, unless you think we should call the paramedics?"

"Let's give her a minute to revive. Where's that water I gave her?"

Another temp handed it over. "Janice, can you hear me?" He elevated her head. "Try to take some of this water."

She moaned something and turned her head away.

"Just a sip. Okay?"

After several scary seconds, she moved her head toward him. She could only get down a little of the liquid, but at least she was coming to. On the other hand, her head felt quite warm. Feverish.

"My mom called a family doctor who lives nearby. He'll be here in ten minutes," the temp told him.

The doctor arrived in seven minutes. By then, Janice was doing somewhat better, although her head still felt warm.

"What was she doing here at the Woodley mansion?" the doctor asked.

Mike filled him in.

"She's been on her feet for hours? She was in charge?"

"That's right. Why?"

"She's exhausted. Plus, she apparently was under a lot of stress coping with the fountain accident. Her body just imploded. She may be coming down with a virus, or it may just be a cold, but either way, she needs to get some rest in her own bed. Let's see how this develops before I order any meds. She may just need to sleep."

"Okay. Consider it done. We'll figure out how to finish up this job without her," Mike said. He had no idea how, but at the moment, his main concern was getting Janice to cooperate and then getting her home. Ned and Shae had their hands full for now. Then he remembered Tim Harriman. Janice and Tim had been dating for several months. How'd he gotten out of tonight's festivities? Whatever, Mike called Shae and asked her to have her dad meet him at Janice's house as well as let Ned know about his mother.

Jay would help him carry Janice to his car and then remain behind at the mansion, taking over for Janice until Mike got back.

Janice delivered safely, Mike headed back to his parents' place. It was already one in the morning.

By two, the group had finished their work and loaded another van. Part of the group left, but a couple of guys stayed behind to unload the items when they reached the gallery.

Ned greeted them at the door. "How's my mom?"

"She was asleep before I even left her place. Tim said he'd stick around as long as needed."

"He may be needed here tomorrow instead. I have an out-of-town gig I can't cancel, and Shae has a major meeting with a new client. I sent her home to get some needed sleep. But if you think this is more serious with Mom, we'll change plans."

"Won't know about your mom until morning. You might as well go. She's got Tim and Jay and Darren and me who can take turns being with her, if that becomes necessary."

"I hate doing this." Ned shook his head. "I wasn't there for Dad when he got sick. I don't want history to repeat itself."

"It's probably just exhaustion and maybe a cold. Don't beat yourself up."

They batted around the question of Janice's care another minute before Ned agreed to go ahead with his plans. By three, everything had been unloaded, unpacked and awaited the artisans' arrival later in the day. Ned drove Mike and Jay back to the mansion before heading off to his new home.

"Thanks, you two. You really came through for Mom tonight. I don't know what we would've done without you," he told them.

"Hey, you wouldn't have needed our help had it not been for the disaster with the fountain. That rests squarely with our mom and her irresponsible decorator."

Rather than return to his apartment, Mike crashed at the

mansion. The downstairs rooms that housed the event were a mess. Jay agreed to stick around for the clean-up crew their mother had scheduled. It remained to be seen if that group could eradicate the devastation left by the water. If not, Jay would be calling in specialists before leaving to meet with clients.

Though it meant only a few hours' sleep for him, Mike wanted to be at the gallery by the time Janice's assistant arrived to prepare her for the day ahead. The lucky woman had missed the showing, Janice told him, because she wanted to attend her granddaughter's winter concert at school. In return, she would now be challenged to perform on all four cylinders today. He hoped she'd be up to it, because he was down to one cylinder himself.

DARREN AWOKE, her body refusing to come alive, most likely in response to standing outside in the cold last night for several minutes. It would be so great to stay in bed a little while longer, but she had to get to the gallery early. Janice might need her help dealing with the other artisans as they checked the status of their pieces.

She arrived to find Mike already there, talking to Janice's assistant. "What are you doing here?" she asked him. "I thought you'd be in bed for several more hours after last night's rescue efforts."

"Don't I wish?" He stifled a yawn, then updated her on Janice's situation. "Brigitte here will call the other artisans who were there last night and schedule times for them to come in and view their things. If she's lucky, we can spread this out over the day to avoid a crush all at once."

"We?"

A sheepish expression came over his face. "Uh, yeah. I have several conference calls I'm putting off until later, but I could really use the help. I'm sure your boss will give you a pass on his project today." He ran through the litany of everyone else's reasons for not being there.

"Just for the record, you are my client, not my boss. What about Brigitte? Doesn't she usually fill in for Janice?"

"From what Ned told me, Brigitte holds down the fort but doesn't negotiate prices, unless the customer is willing to pay the stated price. He didn't feel she could handle the liability issues associated with the damaged items. And if one of the artisans identifies a new problem, someone has to deal with that paperwork."

"But I'm supposed to be at the house to take delivery of your appliances today. If I have to reschedule, I don't know how soon I can get them."

"Call and see. I really need you here."

Nice to be wanted, but things were starting to mount up at the house. "Okay. I'll try." She put in a call to the vendor. They couldn't find her order. Of course. "But I just spoke with someone about it yesterday. A Kyle. I forget his last name."

"Kyle isn't here today," the person on the other end of the line replied. "Spell the name it was under."

She complied. Still no order.

"Try Williams, Darren instead of Woodley, Michael."

Eureka! She could've sworn she'd given them Mike's name. Apparently, *Kyle* zeroed in on only her name.

"Okay, I found it. It says the washer, dryer, and dishwasher are scheduled for delivery today."

"Wait. Only those three items? What about the refrigerator, stove, microwave, and garbage disposal?"

The guy was apparently checking, because the line was silent for a bit. "You sure all those were ordered here? I can't find a record of any of them."

No! No, no, no. "That can't be. I've got a copy of the order. All those items are on there."

"Why don't you give me the product numbers of the other four, and I'll look them up that way."

"I can't right now. I don't have the orders with me."

"Oh. That presents a problem."

"I'll get them and call you back, okay? What's your name?" she asked.

"Brian James, but I've just been reassigned to the flooring department. I won't have access to your order over there."

She pursed her lips. "Okay," she said, keeping her tone as civil as possible since she still needed a name from this guy. "Who should I speak with when I call back?"

"Sorry, ma'am, I can't say. They're bringing in someone to take my place."

"Well, then, Brian, I guess I'll just have to start over with whoever shows up."

She went in search of Mike, who she found deep in discussion with Brigitte. "Well? Did you get the delivery rescheduled for tomorrow?"

She opened her mouth to answer and realized she'd never gotten around to discussing the delivery. But Mike had enough on his mind right now. Brigitte appeared particularly perplexed, judging by the frown on her face. Darren didn't need to add to his problems. At least not yet. She still had a little wiggle room on the house. "Uh, I have to call back later and see what they've been able to arrange."

Brigitte's consternation stemmed from her difficulties sched- uling the artisans at different times. Everyone wanted, demanded, to view their things as soon as possible. "I tried, I really did, Mr. Woodley. But you know artists." Then she remembered Darren. "Sorry, Ms. Williams. Didn't mean you."

Of course, she did. Darren shot right to her things as soon as she arrived. Now that Brigitte had reported the response of the other artists, she could sympathize with them. "Let's see, there were ten of us showing last night. Minus me, that's nine. We could each oversee three, couldn't we?"

Mike considered. "Maybe, if we held a group meeting before we let them see their stuff, so they all hear the same things at the same time."

"I could put together a list of instructions and a packet of all the forms they'll need," Brigitte said, "and you could hand it out during this meeting. But please, don't make me lead it."

That much decided, Brigitte headed off to her office, leaving Mike and Darren alone for the first time in days. Darren suddenly became shy.

Mike pulled her into his arms. "This is better. I've missed you."

"You saw me last night."

"With everyone around. Nearly killed me to keep my distance. But we've got a little time now before the others arrive."

He nuzzled her neck, waking sensations she'd tried all week to suppress. "Tempting, but here? Brigitte could return any minute."

He took her hand and pulled her toward the back of the gallery. "There's a room Janice uses for art classes. Ned and I first met Shae there."

She knew the room. Janice had given her a tour several months ago when she first signed on with the gallery. "It's not very large," she said once they'd closed the door of said room. "And it's packed with canvases and other art supplies."

"The conference table? Or the floor?"

"Will the table support two people?" she asked. The thought titillated. Her sexual experiences were limited to couches, beds and cars.

"Let's see." His voice had already grown heavy. He lifted her to a sitting position along the side of the table. Then she lay prone and waited for him to join her. "Ready or not."

To their relief, the table was quite sturdy, but just in case Brigitte showed up unexpectedly, Darren merely undid her bra and pulled up her top. Mike leaned down and sampled immediately.

"God, I've missed this," he said when he came up for air.

"Me, too."

"Better hurry before we're interrupted." He unzipped her
jeans and pulled them and her panties down to her thighs. He did
the same for his own pants, after fishing a condom from a pocket.
"With you in my life, I now come prepared." He laughed as the
double entendre sank in.

With time at a premium, they went at each other with a
vengeance—kissing, fondling, licking. Though she preferred a
more leisurely approach to lovemaking, the frenetic pace right
now was a huge turn-on. The slight budging of the table with
Mike's thrusts only added fuel to the fire exploding between
them. She'd missed being with him like this the last several days,
but until he was actually in her, she didn't realize how being with
him had come to mean so much.

Spent, they lay next to each other a few minutes, regrouping,
catching their breath.

"This room gives me an idea," Mike said.

"Thought you already followed through on that idea."

"Another idea. For the future. At your studio. What say we
use you as the canvas and let me be the artist with your paint?"

She'd never even considered such an idea, even in art classes
when she was painting nudes. She grew wet again just contemplating it. On the other hand … "Hey, I'm the artist here. I get my
turn painting you, too."

"On canvas, or would you use my body as well?"

"Hmm. I'll let you wonder. Nothing like anticipation to
enhance the mood."

He kissed her again as he helped her refasten her bra. "You're
cruel. Anticipation has already revived my guy."

She scooched off the table and put her clothes on. "Tell him he
has to wait. Time to find Brigitte."

CHAPTER 19

By the time Darren returned home, she was dragging. Her body felt as though it had been pummeled by a meat tenderizer. Couldn't have been her time on the conference room table with Mike. She'd actually felt energized by the time she zipped up her jeans. No, must have been from shuttling between the three, actually four—Brigitte could only handle two—artists she helped inspect their pieces. Maybe there'd been a draft in the gallery.

Whatever, all she wanted to do was go to bed and shut out the world. Her bed, not the couch where she'd been staying with Colby in the house.

Colby was actually home from classes already. What time was it? Four thirty? Where had the day gone?

"Darren? Are you okay?" Colby asked. "Stupid question. Of course, you're not. You look terrible."

"I don't feel well. That's all I know."

"Then let's get you to bed. Take your own bed. I'll move out here."

Who was this person? But Darren wasn't going to object. She

let Colby lead her into her room and pull down the covers. She took a quick warm shower, threw on her most comfortable night-shirt and collapsed into bed.

It was after midnight when she woke. Then, just to relieve herself and down a painkiller. Her head felt swollen and hot. Good grief. Had she picked up something from Janice? No time to debate. Bed was calling her name again.

When she came to the next time, it was seven. She could hardly breathe. *Tell me I'm not sick. Can't afford to be sick.* But there it was. No use ignoring the fact or fighting it. She went back to bed.

The door creaked. "Darren? How are you feeling this morning?"

"Stay where you are. I don't want to expose you any more than I already have."

"Uh-oh. Look, I've gotta take off for class soon. I'll fix you some weak tea and a piece of toast, and I'll leave them just outside this door. I'll try to get back between classes to check on you."

"Don't worry about me. You need to stay healthy so you don't miss class. Don't call Mom. She can't afford to miss work if she gets sick."

"I can't leave you to fend on your own. What about Mike?"

"No, don't bother him. He barely slept the last two nights after everything went south at the showing." She'd brought Colby up to speed on that catastrophe the night before last, when she'd come home and raided the fridge.

"Look, sis, after all you've done for me lately, the least I can do is check in later to make sure you're still alive." She took off, not giving a rapidly fading Darren a chance to reply.

Darren's condition hadn't improved by twelve thirty, when Colby stuck her head in the door. If anything, Darren was worse. The sniffles now required constant nose-blowing, and she had a sore throat. She had Colby take some money from her purse, since

Colby's funds were so limited, and asked her to buy one of those end-your-cold-early remedies when she returned later in the day, although by then her cold would probably be beyond the early stages.

Midafternoon, she got up, reheated the tea and toast she'd not eaten earlier. There was something she was supposed to do. In fact, it was something she was supposed to have done the day before. That much she remembered. But the specifics eluded her. She'd expended all her energy reheating, eating and drinking, so she returned to bed again.

She could really use her mommy about now. Not the current Elise Williams, who would most likely freak at the possibility her older child might be exhibiting the early signs of her father's ailment. No, Darren craved the mommy of her childhood, who'd pat her hair, rub her shoulders and promise her she'd be feeling better in no time.

Mike would provide just as much comfort. And he was a lot sexier than her mother. With great effort, she summoned up the energy to call him. "Hi."

"Hi, yourself." He sounded different, his voice lower.

"I could use some company. Any way you could break away from whatever you're doing and come out here?"

"What's with the voice?"

"Don't know if I picked up whatever got to Janice or what, but I've been in bed all day with a cold. It's winning."

"Geez. I, uh, got the same thing. I was about to call you." He finished off with a very powerful sneeze.

"Do you think it's because we, uh … you know?"

"If that's the case, one of us gave it to the other."

Silence on both ends. On Darren's part, she was determining if she had enough energy to drive downtown to his place. Not to take care of him, but if they already shared the same germs, why not share the same bed and commiserate?

"When does your sister get home?"

"In a few hours. She's stopping at a pharmacy first to buy me some OTC cold medicine."

"Maybe she could drive you into town so we can be miserable together? If I play my cards right, I can convince my parents' housekeeper to drop by with food."

"I'll wait for her to get here with the cold medicine, but I'll take a ride share and tell her you're going to take care of me at your place so she can study in peace this weekend. She doesn't need to know you're laid up as well." She stopped long enough to cough. New symptom. "Won't the housekeeper mention seeing us together to your parents?"

"Do we even care anymore?"

The man had surprised her. No, she didn't care, but she thought he did. "If you're okay, I'm okay."

"Bring clean clothes, your own pillow and whatever meds you've got. See you later."

Mike hung up, a smile on his face as he rolled into the comfort of his pillow. He should call Tammy, but his call from Darren had taken its toll on his energy.

He almost didn't hear the buzzer announcing her arrival some time later. He hadn't slept the sleep of the dead since college, when he'd collapsed for hours after finals.

If he looked as bad as Darren, they were both truly sick. Her hair hung in limp strands, the area surrounding her nose was red and her eyes looked droopy.

"Wasn't sure I'd make it," she told him in a non-sexy hoarse voice. "The ride share driver was afraid to take me at first until I put on a mask."

"Want something to eat? Tammy, my parents' housekeeper, left tons of homemade chicken soup, bread for toast and gallons of orange juice."

She clutched her stomach. "Uh, thanks, not right now. But could I have a glass of water. Need to take this medicine. Want some?"

"Already medicated, thanks to Tammy."

She lifted her bag. "Where can I change?"

He pointed to the bathroom.

She stumbled into the room and closed the door. She definitely was out of it, or she would've stayed and given him a show. A few minutes later, she emerged in a loose-fitting pink plaid flannel nightshirt. "Only thing still clean."

"Sent my stuff back with Tammy."

"How do I"—she stopped to cough—"get my own Tammy?"

"Want me to talk to my mom?"

She held up a hand. "Never mind."

"Per Jay, she tried to call Janice yesterday, but Tim wouldn't put her through." He swiped at his leaky nose with a handker-chief. "He even told her she'd made Janice sick."

She didn't answer until she spotted the tissue box and wiped her own nose. "Repentant?"

"Sent Tammy over with a basket of muffins."

Her laugh in response sent her into a coughing spasm. "Better quit talking."

They lumbered into the bedroom and both went for the same side. "Want to flip a coin?" he asked.

"No. It's your place. I'll switch."

Some host he was. "Stay here. You came all the way here, least I can do." He waited for her to settle, then tucked her in. By the time he reached his side, she'd already closed her eyes. Within minutes, the soft shushing of her breathing told him she was asleep.

A few minutes later, he was out to the world as well.

Around nine that evening, hunger got the better of him. Dark shadows enveloped the room, but in the light cast by his clock radio, he could make out Darren, still asleep. He gazed at her a few moments, an unanticipated delight engulfing him. Not his fella coming alive, but instead, a warm, comfortable feeling. What the hell? His body had been overtaken temporarily by the forces of the common cold, and yet here he was, his spirits consumed with … love?

How much medication had he taken? Enough to make him hallucinate? Conjure up feelings that didn't exist?

Maybe it was hunger. He wandered out to his kitchen and warmed a mug of soup in the microwave. He downed half, then went to stand before one of the living room windows that faced the street below, where he sipped the rest. Nine o'clock on a Friday night. Still a lot of traffic. How many of those drivers were in love? How did they know?

He'd never trod this path before. Maybe back in college he might have entertained a fleeting belief he was smitten, but those feelings were simply the fodder of a teenager still awakening to sexual maturity. This was different. They both were sick, for God's sake, both of them sneezing and wheezing and barely able to finish a sentence without coughing. And yet … and yet with her beside him in his bed, he felt well.

AT TEN THE FOLLOWING MORNING, Darren and then Mike were awakened by the ringing of her phone. It took four rings for her to pick up, but the caller was still on the line. "Ms. Williams?"

"Yes?" Her voice sounded like a foghorn.

"Brian James. You called the other day about the appliances ordered for Michael Woodley?"

She remembered something about the call. Something she was supposed to do. And hadn't. "Uh, right."

"You were going to call me back with the product numbers of the items ordered?"

The product numbers! With the onset of her cold, she'd completely forgotten. She sat up in bed. "Oh. Sorry. I, uh, came down sick and totally forgot."

"I wondered what happened. When you didn't call, I did some more checking and finally found all the items."

"That's terrific," she said with as much enthusiasm as she could muster.

"Uh, there was a bit of a slipup placing all the orders. If these are the right product numbers, I'll expedite them immediately."

Her brain struggled to understand what he'd just told her. "What, what does that mean, Brian?"

"Three items are here in our warehouse and can be delivered as soon as you're ready. The other four, uh, should be here in, uh, a few days."

She rubbed her eyes, as if clearing them would clear her brain. "A few days? What does that mean? Two? Three? A week?"

"We're shooting for three but can't guarantee their arrival date for sure."

"I see," although she didn't. Okay, the house wouldn't have appliances until sometime next week. There was still time. In the meantime, she needed to come back from the dead. "Call me when they're in and you have a specific delivery date. And Brian? Email a copy of this new order to me and make a note in your records, just in case someone else gets assigned to your department by the time these things arrive, so whoever takes delivery knows the circumstances."

She hung up to find Mike now wide awake and staring at her with a combination of awe and fear. "What?"

"You must be feeling better. That's the most you've said since you arrived."

She massaged her temples. "I'm more stuffed up than ever. The situation just called for my utmost attention." She sought her pillow again. "And that little display of fire cost me what little energy I had." She explained the appliance slipup.

"Where does that put you with the rest of the decorating?"

"Oh my gosh! I haven't been able to check the house for a couple of days." She related how she'd already returned two items. "I need to make sure that hasn't happened again, or that boxes are sitting on your front porch unprotected."

"Surely, the vendors would have contacted you if there was no one there to accept delivery?"

"Not necessarily. These people have their own system of notification, which defies the understanding of mere mortals like myself."

Her head came off the pillow, but Mike pushed her down again. "No, you don't. You're in no condition to go out there. We'll find someone else."

"But it's my job, Mike. I'm letting you down."

"You kidding me? In the last two days, your artwork has come under attack. You rescued my mother from the elements, calmed Janice and helped fellow artists inspect their pieces for water damage. How could I expect you to do more?"

"But what about your house? If I can't get my arms around this delivery situation, it won't be ready in time for your Christmas dinner."

"Don't worry about finishing the house on time. I issued that invitation out of frustration with my mother's meddling in my life to get her off my case. Today, my reason seems pretty pathetic. We'll deal with whatever happens."

"That deadline has been sacred to you. What changed your mind? Did you take too much cold medicine?"

"The only thing that's changed is our health. Our first priority is getting better. We can't let little things like missed deliveries interfere with recuperating."

A new hacking fit cut off her reply. He brought her some water. She sipped and the coughing gradually subsided. "Okay.

No worrying today, since I doubt I could get myself out to the house under my own power. But come the beginning of the week, I'm back at it, no matter how horrible I feel."

"I hope that won't be the case. If you worsen, I'm calling a doctor, and you're not going anywhere, except maybe to a hospital."

CHAPTER 20

little less than three weeks to D-Day, Done with the House Day. She could do it, Darren kept telling herself as she packed up and left Mike's loft on Monday morning. No more sore throat. Sneezing had subsided, along with having to blow her nose every minute. Instead, the congestion had moved to her sinuses, which throbbed every time she moved her head. She'd barely eaten anything over the weekend, so her energy level had plummeted.

Physical ailments aside, her spirits were remarkably positive. Could it be because she'd shared Mike's bed the past three days without having sex with him? Kissing had even been restricted to a minimum, because they didn't want to share germs. They'd seen each other at close to their worst and apparently survived, even with her going without a shower or washing her hair for two days.

She'd been so sick when he'd first suggested they take care of each other she'd acted on autopilot. Had her faculties been in better shape to think through the wisdom of spending this time together, she probably would still be home in her own bed. But now, three days later, they'd developed a new level of camaraderie.

Time to get back to business. She gathered her things, kissed a still-sleeping Mike on the forehead, and headed out of the building to catch her ride. She rarely allowed herself the luxury of a ride share, but she hadn't trusted herself to drive a few days back.

Colby was zipping her book bag when Darren arrived. "There you are. I was starting to wonder about you."

"I've been at Mike's. You knew that. Sorry I didn't call, but I spent most of the last few days sleeping."

"And turned off your phone. Not that I blame you, but I had to reassure Mom you were fine when she couldn't reach you."

"I didn't turn off my phone." But when she checked, sure enough, it had been powered down. Mike must have turned it off sometime after the guy called about the appliance order. Probably right after he'd told her not to worry about finishing the house in time. Sweet, but he shouldn't have done that. "I'll call her as soon as it recharges."

"Feeling better?"

"Yes, I am. Mike took good care of me."

"I'll bet he did," Colby said, her eyes twinkling. She left before Darren could think of a fitting reply.

By the time she'd showered, washed and dried her hair and eaten a small breakfast, as much as she could get down, Darren's cell had recharged. Only then did she note the number of waiting messages. Two from Colby, two from her mother, and another four from unknown numbers. Two of the latter had left messages. Both were vendors attempting to deliver items on Saturday. Both asked her to return their calls immediately.

The first vendor acted insulted because she'd failed to show up on Saturday. "How was I supposed to know?" she asked.

"Called ya before we took off. When that didn't work, I sent an email."

"What kind of advance notice is the same day?"

"Hey, lady, we're now in peak holiday season. Everyone wants their dining room tables for all their parties and family get-togethers."

"How soon can you come back with my table?"

"No can do. That table's a popular number. Had to send it back to the factory."

"Already? Call it back. I need that table."

"What's it worth to you?"

"You're upping the price? That's not legal."

"Call it a restocking fee. Fifty bucks more. You want the table or not?"

Maybe if she planned to continue her career as interior decorator, she might someday learn how to deal with such blatant fee padding, but she needed this table now. It was worth fifty dollars and her pride to get it on time. Still, it would be three more days before it could be delivered.

She hung up. Did she have the strength to make the next three calls?

The master bed was the next item on her list. The call went about the same way as the first—except the "restocking fee" this time was seventy-five dollars. But at least it would show up later in the day.

Once contacted, the other two deliveries also claimed to be too busy to deliver right away. One "committed" to Wednesday, the other a day later. At least they didn't up the charge like the first two.

The rest of her week went about the same, except on Wednesday Mike called to say he was leaving town for a few days. He'd been invited to sit in on a congressional hearing on interstate commerce in Washington, D.C. The topic touched on some of his business concerns, and he felt he needed to be there to protect his interests.

"Are you feeling well enough to travel?" she asked.

"Have to be. But I'm glad I took last weekend to rest. You're a good caregiver."

"Giver? I slept most of the time."

"You set an example for me. I probably would've been out playing racquetball with Jay had I not wanted to be with you."

He'd be back late Saturday, so she looked ahead to Sunday, when they could see each other again.

GRADUALLY, items arrived at the house. She'd learned to inspect them on the spot to assure they were in good shape. In between deliveries, she worked her way down the massive list of household items with which she'd need to stock the house—kitchen items, cutlery, dishes, small appliances, bedding, linens and so on. Since it had taken so much effort to pry color and style preferences from Mike, she didn't bother to ask about these. She'd save all the receipts and return what items she had to, but she suspected he'd be fine with most.

As it turned out, Mike no sooner returned from the Capital when he had to leave again for the West Coast on Monday morning. Their time together was short, but she cherished it nonetheless, although it shocked her how much she missed him once he left.

Eight days before her deadline, she received a frantic call from a healthier Janice. "You've got to come rescue me. How soon can you be here?"

"What's up?" She really couldn't spare the time. Three more deliveries were scheduled for late afternoon.

"It's that woman. Frances Woodley. She showed up wanting to make amends for the debacle she created at our showing."

"That's good, isn't it?"

"Not the way she's doing it. Please, Darren, I'm begging you. I don't know what I'll do to her if there's not someone here to referee."

The last thing Darren wanted to do. Plus, she really didn't want to make any more trips into town today than necessary. Though the calendar said the beginning of winter was a few days away, temps had already plunged, and the sky was a nasty gray. "Okay. Hold the fort until I get there. I'm out at Sullivan's Creek."

"Okay, but hurry."

Darren left it at that and ran to her car. Her gas budget was taking a hit while she worked on this project. Hopefully, Janice had tallied up the sales from the showing by now, so Darren could get paid.

She arrived at the gallery to find Brigitte taking notes as Mrs. Woodley appeared to be pointing out items she wanted to purchase. That was a good sign, wasn't it?

Mrs. Woodley stopped short. "How many does that make?"

Brigitte counted up. "Uh, three at the moment, not counting the other three you selected and then eliminated."

"Right. Well, I want to do my thing to make things right, but I must get what will work for me and Mr. Woodley." Then she spotted Darren. "Darren, dear! How nice to see you again."

"You seem to be no worse for wear. I'm glad you're doing better." Where was Janice? She'd gotten the impression Mrs. Woodley was beating up on her. Everything here looked quite civil.

"I stopped by to square things with Janice. With everyone around me freaking out that night, it seemed prudent for me to get out of the way when that ill-fated accident occurred. I only learned later that Janice dealt with the aftermath, with the help of my sons."

The woman had such selective memory. But she was Mike's mother. "I'm sure Janice appreciates your support. Where is she, by the way?"

"She mentioned something about a headache and needing to find painkillers," Brigitte said.

Headache. Sounded about right. "I, uh, stopped by to see how she's feeling. She, uh, took sick the day afterward," Darren said.

Two fingers, nails expertly manicured, touched Mrs. Woodley's chin. "Oh. I hadn't heard. Is that why the headache? She returned to work too soon?"

She sounded so ingenuous. Had she no clue the effect she had on Janice?

"I'm feeling better," Janice said, coming up to them.

Darren turned away from Mrs. Woodley long enough to send her friend an expression that telegraphed "coward."

"I think those are my final choices, my dear,| Mrs. Woodley said to Brigitte. "I'll make arrangements to have them picked up later this week. Perhaps we could speak privately in your office, Janice?"

Janice's eyes went wide, then sought out Darren's. "All right, but since Darren has been involved in our collaboration since the beginning, I'd like her there, too."

Janice, don't do this to me.

Mrs. Woodley kept her smile. "Of course." Janice led the other two to her office. "That regrettable accident with the fountain caused serious damage to my floor. I brought copies of the receipts from the repair people." She reached in her purse and retrieved a stack of paper and attempted to hand it to Janice. "I'm sure your event insurance will cover these."

Janice didn't take the receipts. Her shoulders went back and her chin protruded an inch more. "We talked about this as we put the event together, Frances. You agreed to take out event insurance for your property, since the event took place *on your property*, and it was your idea to stage the showing *on your property*."

In the back of her mind, Darren recalled a similar discussion between Mr. and Mrs. Woodley the night of the showing and remembered Mrs. Woodley admitting she'd decided to pass. Now she was putting the screws to Janice? Not good.

Frances Woodley took a step back, her eyes going wide and innocent. "But surely your insurance covers damage to wherever your showings take place?"

"Even if it did, which I'd have to check," Janice replied in a flat tone, "I'm not going to pay for your damage. We discussed the details ad nauseum before the event, including the room layout. I was quite clear about the amount of space needed for the crowd to move safely through the displays. You never mentioned bringing in a fountain. Had you brought it up, I would've vetoed it strongly. It was dangerous, as it proved to be."

Mrs. Woodley's expression froze. Darren waited for her temper to erupt, the indignation of the society matron. Instead, unexpected tears burst forth. "You make me sound so, so irresponsible. I just wanted things to be perfect so I'd gain the attention of all those other women in the room. So they'd be my friends."

"I, uh ..." Janice said.

Darren just stared.

Mrs. Woodley sniffed, then attempted to wipe away the tears streaming down her face. "You don't know how bad it's been, coming back to town after all these years away. So many of my friends no longer live here. Or ... died. We might have the largest, fanciest house in town, but no one seems to care. No one wants to have anything to do with us, including my sons."

Was this a ploy for sympathy or genuine angst? Darren had no idea what to do. Janice took the lead. "And this was your way of gaining friends? You're smarter than that, Frances."

"I, I ..." Apparently Mrs. Woodley wasn't expecting such candor.

"It's been a little over two weeks since the showing. How many of the guests have you contacted to apologize for the way the evening turned out?" Janice asked.

"Contacted? Uh, I've not had time to call people. I've been overseeing the damage done to my house."

"Uh-huh. I spent several hours with your sons and my son getting the various artworks returned to the gallery without further damage. I would have stayed longer to inventory every piece to make sure they all came back intact had I not taken sick. I appreciate Mike's help the rest of that night and the next day. Darren also helped. Once I was feeling better, I called every guest to express my concern."

"Thank you for doing that. And thank you, Darren."

Darren nodded, but she didn't want to interrupt Janice's diatribe, uh, dialogue. Mrs. Woodley hadn't yet caught on.

"I didn't tell you to gain your thanks. It was an example of something you should have done of your own accord."

"But …"

"A person who has friends cares for them, for their welfare. The way you came off, all you appeared to want from them was to show off and gain their acclaim."

"I just wanted them to call me, invite Joe and me to dinner, include me in their parties."

"That takes time, Frances. You have to build relationships one by one. I remember when my husband, Dan, passed away. He'd been the social part of this gallery. I hung around in the background. But if I was going to keep the doors open, I had to assume his role. It wasn't easy, because I didn't consider myself a people person. I felt inferior to the kinds of people who made up our client base. But over time I did it. So can you."

"You don't understand. I don't have time." Her voice had risen. Then she seemed to realize she'd said too much. Shook her head. "Never mind."

"No, tell us what you meant," Janice said. "Why don't you have time?"

Mrs. Woodley stopped, took a breath. "I, uh, meant all the holiday parties have already been set up, guests invited. Even if I called a few people today and things went well, I doubt they'd invite me now."

Janice's eyes softened. She laid a hand over Mrs. Woodley's. "At least give it a try? You never know what might happen."

Darren needed to say something to back her up. "Listen to Janice, Mrs. Woodley. She's reinvented herself successfully. You can, too."

The distraught woman seemed to consider their advice. "I guess it wouldn't hurt to try."

"Good! I'll have Brigitte give you the list of telephone numbers before you leave."

Once they'd turned their visitor over to Brigitte, Janice released a drawn-out breath. "Thank you so much, Darren. She totally changed her tune, once you showed up to lend me support."

"No, dear friend. That happened when you forced her to admit what's been driving her. I had no idea she was so lonely. You knew exactly what to tell her."

"Just so she follows through. And if she does, just so someone on that list befriends her."

From here on, it was up to Frances Woodley to find friends. Darren had her doubts, given what she'd observed about the woman so far. But then, who'd have expected her to break down and even tell them what she had? Did Mike know or suspect any of this? If he didn't, should Darren tell him?

And what had Mrs. Woodley meant when she said time was running out? Clearly, she'd simply pulled a flimsy explanation out of the air when Janice pushed her on the statement. Was that something Darren should also share with Mike?

As much as she cared about the guy, and she was no longer denying those feelings, with that change in their relationship came complications like these. Darren didn't like complications. She'd spent too much time and lost too many tears after Gordy's death. That's why since then she'd deliberately steered clear of any kind of commitment that might further confound her life.

MIKE HAD BEEN ready to leave the coast to return to the Midwest when he received a call from his brother, Gardner, inviting him for drinks. They arranged to meet in the bar of the hotel where Mike had been staying so Mike could take off for the airport afterward.

Gardner—or Gard, as his brothers called him—had already arrived and settled in a booth. He was the baby of the family, four years younger than Mike. Unlike himself and Jay, Gard still looked very much the college preppie, even though he'd been out of school a few years. However, there were circles under his eyes, and as Mike approached him, Gard's eyes reflected a nervousness Mike had never seen. At meeting with him? What was up?

Gard rose as Mike approached. They shook hands and briefly embraced. "Been a while, bro," Mike said. "Good to see you."

"Glad you agreed to meet me."

They sat. Gard was already nursing a beer. After Mike ordered the same, he waited for his brother to broach whatever subject had prompted this get together.

"Doesn't look like Lilith and I will be in Des Moines for Christmas. I know it's tradition for all the Woodleys to spend Christmas together, but this year it's time for Lilith and me to spend it with her family. Her parents are coming out here instead. So I thought I'd catch you now while you were in town."

"Do Mom and Dad know you won't be there?"

"Talked to Dad today. Asked him to break it to Mom."

"Coward." Mike offered the hint of a smile.

"There's more. Wait'll you hear that part, and then you can call me a coward."

As he suspected, there was something more to this meet than

just to see each other. Once he finished his beer, he gave his brother his full attention. "Okay. Shoot."

Gard sucked in his lips, took a huge breath. "Understand Jay has left Woodley Industries and is now working for you."

"And doing quite well." He owed Jay that much.

"Also, ever since they've been back in town, Dad's been applying pressure for you to come back."

Mike wondered how Gard was getting his info. Probably Jay. "I've turned him down flat every time, so if you're worried I'd be cutting in on your territory, you can forget it."

"Funny how life turns out sometimes," Gard said. He folded his hands on the table and settled into his seat. "The person with the skills and know-how to lead the company into the future doesn't want it. And the three who are now or have been part of the corporation can't cut it or don't want to be there, either."

"Interesting. Jay's already gone. We both know Dash is an idiot who Dad's put up with to make Harper happy. Does that mean you're the one who wants out?"

"I've tried to do right by Dad, Mike, I really have. But it's just not my thing."

This was a surprise, more so than Jay's defection. "What is your *thing*, then, or do you know?"

Gard's disposition changed in front of Mike. His whole face softened into a smile. "Oh yes. I want to be a chef in my own restaurant."

"That's, that's great, bro. Have you told Dad?"

"I'd been planning to tell him at Christmas in person. But now that our plans have changed, I want to begin the year with a clean slate. But I don't want to leave Dad in the lurch with the only remaining family member being Dash."

And there it was. The reason for this meeting. The hammer had slammed down on him so fast and unexpected his only recourse was to relent and step up to the plate. "This was a setup, wasn't it? Dad really does know, and the only way you can get your walking papers without raising his ire is to convince me to take over. Pretty low, man, especially for you. You've always been in my corner."

Gard backed away, as if he'd been stung. "No, Dad doesn't know. I thought I could make things go smoother if I could deliver you in my place. You've had your chance in the world, Mike, and done really well. Now it's Jay's and my turns."

"Then do it. Without sounding too sappy, I agree, you both have to follow your hearts and do what you want to do. Maybe it's time for Woodley Industries to find new leadership outside the family. We can all still stay on the board and direct things from there."

"I don't know. Dad's got his heart set on at least one of us picking up the mantle from him." He paused, as if debating whether to add something else. "Speaking of Dad's heart, how does he seem to you?"

A tiny dagger of ice pricked at Mike's own heart. "Why do you ask? Do you know something?"

Gard shook his head. "Not really. But when I visited him in Michigan last summer, I came upon him and Mom in this heated argument. They didn't know I was there, and Mom was chiding him for missing some appointment. He kept pooh-poohing its importance, and then out of the blue, he clutched his chest and had to sit down. By the time I got to him, he was breathing normally again, but his face was still pale."

"I witnessed something similar not long ago. When I pushed to know what was going on, he dismissed it as nothing." Was this big campaign to get him into the company part of his dad's desire to see one of his own at the helm before he had to step down due to poor health?

"Look, I'm going ahead with my project, whether you come back to the company or not," Gard said. "I have a line on a place, but first I need advanced culinary training. I've been taking courses as I can, but now I have to really get serious."

Mike considered. His little brother was going to be a chef. The more the idea bounced around in his head, the more he saw how right it was. "What about Lilith? She okay with this new career bent?"

"She's the one who's been prodding me to take the leap. We've been saving up for the salary cut for months, and she's doing well in her own job."

How about that? All this time, Mike thought he detected trouble between Gard and Lilith, but the real problem was that his brother was unhappy in his job. Lilith had been the one to see it.

Time to go. Mike stood. Gard rose also. Again they embraced. "Good luck," Mike said. "You'll do well." He twisted to head out and then returned to his brother. "I'll talk to Dad. I won't change my mind about joining the company, but it's time he came clean about his health."

The question about his dad's health plagued him throughout his flight home. Was that why they'd moved back to Iowa, so his dad could return to his roots? His mother had left her social world in Michigan and now, given the outcome of the showing, seemed to be floundering to reestablish herself in the community. Had she given up her life there for his dad's peace of mind?

Was his dad's health the reason why the man kept prodding him to join the company? His dad had said he wanted to leave the company in good shape when he stepped down, but Mike assumed the man was speaking in nonspecific, future-related terms.

If his dad's health truly was in jeopardy, did he owe it to his dad, his family and Woodley Industries to step up and take the lead? Could he turn his back on his own dreams?

He gazed out the plane's window. Not much to see except the continuously changing cloud formations. It had been nearly a decade since he used the bulk of his trust fund to bail Ned out from his burdensome contract in Europe, the act which had angered his father so much he was invited to leave the company.

The rest of his family had supported Mike's father and kept their distance from him. That's when he'd struck out on his own, shutting them out as well.

Though the family had never treated him as an outcast, he'd learned to survive on his own without them. Only in recent years had relations begun to improve. But in the intervening years, the idea of family had soured, certainly wasn't as important to him as it was to Darren, who'd been willing to take on a task in which she had no experience to pay off a gambling debt that wasn't even hers.

As his flight neared its destination, he realized he wasn't resisting his dad's offer because he'd lost his family loyalty. Like Jay, and now Gard, heading up the family business wasn't his dream. If he caved and did as their father wanted, his heart wouldn't be in the job. He would be cheating himself and everyone else, including the family business.

But there was someone else who had dreamed of heading the company someday. Someone who'd stepped aside out of loyalty to her spouse and because her parents had pressured her to lead a different life than the one to which she'd aspired. Harper.

With this new turn of events, would his sister be willing to put her own interests above her husband's? Only one way to find out.

CHAPTER 21

t was December twenty-third. Darren had today and the next day to finish decorating Mike's house. Despite the headaches of the delivery schedule, most of the large pieces had arrived and were in place. However, a few critical pieces, like four of the twelve dining room chairs, were still missing in action.

"What's going on?" Colby leaned against the bathroom door as Darren finished brushing her teeth.

"Sorry. Didn't mean to wake you. I was searching for a tube of lipstick I was sure I'd tucked away in the closet and knocked over a box of other toiletries."

"Leave them. I'll clean up later, after I've finished my beauty sleep. It's my first day of winter break, you know."

"Lucky you. What I wouldn't give to stay in bed. Maybe later in the week, once Christmas is over and Mike's house is done."

Colby stifled a yawn. "Still working on it?"

"I had no idea there would be so much last-minute stuff. All my energies have been directed at tracking down orders and sticking around the house to take delivery, which has eaten into the time I need to shop the local stores for household items. I still can't get away this morning, because they're bringing Mike's new desk and I need to be there to show them where to place it. Mike left strict orders where it was to go."

"That sounds so … anal. He comes across to me as so even-tempered."

"Mostly. But he also knows what he wants and how he wants it."

Colby widened a sleepy eye. "Does that include you?"

Her sister was no slouch. She had to know Darren's stay at Mike's apartment was more than just two friends caring for each other. "Maybe. But don't get excited. It's not like I'm furnishing that house for myself. Mike's not into commitments."

"Darren, the man didn't go to bat for me, put himself in jeopardy, because he's just a nice guy. He did it for you. If you haven't figured that out yet, you've been smelling too many paint fumes."

"That was weeks ago. We hardly knew each other then."

"Think about it. Something was going on. In the meantime, my bed is calling. But once I'm up and have more time than usual on my hands, if you want me to do some shopping for you, let me know."

"I can't ask you to do that. This is your vacation. You need to relax, not fight the holiday crowds."

Colby headed back to bed. "Suit yourself. But time's running out. I'm here, if you change your mind."

What a nice gesture. Colby wasn't one for shopping. But ever since the gambling group had been arrested and Colby's record made good at school, a different Colby had shown up. One who was less into herself. But Darren had been looking forward to selecting the household goods on her own, as long as there was still a little time remaining.

Had Colby picked up on something even Darren hadn't discerned, that she wanted her own personality reflected in the new house? Even if her sister was right, Darren didn't dare think about it. Taking up residence in Mike's house wasn't in the cards.

She didn't have time to daydream about the possibility now. She had a full day ahead.

And a full day it turned out to be. The guys with the desk didn't show up until late morning, even though they said they'd be there by nine. When they did arrive, they only had one of the three boxes containing the desk. It took another twenty minutes of searching their truck, loaded with other holiday packages, to locate the other two boxes. With the desk now in place, she could finally decorate one room. One down, the rest of the house to go.

While she was carrying more boxes of accessories in from the garage, she took a call from the guys delivering the dining room table, which due to the crush of the holidays, hadn't arrived the previous week as promised. They were in transit from Colorado and had made it as far as western Nebraska before they had to pull up due to the weather, the first major snowstorm of the season.

"When can you get the table here?" she asked, trying to keep her voice calm.

"Can't say," the driver said. "This thing is brutal. Several vehicles already off the road. Didn't want to risk it with this cargo. We'll try to leave at daybreak tomorrow."

Tomorrow. It had to be there by then, because that was all the time left. She could do this. She had to, for Mike's sake.

The rest of the day she spent placing the various decorative objects she'd been collecting. But to do the job right, the artist in her made her take her time deciding the perfect spot for each item.

Absorbed in what was turning out to be one of the most fun parts of this job, she almost missed hearing the doorbell. Her heart came alive when she saw it was Mike.

"I haven't forgotten my promise to stay away from here until you say it's time. But this is an emergency."

Her eyes went wide. "Emergency? Are you okay?"

Damn, shouldn't have scared her like that. "Sorry. Yeah, I'm fine. It's my family. Well, they're okay, too, for now, anyhow." God, he was rambling, partly because he hadn't seen her in days and partly because his plan could affect her too. Maybe. Down the road. Well, maybe. "I won't come in. I'll save the big reveal 'til tomorrow. How 'bout you come out here? Join me in the car."

She grabbed her jacket and followed. As soon as they were both seated inside the still-warm vehicle, he pulled her into his arms and kissed her long and hard. When he finally came up for air, he took in her essence and felt better than he had in days. "I've missed you."

"That's the emergency? Your libido?"

"Uh, not exactly, but holding you in my arms again took priority."

She laid her head against his shoulder. "I've missed you, too."

He skimmed his hand down her back, pressed her to him. "You feel so good."

"Is this your idea of a booty call? As much as I'm up for it, if it is, I've got to get back to the house, or I'll never be done in time."

"Do I have my own bed? And a fridge?"

"They've been here for days. Why?"

"As long as I've got them, the rest will fall into place." The thought of trying out that new bed was making him go hard. Couldn't go there right now. He needed her input.

Even when she related how the guest of honor at his Christmas dinner, the table, might be absent, that part no longer seemed such a big deal. What was important was what he had to say to his family at that dinner.

He told her about his meeting with Gard and their suspicions about their father's health. "Hmm," she said. "That reminds me of something I was going to tell you the next time we were together." She related his mother's time's-running-out statement at Janice's gallery. "Do you think she might have been referring to your father?"

"Meaning, if he is sick, it's serious, and his time is limited." He spoke the words more to himself than to her, trying out the idea.

"That's just a theory, Mike. Your mother explained that time was running out to receive invites to the key parties of the season, but neither Janice nor I were convinced. It was like she suddenly realized she'd said too much and was attempting to cover her tracks."

"I'm going to work on the assumption something really is wrong. It explains my dad's insistence I join the family business and eventually take over from him." He went on to tell her about Gard's decision and how that left only his sister's husband still in the company to represent the family.

"Are you considering your father's offer?"

"Do you think I should?"

She blinked. "That's your decision, Mike. Why do you ask?"

How much did he want to say? That her opinion was critical to his decision? If he said that much, it was like admitting she was the most important person in his life. She was, despite all his resolutions about commitment to the contrary. But while her mind was tied up on the house, he didn't want to heap this confession on her.

"I value your opinion. You have enough distance from my situation to recognize possibilities and pitfalls that I don't."

"You no longer have to prove yourself to your family. You never did, only you didn't believe that. You must do what's best for you."

"Back up. You think I'm still trying to prove myself to my dad and the rest of the family?"

"That's why this Christmas dinner is so important to you, isn't it?"

He started to deny her claim but stopped. Maybe, in the beginning. He'd been telling himself it was simply to get his mother off his back. Did he really care what his family thought of him? "I'm not like you, putting my family's welfare above my own. Nor do I care what they think of me. I'm my own person, independent of them."

"Really?"

"Yes, really. What are you trying to tell me?"

She didn't answer at first, like she was framing her response. "When we first met and you kept rejecting my work, I attributed it to your not knowing your own mind. I had the same thought when you had such difficulty explaining how you wanted the house decorated. I was wrong on both accounts. You rejected my work because you wanted to see me again, and you got a sort of perverse pleasure in hassling me, which was the beginning of the dance between us."

Man, this woman was sharp. He loved her for that. "Why couldn't I define my tastes about the house?"

"It wasn't until I saw paint on the walls that an incredible thought struck. Even with all the current embellishments you added to the house, the color scheme, even some of the furnishings are very similar to your parents' home."

No. Where was she getting this idea? "Meaning?"

"You tell me, Mike. I think as much as you claim your independence from your family, you want to build a home like theirs."

"That's crazy. I couldn't wait to move out of that place when my parents returned. Why recreate it here?" He'd made such a big deal with his mother when he told her he didn't dance to her mambo.

"You told me when we first met you weren't close to your family. You neglected to add you once were quite close, when you were growing up in that mansion. Even though your father didn't disown you, his rejection crushed your spirit more than you've ever admitted to anyone, including yourself."

"When I asked for your opinion, I didn't think I'd get this lengthy psychoanalysis."

"I've come to care for you, Mike. More than is probably wise, given your preference for no entanglements. But there it is. I couldn't help myself, any more than I could back away from telling you my thoughts."

He lifted a strand of her hair, dangled it between his fingers. "I care for you, too. But this theory of yours, it's mind blowing. It throws the decision I thought I'd made into question."

"You already knew what you wanted to do? Why did you ask me, then?"

"You're so into helping your family, I wanted to know if you thought I should do the same, because I'd decided the best course for me was to stay true to myself and refuse the offer."

She seemed to mull over his decision. "As much as I believe in helping family, sometimes you have to take a pass and let them deal with their problems on their own. Given the situation you've described, I'd say you made the right choice."

The breath he'd been holding escaped him. "I was hoping you'd see it that way." He took her in his arms again and held her tight. But her rationale concerned him enough to pull away. "What you said made sense, but what about you? You've put your career on hold the last several weeks because you needed the money from finishing my house to pay off Colby's gambling debts."

She backed away. "That couldn't be avoided. Who knows what they would've done to her if she'd told them she couldn't pay."

Who knew what might have happened if he hadn't forced Colby and Darren to go to the school and the authorities? "Okay, I'll grant you that much. But then you had her move in with you, when you have neither the room nor the same lifestyle as your sister. She's a slob, Darren, and you're constantly cleaning up after her."

"That was to save rent money."

"And have her close so you could watch over her."

She pursed her lips. "Okay, you're right. I had to make sure she could resist the temptation to gamble again. Her counselor couldn't do it all."

"Then there's your mom. You give up your Thanksgiving holiday every year to help her at the restaurant."

"I don't mind. Helping at the restaurant gives meaning to the day."

"How about the times you drop everything to go be with her because she's feeling blue? Or help her make rent for the month?"

"She needs me."

"Really?"

He could feel her body tense. He'd overstepped. Too bad. Time for her to face her demons as well. "Or do you need her to need you?" He let his question settle in the air. Sink in.

She didn't speak for several beats.

"I'm no shrink, Darren. Hell, I even accused you of psychoanalyzing me, but I'm wondering if this need to take care of your mother and sister doesn't somehow stem from your dad's death. You told me your mom went into a funk after he died, barely able to cope. Perhaps you felt you had to step in for him and take care of both her and your sister?"

Her eyes flashed a dark fire he'd never seen. "That's, that's preposterous. I hurt just as much as Mom and Colby after Dad passed away."

"I'm sure you did, but maybe you got through your grief by taking care of the other two. Over time, you took that on as your role."

She shook her head vigorously. "You're so wrong. I would've gladly stepped aside if Mom or Colby took the lead, but they didn't. Someone had to."

"Your dad's death hit you just as hard as it did your mom and sister. I suspect you were just coming out of that period when you met your fiancé. Then he died, too. It's no wonder you've steered clear of any further serious relationships. You're only so strong."

"How dare you bring my family and fiancé into a discussion of your family?"

"Because we're not so different in our family relations after all. We've both been hurt. We just reacted differently."

"You've gone too far. This discussion is over." Her tone had gone more deliberate. She slid across the seat, opened the door and was outside before he realized what was happening. "Don't worry about your house being finished on time, Mr. Woodley. I'll take great pains to assure you have just the right setting to impress your family. Merry Christmas."

"Darren! Hey, I'm sorry if I went too far. I thought you needed to hear my observation."

But Darren was almost back in the house before he finished. If he followed her, he'd be breaking his promise not to enter the house before the twenty-fourth. He tried calling. She let the call go to voicemail. He repeated his apology, then hung up. He'd try again later. Maybe with a little time, she'd understand what he'd been suggesting.

Damn woman. She could dish out the advice but couldn't take it when it was aimed at her. He thought they'd grown close. Close enough he could tell her what he suspected about her relationship with her family.

Proved his point about relationships. Couldn't get too close.

He revved up the car and sped out of Sullivan's Creek.

DARREN SLAMMED INTO THE HOUSE, ready to throw something. She didn't dare touch anything for fear of demolishing all her hard work. It'd serve him right, but she wasn't about to sell her work short. She'd have to find some other way to release her anger. She remembered the empty boxes and cartons in the garage. At some point, she'd planned to tear them down for stacking. Might as well attack them now.

She tried not to think about Mike's comments while she ripped apart the cardboard, but his words kept ringing in her head. One comment, in particular, wouldn't go away. That she'd shied away from serious relationships because she couldn't bear the thought of losing someone else.

Okay, that was true. She'd realized the truth of it when she'd finally enjoyed intercourse with him. She'd actually come to see a future with him, if he ever got over his own fear of commitment. Forget that now. She'd allowed him to get close, and he'd used that intimacy against her.

As much as she wanted to escape this house that screamed Mike, she wasn't going to renege on her responsibility. He'd prob-ably read some deep-seated psychological need into that feeling also, but let him. This was who she was. She finished what she started.

Who was she kidding? She wasn't going to finish what she'd started with Mike. That was over. Somehow, she'd get through the next few hours, the next few days. Then move on. Without him.

She resumed the task of situating objects in the perfect spot. Again, slow going. Before she knew it, darkness fell. She hadn't eaten in hours. Why hadn't she thought to bring a lunch? Because her mind had been preoccupied ticking off all the tasks ahead of her for the day. If she drove into town to pick up something, it would be late before she got back to the house. Instead, she opted to go home and get a good night's sleep before throwing herself into final preparations the next two days.

Colby was sprawled out on the sofa, munching popcorn and watching a TV show. "Binge watching. Discovered this incredible show I've only heard about while I've buried my head in law books. Why don't you take your own bed tonight? I'm ensconced here while I finish the last two episodes."

Sleep in her own bed? Didn't have to ask twice. "Thanks. I'll grab a bite, then call it a night."

"Wasn't sure when I'd see you. Did you finish?"

Darren updated her on the day's progress, or lack thereof, but omitted any mention of her break up with Mike. "Won't know until morning if the dining room table will get here in time with all that snow out west."

"That snow is headed our way, according to the TV weather people."

Great. One more complication. "When? How much?"

Colby tilted her head, as if trying to remember the details. "Supposed to start late tomorrow and build intensity the next day."

Darren sank into a nearby chair. "This can't be happening. I need every last minute tomorrow to finish the house."

"My offer to help still holds. Just tell me what to do."

"Thanks, but …"

"Look, I'm bored already. I'm watching this show because I don't know what else to do. You'd be helping me stay sane."

Colby would be such a great help, but Darren couldn't bring herself to turn over even the slightest bit of responsibility to someone else. Especially her sister.

Hold the phone. Wasn't this exactly what Mike told her she did? She'd denied it strongly. Was she deliberately making things more difficult for herself by resisting Colby's offer?

Time was so short, she couldn't afford any screwups.

Was that how she saw her sister, as a screwup? Colby was an adult. Smart enough to get into law school. The school had seen fit to forgive her. Had Darren not yet reached that point?

Okay, Mr. Woodley, you think you're so smart. I'll just prove you wrong and let Colby help me.

"Maybe you could shop with me and run things back to the car." She fully expected Colby to reject the suggestion.

"Okay. But don't you still have things to do at the house?"

Reluctantly, Darren had to agree. "Right. I have to launder towels and bedsheets and make the beds along with final decorating touches."

"You don't trust me to get what you want, is that it?" Before Darren could respond, Colby went on. "No, that's not it, because you'd be on the phone making me send you photos. You just want to have the fun of doing this yourself."

Darren closed her eyes briefly, trying to wish away this confrontation. "Okay, you got me. I've been looking forward to this part more than I realized." Finally, Darren gave in. "Okay. I'm down to one day. I need the help. But you can say so long to sleeping in. You'll need to be at the stores by nine."

"I'll be fine. Why don't you bring Mom in on this, too? She could do the laundry and make beds so you can focus on the final touches."

Laundry and dishwashing weren't her strengths. Darren could really use her mother's assistance. "Doesn't she have to work? I don't want to cut into her wages."

"Then pay her. More than she'd get at the Blue Iris. She'd love to be part of all this with us."

Why not? It was truly time to bring in the big guns. She called her mother, who went absolutely bonkers at the idea of joining her team. "It's not the fancy stuff, Mom. Mainly washing towels and sheets and making beds."

"Something I know how to do."

THE NEXT MORNING, even though Darren was up early to set off for the house, Colby was awake and dressed before her. As Darren drove toward Sullivan's Creek, she received a call from the guys delivering the table. The storm had dumped over ten inches where they were staying, and the interstate had been shut down for the next several hours until at least one lane had been cleared.

If, and it was a big *if*, the roads were cleared soon enough, he thought they could make it to Des Moines by the end of the day. All Darren could do was encourage him to do his best. As much as she wanted that table, it wasn't worth the men risking their lives to deliver it.

"Maybe you should consider a backup, dear," her mother said.

"Backup? You mean another table?"

"Exactly. You could rent one about the same size, and once it has a tablecloth over it, no one will know the difference."

"Could I get one yet today?"

"I'll call the Dortmans. They know people."

Maybe it had been a good idea to include her mother.

Fortunately, her mother had thought to bring the detergent and fabric softener Darren forgot. They would have wasted precious time driving back to town to buy some before they could get started. "I know you do your own housekeeping, but you have so much on your mind right now, I thought this detail might have slipped your attention."

Okay, it had been a great idea to include her mom.

The highlight of the morning was the arrival of the four missing dining room chairs. Darren held her breath as she examined each of them. Not a scratch. Now she had twelve chairs but no table, but thanks to her mom's connections, a backup of the same dimensions was on its way and slated to arrive by noon. She stayed tuned to one of Mike's new TV sets, listening to weather reports every so often.

Colby arrived a little after one, her car piled high with boxes and packages. She'd also picked up lunch for the three of them, compliments of the Dortmans. She handed Darren a turkey sandwich. "This place looks great, Darren. Can I get a tour before you put me to work?"

Music to her ears. "Sure. But you don't need to stick around."

"Have you washed the dinner plates and silver yet?"

"Uh, no."

"I also brought dish detergent," their mother said. "And I want in on the tour, too."

"Then you'll both be the first."

Colby returned a broad smile. "Mike hasn't even seen this?"

"Part of our deal. I didn't want him making changes up to the last minute. I sold it as my big reveal, as they do on home improvement shows."

As they toured each room, Darren asked Colby and their mother's opinion on furniture placement and the items accessorizing the room. Impressed, Colby could only come up with a few changes, all minor.

Their mother simply shook her head, mouth open. "I love your paintings, dear, but this house. It's so you."

Really? She'd tried so hard to make it reflect Mike.

They spent the rest of the afternoon putting things away, dusting, vacuuming and whatever else was needed to get the house ready. The snow started falling around two. Large, fluffy flakes dotted the front yard of Mike's house, but the street was still warm enough that the precip melted there. That phase didn't last long. The white stuff started to collect everywhere.

"I totally forgot about signing up someone for snow removal. What are we going to do? It's only going to accumulate more before tomorrow. How will Mike's family get in without having to tromp through the stuff?" She turned to her mother. "By any chance, is there a snow shovel in that bag of yours?"

"Afraid not." Her mother looked to Colby.

"There are a couple out in the garage," her sister replied. "Mom texted me."

Oh yes. Asking her mother and sister for help had been a golden idea.

CHAPTER 22

As fast as she shoveled, Darren couldn't keep up with the snow. After she'd been at it a half hour, Colby joined her.

"Rest. It's my turn."

Darren gratefully submitted. "Thanks."

As she started for the house, two cars pulled up. Jay emerged from the first. Mrs. Woodley and an older man followed him. A couple Darren didn't recognize got out of the second car along with two children.

"Looks like we're just in time," Jay said as he approached.

It took a few seconds for their visitors' identities to sink in. "You're not supposed to arrive until tomorrow."

"We kept watching the weather and didn't think we'd make it through the roads tomorrow morning. So, whether our host likes it or not, we're here for a Christmas Eve sleepover."

"Hello, dear," Mrs. Woodley said, coming up to her. "Isn't this exciting, a housewarming and Christmas dinner all in one? You remember my husband, Joe? You took care of me until he arrived the night of the showing?"

Darren didn't know what to say. "Hello" seemed too trite. Where was Mike? Did he know about this? If he was on the way, she had to get out of there before he arrived.

The couple she didn't know prodded the two younger ones to move along. For their part, the kids, though struggling to make their way through the snow, were still having a great time playing in it. All four came up to her.

"You must be Darren Williams," the woman said. "I'm Mike's sister, Harper Woodley Morgan. This is my husband Dashiell, Dash, and our two children, Brandon and Hailey."

Colby shoved Darren ahead as the seven visitors started for the front door. "Go with them."

Then it hit Darren. They were going to see Mike's house before he did. Darren pulled Colby aside. "Call Mike. Tell him." As Colby nodded, Darren rushed to beat the others to the door. "Uh, this will be quite a surprise to Mike."

Jay pulled up to her. "I know, I know, we're seeing this before him. But we talked it over and decided it was more important we get here now in one piece."

He had a point. But Mike still wouldn't like it. Why did she care? They were done. But, damn, she did care. She scurried past him to make sure everyone was removing their shoes or boots.

She needn't have worried. Her mom had taken up footwear removal duty and had already hauled out two mats they'd stored in the entry closet just hours before. "Hello, everyone. Welcome to Chez Woodley. Oh, that's your place. Welcome to Chez Woodley West." All her years as hostess at the Blue Iris were in force.

"Besides our bags, we brought enough food for tonight, morning, and tomorrow's dinner prepared by our housekeeper. She was thrilled to have the day off tomorrow," Mrs. Woodley told Darren's mother.

"Then let's start with the kitchen for your tour," Elise Williams said.

"Dash and I will take over snow removal as soon as we bring in all the goodies," Jay said to Darren and Colby. "You two get warm. Then you can show Mom and Dad and Harper what you've done with the house."

"I don't suppose I could talk you all into waiting for the grand tour until Mike gets here? He hasn't seen it yet himself."

Mrs. Woodley pulled up on her way to the kitchen. "Oh my. We don't want to rob him of that honor. We'll put the food in the kitchen, but we'll leave the rest of our things here."

Colby gave Darren a high sign. "He should be here soon," Darren said. "He had no idea you were coming today."

Harper brushed snowflakes from her jacket sleeves. "This is exciting. We never have snow in Florida, and I barely remember it from when I was growing up here."

"Then this should be a real highlight of your trip," Colby told her.

Later, Darren would be hard pressed to recall what happened in the next half hour. The women and kids removed their outerwear. Darren's mother made hot chocolate for everyone—had she brought that along also? Mr. Woodley sat stiffly in the leather club chair in the living room. And the metallic clink of shovels on the driveway resonated throughout the room.

Darren's mother whispered in her ear. "Unclasp your hands."

Only then did Darren realize from the red streaks on her hands what she'd been doing.

After what seemed like hours but was only thirty-four minutes, tires screeched to a halt on the newly cleared driveway. Mike had arrived. Showtime.

Darren attempted to blend into the furnishings. No one knew she and Mike were quits. No one, except Colby and maybe Jay, knew they were ever together. Mike would blame her for this, and she wasn't up to defending herself against the follies of the weather and his family. After all, they'd thought ahead, not wanting to spoil Mike's Christmas dinner. Would he take that into consideration before chewing her out?

MIKE HAD BEEN PICKING up a special-order purchase flown in from New York City at a mall on the west side of town when he received Colby's call. The family had already shown up at the house? Before he even got to see Darren's work? Damn. Triple damn!

The snow was well over a foot deep by the time he reached the parking lot. Good thing he'd worn his cowboy boots today. Too bad he hadn't planned to stay overnight in his new bed and packed another set of clothes. Once he got out there, which looked like it would be a chore in itself, he probably wouldn't be able to return until sometime tomorrow, if the roads got cleared.

Why hadn't he thought ahead and contacted his mother about modifying their schedule? Because all he'd had on his mind the last twenty-four hours had been Darren and making things right with her. God, he hoped he hadn't blown it. He'd finally let a woman get under his skin and convince him there was more to life than serial dating and what had he done? Insulted her to the point she had to run away.

He had to focus completely on the road. Just finding it and staying on it with the accumulating snow hiding the lane lines was a challenge. The wipers got a workout keeping more than a few inches of windshield visible. After a bit, so much snow amassed behind the blades, they barely moved. At least the road hadn't yet grown slippery. The real problem was burrowing through more than a foot of the stuff, which now was higher than the car's bottom.

With four cars already in his drive, he couldn't park in the garage. By some miracle, the drive had been cleared, although more snow was already making that a thing of the past.

He tucked his purchase inside his jacket and made a run for the front door. Forget the garage. He was going to see his house the way Darren had promised. As he passed the front car in the drive, now almost hidden under the snow, he realized it was Darren's. She was still here. He hoped she'd finished the house. Not that he cared, but who knew what his mother's impression would be if the decorating wasn't finished.

As he came through the door, he was struck by how warm and cozy the place looked from the last time he'd been here. It also hit him that Darren had been right. As now furnished, the house did echo his parents' home, in a more modern, scaled down version.

His mother flew to his side. His dad hung back. On the sidelines, Jay offered an expression of commiseration. Harper and Dash and the kids off to the side allowed his mother to pass. Colby? Mrs. Williams? Where was Darren? Finally, he spotted her, hanging back, staring at the floor.

Be nice. They meant well. "Hi, everyone. Welcome to my new home."

"We were worried you wouldn't make it through the storm," his mother said.

"Almost didn't." No need to mention he'd almost driven off the road a couple of times. "This is going to be a record breaker. Different holiday than we planned, huh?"

"Hope you don't mind our early arrival. If we waited until tomorrow morning, we didn't think we'd make it," Jay said.

Mike forced a smile. "Good thinking. Not sure how the food will get here, though."

"We took care of that." His mother filled him in on Tammy's contributions. "We'll have to do our gift exchange another time, because we had to leave those behind to accommodate the food and our bags."

"Sounds like you thought of everything," he said.

His sister handed him a mug of hot chocolate. "Even this. Here, warm up."

Jay wiped a chocolate smudge from his lips. "We've been waiting for your arrival before touring your new place."

Their dad slid an admiring hand over the bannister of the stairwell. "But from what little we've seen, looks like Ms. Williams has done a great job. Your mother is already licking her chops to hire her to give our place the same look."

As the irony of his father's words hit him, he involuntarily shot a glance at Darren and caught her eyes on him. Her lips curled up on one side at his dad's statement. "You'll have to negotiate with Darren, Mom. She's anxious to get back to her paints and easel."

"Well, my dear," his mother said to Darren, "we must talk about your future plans while we're all here together."

"Actually, we were about to head back to town," Darren replied, eyeing her mother and sister.

Mike caught himself just before he told her absolutely not. If he had, she might have chosen to leave just to spite him.

His father, who was staring out the front window, spoke up. "I don't think that would be wise, my dear. Looks like over a foot and a half out there now."

Darren bit a lip. "But we can't stay here. This is your family time."

"If I recall," Jay said, "you included Mike and me in your Thanksgiving. Turnabout's only fair."

Mrs. Woodley placed a hand on Elise Williams' arm. "Please stay. There's plenty of food."

"We didn't get quite finished setting up the bedrooms. We could take care of those if we stayed," Darren's mother replied.

With everyone chiming in to discourage the trip back to town, Darren relented.

Mike held up a hand. "Since that's been decided and before anyone makes any more beds, I want to see my new home."

"Good idea," Jay said. While Mike stayed in his place, Jay went to Darren and took her hand. "Lead the way, my lady."

Even though he'd approved the selection of every object in his house, Mike had no idea it would all come together so well. He couldn't believe this was his new home. It was everything he could have ever wanted and then some. Darren had even hung the two pictures she'd done for him in his office.

Everyone else approved as well. Even Mr. Woodley, who stopped at the wall leading into Mike's office. "Where did you find these family pictures? They're so dramatic in black and white."

"I'm glad you like them. I have an in with your housekeeper. Even Mike didn't know about those."

Mike approached her, tried to use the opportunity to get back in her good graces, knowing full well the message she'd been trying to send with the emphasis on family. "These are great, Darren." Though she slid away, she seemed pleased. "You knew exactly what this entrance to my private workspace needed."

Each new room surprised him with her special touches. In his office, it was a room-sized basketball hoop. How did she know he'd been on the high school varsity team, along with Ned? Ned. Wow, she'd done her homework.

The kitchen boasted a gourmet milkshake machine. When had he ordered that? The dining room was already set for dinner tomorrow with seven settings of the china and silver he had selected. But where did she get the table? Wasn't his stuck somewhere in western Nebraska?

The piece de resistance was the master bedroom. Though he loved the flat-screen TV hidden behind a mirror, it was the throw decking the end of the bed that floored him. Darren's personal handiwork. "Made it years ago when I was learning to knit. Almost forgot I had it until I needed something just that shade of blue to make the room pop."

Blue. Her personal message. Something made with her own hands in the color he saved for when he wanted to be alone. Or maybe alone with her. "I'm speechless, Darren. I've always believed in your artistic talent, but you went beyond anything I could've anticipated."

She returned a half smile, then, as if suddenly reminded of their recent parting of the ways, nodded, backed away. "Thanks. I give every project my all."

During their tour of the other bedrooms, they discovered Darren's mother and Colby stretching a fitted sheet over the mattress pad. "Oh shoot, we tried to stay ahead of you."

"We'll all pitch in to help," Harper said, grabbing her husband and making him help smooth one corner.

To Mike's surprise, his mother joined in as well, stuffing the pillows into cases. "While we're here, we might as well decide on sleeping assignments. Of course, you get the master, dear. That leaves the other three bedrooms for the rest of us. Brandon and Hailey brought sleeping bags."

"I'll take the sofa bed in my office," Mike said. "Jay, could you sleep on the davenport in the living room? Maybe the kids could join you there? That would leave the four bedrooms up here for the rest of you. I'm giving the master to Darren. She deserves it after all her hard work."

Darren shook her head. "Perhaps your parents would enjoy it more."

"No, dear, Mike's absolutely right. You've been working up to the last minute. Take the master," his mother said.

Harper cut off any further refusal on Darren's part. "Who's ready to eat?"

After an early supper of cheese and broccoli soup, green salad and still-warm bread, Mike attempted to pull Darren aside. Begrudgingly, she followed, only as far as the corridor leading to his office. "Can we talk? Later? I need to discuss something with my brother and sister first."

"Your dad's health?"

"Yeah. I want to give my dad a final answer to his offer while he's here."

She touched his forearm. "Good luck."

At least she was still speaking to him.

He waited for an opportunity to get with Harper privately, which came when she returned from taking a garbage bag to the garage. Jay caught his signal and followed them to Mike's office.

Mike updated them about his visit with their brother in California. "We think that's why Mom and Dad moved back here. So Dad could spend his last years in his hometown."

Jay turned from examining Darren's two paintings. "I suspected as much, but Dad would never admit it. Mom just changed the subject whenever I asked."

"I had no idea Gard wanted to be a chef," Harper said. "Nor that you'd leave the business to help Mike sell lots here in Sullivan's Creek. Very nice development, I might add, from what I could see between snowflakes."

Mike gazed around the room. "Thanks. I never envisioned myself living here year-round when Ned began this project, but as events turned out, it was one of the best decisions I ever made. Snowstorm notwithstanding."

"If you're all correct about Dad's health, it begs the question of the Woodley Industries' future. Dash is still there, but I know how Dad feels about my husband's abilities to lead the family business. So that leaves you, Mike, to take the reins. Is that why you called us in here? To obtain our blessing?"

"Dad's been after me ever since he got back to town to join the company. I've turned him down repeatedly. I almost gave in when I learned about his health, and then the best solution came to me. Why not let the Woodley who is not only most qualified to run the business but also wants to do so take over? You, Harper. What do you say?"

His sister dropped onto the sofa. "Me? I haven't worked there or anywhere since before the kids were born."

"You're a quick study. Look how fast you picked up on what I was getting at."

"What about Dash? I couldn't ask him to work for me."

"Talk to him. Tonight. I know you want to do this, sis. I also know you'd be great." He switched his attention to Jay. "What do you think, bro? You're the oldest."

"Maybe so," Jay said, "but you're the smartest. You figured out a way to make us all happy." Then he remembered their sister. "That is, if you say yes, Harper."

Harper seemed to be thinking through Mike's proposition. They needed something to clinch her decision. "You want to stay in Florida, avoid a diet of this type of weather. We'll convince Dad it will work. You want a place to stay whenever you come to town, I'll build you a house out here, so you wouldn't have to be directly under Dad's nose." He'd plucked the idea out of thin air, but he liked it. "In fact, while Jay's getting back on his feet, he can stay there, too, so he can use it as a model whenever he's showing homes."

Jay thumped him on the back. "You really are smart. I was going to hit you up with a similar idea. This makes it much easier."

Harper rose. "I'll talk to Dash. Tonight."

"Then you're interested?"

His answer was a kiss on the cheek. "The only reason this opportunity has arisen is because none of you boys wants it. But maybe you all intuitively realize the best person for this job is your sister. I do want it. I've always wanted it. I just have to make sure my husband is okay with this too." She left the two of them behind in Mike's office.

"What'd'ya think? That bastard for once gonna let his wife come first?" Jay asked.

"Depends on Harper. She's held back and let him be the big cheese for so long, she's either ready to take her turn or she'll continue on the same track. The little spitfire we used to know is still inside her somewhere. It's up to Harper whether or not she lets her emerge."

"And if she doesn't?"

Mike released a sigh. "I've made my decision, once and for all. I'm not joining the company. If Harper passes, we should get ready to say good-bye to Woodley Industries as we know it."

CHAPTER 23

Only sheer determination kept Darren from nodding off. Her body felt like every bone had been broken. Worse, though, her brain could barely function. Keeping her cool around Mike with an audience of both her family and his took great effort. She was glad, relieved, the house was done. Even happier, it had received everyone's, including Mike's, approval.

Now though, all she wanted was to escape. Be alone with her thoughts. But Mike had asked to speak with her. Probably wanted to end things between them on a high note. Okay, she was a big girl. As difficult as it was to be in the house they had created together and no longer be part of his life, she could do this.

She watched Mike's sister emerge from the office area and immediately pull her husband off to the side. Mike and Jay didn't appear for a few more minutes.

When he did appear, Mike approached her. "There are a few details about the house I need to run past you, Darren. Would you mind joining me in my office?"

"Uh, sure."

He closed the door behind her. "Sorry about this crush of family. You must be exhausted."

"I like your family. And Mom and Colby are beside themselves getting to stay overnight in this house."

"I know I told you before, but you did a terrific job. I couldn't be more satisfied."

Was he leading up to something, like a bonus, or a kiss-off? She kept her response neutral. "I'm happy it turned out so well." No point apologizing for clearing the finish line at absolutely the last minute.

He gestured for her to join him on the sofa. She complied, but each inch closer to him tugged more on her heart.

"I went too far the other day when I said you need to be needed. That's my opinion, but I didn't have to share it with you. I guess I, uh, just thought we'd gotten close enough to confide such things."

"In all fairness, so did I. I certainly didn't hold back when it came to your feelings about your family."

"Yeah, well, turns out you were right. My family wasn't as screwed up as I thought. Even Jay, despite his divorce, because of his divorce, is a new man. I've never seen him so happy."

Neither spoke as they each digested their confessions.

"So you, uh, thought we'd gotten close? Like, uh, friends?" he asked.

Was that the way he saw their relationship? Friends? Oh hell, they'd reached the point of no return. Why not come clean? "I felt we'd become more than friends. More than just sex partners, as nice as that was. I've, uh, fallen in love with you." There. It was out. Let him deal.

He took her hand. Kissed it. "You beat me to the punch. But just so you know, I'm in love with you, too. God knows I've fought it, denied it, but when I thought I'd hurt you, lost you, the other day, I felt like part of me had been ripped out."

He placed his palms on her cheeks and brought her mouth to

his. The kiss was tender yet strong, the connection of their lips sealing a new bond between them. One that would not end soon. If ever.

When he sat back, his eyes bored into hers, willing her to see their future together.

"When I said I didn't believe in commitments, I was full of crap. Didn't know it at the time. Had to open my eyes and see my family for who they really are. I've avoided the kind of relationships I thought were ruining them until I realized they were the smart ones."

This surprised her. He'd been so sure of his stance. "I guess I went along with you because I didn't want to lose someone close again."

"That's still possible someday."

"Agreed. If and when that time comes, I'll have to deal with my grief all over again. But the hurt has healed. I'm stronger because of it, and I'm willing to take the chance."

"This is weird, isn't it?" he said. "Being snowbound with the very people who I've been avoiding. I was so frustrated when I arrived earlier, because I felt like I'd lost control of the event I'd set in motion. But ever since I've been here, this has been the best holiday ever. Even better than the Thanksgiving I recently shared with your family. I feel at peace with the world and myself."

"Now that we've talked, I feel the same way."

"There's a Part Two to this discussion," he told her, "but for now, I just want to sit back and take it all in."

"Sounds good to me."

～

EVEN THOUGH HE slept on his new sofa bed instead of his new bed in the master and there were still several pieces of his life undecided, Mike got a good night's sleep. Must be the comfort offered by his new home. The weather didn't affect either the furnace or electricity, although the weather woman said fifteen inches had fallen. He was glad one of the improvements he'd insisted on was a private bath off his office. Came in handy this morning.

He wasn't the first one up. Darren's mother had taken it upon herself to prepare breakfast. "You're my guest, Mrs. Williams. Just because you work in a restaurant, no one expects you to take care of all the meals," he told her when he wandered into the kitchen.

"That's very kind of you to say, Mike, but I don't usually sleep beyond six thirty. I was at a loss what to do once I'd dressed, so I made myself at home in your kitchen, which, by the way, is a dream. It's so well laid out."

He hardly paid attention to Darren as she went over the kitchen layout with him. As he'd told her at the time, as long as the microwave and stove top worked to warm food and the fridge cooled it, he'd be happy. That was before the last few days. Now he had to smile to himself that Darren's mother had given her approval. "Your daughter deserves all the credit."

He tried to stay occupied while he waited to hear from Harper, dragging Jay out to the driveway on snow-removal duty. Would've pressured Dash to lend a hand as well, but there were only two shovels, and he didn't want to risk a run-in with the guy, had Harper's talk with him gone sour.

Brandon and Hailey, of course, wanted to build a snowman now that the snow had stopped. Harper and Dash had their hands full convincing them there was too much of the white stuff. In the end, wearing their ski clothes, they were allowed to go outside to "explore." Grandpa Joe volunteered to watch over them. They couldn't go far, but they weren't used to the cold.

From the sidelines, Mike watched his father demonstrating how to make their way through the stuff by sliding into it with their hips. Actual steps were near impossible, especially for the two small bodies.

Brandon pulled at his grandfather's jacket. "You look funny, Grandpa. Your face is getting really red."

"Just like Santa Claus," Hailey said.

"Ho, ho …" Grandpa Joe's third "ho" released a coughing fit. Much like the one Mike witnessed in his loft.

Both kids attempted to get to him, but it was a struggle. "Grandpa?"

Mike exchanged a look with Jay, whose furrowed brow mirrored how Mike must have appeared. Both men fought their way to their dad. Each grabbed an arm and dragged-lifted him back to the house. "You guys need to come in also," Mike called.

Once they got their father inside, they quickly removed his muffler, hat and jacket and had him sit in the first chair in sight. His dad continued to hack away for several more minutes.

Their mother, running into the room to investigate the sounds, disappeared for a bit and then returned with a glass of water and a vial of some kind of medication. "Here, Joe. Take this. I told you all that snow would be too much for you."

Their dad, usually one to spurn any kind of medication, obediently accepted a tablet and gulped down some of the water. His body seemed to recede within his clothing, as if a shadow of his usual self.

Mike and Jay stood by, helpless, and waited for their dad to regain his usual brusqueness.

"Do you want to lie down?" their mother asked their dad. "Your, uh, you-know is in our bedroom."

Their dad held up a hand but still didn't speak. His face was no longer as red.

The kids had ripped off their boots and gone to find their parents. Harper and Dash accompanied them to the living room. "Dad? Are you okay? The kids said you started coughing outside and couldn't stop."

Darren, her mother and Colby peeked in from the kitchen but kept their distance.

Mike's mother rose and faced her children. "We're sorry for all the drama, kids. Your dad has battled a chest cold for days. I knew he shouldn't go outside, but he so rarely gets to be with his grandchildren, I couldn't hold him back."

"No, Franny. Time for the truth." His voice was almost back to normal. "Wish Gardner and Lilith were here also, but this will have to do."

"Not today, Joe. It's Christmas. This is Mike's day. We can't spoil it."

"Forget about it being my day," Mike said. "We all want to hear what Dad has to say."

Harper motioned to Darren to come closer. "Would you mind taking the kids to the kitchen and finding them a snack?"

Darren nodded, escorted the kids, and then it was just the immediate Woodley family assembled in Mike's living room.

"I'm not a well man," Mike's father said. "I have a rare form of chronic obstructive pulmonary disease, or COPD, as it's more popularly called. I've never been a heavy smoker, which is one of the major causes, but apparently in my early days, I was around chemical fumes that ate their way into my lungs only to act up now, after all these years."

Mike started to say something, but his father once again held up a hand. "Medication, like the pill I just took, helps, but this disease gets progressively more acute until, well, until my body can no longer fight it off. The time has come for us as a family to plan for the years ahead as they affect Woodley Industries."

Damn! His worst suspicions confirmed, Mike sensed this family confab was going to end with his dad making another plea for him to join his team. How was he going to turn the man down now in the midst of this terrifying revelation in front of the rest of the family?

He sought Harper's attention. Her face was puckered up from their dad's announcement, but when she caught his eyes on her, she straightened her shoulders, pursed her lips, and offered a nod so inconspicuous, only he could interpret its meaning.

Would her decision be enough?

As the oldest, Jay took the lead. "Does this mean you're stepping down as CEO, Dad?"

"I consider myself a young man still. Hadn't planned any major shake-ups in leadership for years. But this COPD changes things." He turned his attention to Mike. "I'd hoped I wouldn't have to ask you under these circumstances, Michael. I wanted you to decide to join me of your own accord. But we can no longer avoid this decision."

Mike said a silent prayer he'd do this right. His words could possibly hasten his dad's deterioration. "I appreciate your confidence in me, Dad. I also know how much you've worked to bring the corporation to its current level. But I'm not your man. My heart wouldn't be in it, and I can't believe you'd wish a life of forced service out of loyalty on any of your children."

His dad's eyes flickered, his breathing increased. But now it was Mike's turn to hold up a hand. "We're all committed to the corporation's future, Dad. We all want to see the best person for the job, the best leader, step in when you step down." He turned to his sister. "That would be Harper."

"Harper?" Joe Woodley's perplexed eyes sought his daughter's. "You want the job?"

Harper came forward. "Yes, Dad. I may have stepped aside when I married Dash, but I have the education and the interest. I did a pretty great job when I interned."

"But you've never managed a division or supervised people."

"Maybe not, but don't discount all the time I've invested in countless charitable organizations. I learned to achieve buy-in and loyalty by virtue of cooperation, a much more difficult way to lead. Plus, I've got all of you to help me when I need it."

"What about Dash?"

Dash joined his wife. "I've always known I'd only get so far up the ladder. I'll stick around and help Harper any way she needs, but our plan until the kids are ready for college is for me to work part-time and be there for the kids when they're home."

"You're okay with that, Dash?" Mike's mother, the one responsible for convincing her once suggestible daughter that a woman's place was in the home, asked the question.

"Yes. Actually, it's a relief. I've missed being around the kids during their early years. I wholeheartedly support Harper's desire to step in for you, Joe."

When his dad brought up the issue of Harper directing things from Florida, both Mike and Jay described their plans to build a home for Jay where Harper could take up residence when in town.

"Sounds like you've all discussed this without my knowledge," their dad said.

"You didn't leave us much choice, Dad," Jay replied. "Mike, Gard and I suspected you had some kind of health problem. We didn't know the extent until today."

"Let's put aside the question of your successor for the moment," Mike said. "The real issue here is your health. Your announcement has thrown all of us, but at least we now know what you're facing. Mom, Dad, you no longer are fighting this alone. We're all here for you."

Jay and Harper added their support. Their mother dabbed at her eyes. All six, including Dash, folded into a group hug. When they pulled apart, their dad's eyes were misty as well.

Joseph Woodley seemed to gather himself, sat up straighter. "Enough bad news for now. It's Christmas, a day of celebration of new life, not the end of another. Harper, we'll talk tomorrow, before you fly back to Florida."

Harper nodded. As she took her husband's hand, her eyes glowed.

Joseph Woodley rose from his chair on his own accord. "I may be sick, but I'm still hungry. Time for that meal you promised, Michael. Let's test out that new table."

Mike didn't have the heart to tell him the table was a stand-in. Maybe he'd just keep it.

While the others finished warming the turkey and stuffing, sweet potatoes, and brussels sprouts, Mike excused himself and sought temporary quiet in his office. He hadn't been sure how to bring up the subject of his dad's health, and thanks to his dad's insistence on playing outside with the kids, that issue had been taken out of his hands. Even appeared his dad was receptive of Harper taking the reins.

That left one more obstacle to be addressed today. Obstacle? Nah. But there was still one more item on today's to-do list. Was he ready? God, yes!

With eleven at the table and this being his house, his event, they placed him at the head. His mother sat to his left, Darren to his right. Perfect.

Jay, Harper and Dash insisted on kitchen duty, since Darren, her mother, and sister had handled breakfast. Mike sat back and took in the scene, surrounded by most of the key players in his life. Too bad they hadn't invited Ned, Shae, Janice and Tim, but they were down the way in Ned's house celebrating their first Christmas together as well. Good thing Gard had already talked to their dad about leaving the business. Made putting forth Harper's name go smoother.

He hardly tasted Tammy's delicious food. His mind was focused on the end of the meal, when they'd feast on dessert and coffee and settle back to reminisce about Christmases of the past. He touched the breast pocket of his jacket. Still there. Waiting.

When the others were involved in another discussion, Darren leaned toward him. "I planted myself near the door, so I could overhear your family pow-wow. I hope that's okay. I had to know if you'd change your mind and sign up for Woodley Industries. Putting your sister forth as the candidate was brilliant."

"She's the best person for the job. She'll do great."

"But it took you to solve the problem. That's your role."

What a perfect cue. "I have another problem that needs solving."

She cocked her head. "Oh? What's that?"

"Maybe you can help." He clinked his water glass to draw the others' attention. "I just asked Darren to help me solve a problem. She's helped me realize I want to be closer to my family. Problem is, I dug myself into a hole when I told her I was a no-commitments type of guy."

He took her hand in his. "I've already told you I realized that was a crock. But I need you to help me climb out of that hole."

Darren wasn't saying anything, but a hint of a smile at the corner of her lips suggested she had some idea what was coming.

He retrieved the tiny box from his jacket, rose, and went down on one knee beside her. He opened the box for her to see the diamond ring he'd had flown overnight from his jeweler in the Big Apple. "Marry me, Darren. I'm ready to commit the rest of my life to you. This house is as much you as it is me. Become my wife and live here with me."

A hush descended around the rest of the table, confirmed only by his ears. His eyes were completely on her.

Darren's mouth appeared to be forming words, although all that emerged was, "I, uh ..."

"Just say yes," he said.

"Yes. Oh yes," she replied, going on her knees as well, her arms around his neck.

They shared a chaste kiss in front of the family. "Merry Christmas, everyone," he said as he placed the ring on her finger.

"How come she gets a gift when we all have to wait?" Hailey asked.

Joseph Woodley raised his glass. "You're wrong, darling granddaughter. Your uncle just gave the rest of us two very special gifts—not only a new member for our family, but he also rejoined the fold. Who could ask for a better Christmas?"

AFTERWORD

Dear Reader,

Thank you for reading this book. If you liked it, won't you please take a minute to leave a review?

To learn more about the eleven contemporary romances and two novellas I've written, sign up for my newsletter at https://www.subscribepage.com/BBContempRom

I've also written two cozy mystery series, the Mah Jongg Mysteries and Nailed It Home Reno Mysteries. You can learn more about them on my website, www.barbarabarrettbooks.com.

Follow me on Facebook: https://bit.ly/2aXZvG9
Follow me on Twitter: https://twitter.com/bbarrettbooks

SNEAK PEEK
THE SLEEPOVER CLAUSE

Finished the Sullivan's Creek series? Why not check out the first book in the Matchmaking Motor Coach Series, *The Sleepover Clause*?

ANOTHER MAN STOOD at one end of the desk. Shorter and blonder than Mitch and Graham, he had the same business-like blue eyes as Graham, set wider apart. He offered a broad smile. "Ms. Carpenter. I'm sorry I missed you yesterday. I understand you had a slight accident."

Though she extended her hand, she wasn't ready to be gracious. "Perhaps if you'd been here, my best pantsuit would still be part of my wardrobe."

The man winced, as if she'd socked him. Then she noticed the cane.

"I'm Geoffrey McKenna, Geoff, the middle brother," he said, recovering and shaking her hand. "I've spent my life keeping these two out of trouble, but yesterday got by me. Have a seat, won't you? We have a few ideas we'd like to run by you."

This was more like it. Jenna must have really come down hard on them. She sat in the chair Graham offered. "Ideas? Not really necessary. That's why I'm here."

"Oh, we know," Graham said, settling himself against the other side of the desk. "But since you're not familiar with Iowa or this business, we thought a little structure would help you settle in."

Structure? What were they up to? She inched her spine higher. *Be gracious.* She widened her mouth into a smile, jaw muscles she didn't know existed clenched. Nothing was more disarming to a group of men than a woman who could smile while she cut the floor out from under them. "Structure. Tell me more."

"We're working on a finely-tuned completion schedule here," Geoff McKenna said.

"The vehicle has to be in L.A. ready to go on July 22," Graham added. "That gives us six weeks to do everything, including test driving and delivering it. You have no more than four weeks, starting now, to finish your part. Were you aware of those deadlines?"

Was she aware of them? If they only knew what she'd been hammering out on her computer at two this morning. The time-line was so tight, her work was planned almost down to the hour. She lifted her eyes to Graham McKenna's. "Yes, I was. And I'm prepared to meet them. With suitable working arrangements," she thought to add.

"Our point exactly," Mitch said. His nostrils flared just the slightest, reminding her of a race horse itching to hit the track. A stallion. A sleek, tobacco-colored thoroughbred.

"Fine. Why don't you tell me what you have in mind, and we'll see how *your* ideas play into *my* plans."

The three exchanged glances. Guilty ones. Her skin prickled. Something was definitely going down here, probably not to her liking. She had to be on guard.

Good thing she was too. For the next half hour, they negoti-ated about every possible action she could take while working under their roof. When she could be there, how long she could work, no music, no hotplates—like she ever cooked—and no shorts or tank tops. She shook her head, said "No" more than once, and actually snorted on one item. She saw through their machinations and wasn't going to let them snow her.

Finally, her tolerance dissolved. "How many items are left on that list?" The three men went into a huddle and compared notes.

"I think we're done," Graham said at last. He read off the lengthy list of conditions.

"You can have access to the vehicle at hours other than what we've agreed to with our advance approval," Geoff added. He looked at his brothers. "Anything else, guys?"

The other two shook their heads and started putting their notes away.

Aubrey waited a beat and then unzipped her leather carryall and removed a folder. "Now, I have a few ideas of my own I'd like to discuss."

Mitch had already risen in anticipation of her departure. "What?"

"My list," she said innocently. "I've been patient and flexible about your stipulations. But I have a few concerns of my own to discuss. Starting with my office."

"Office?" all three men replied, once again exchanging looks.

She was hoping for that effect. "Yes. I don't need much space, but I do need a place to work on my laptop, make private phone calls and store my files. Surely you can spare me a few extra square feet?" she asked with a sweep of her hand.

Geoff raised his brows, Graham shrugged and Mitch emitted a sound like a low snarl.

"I guess we could put her in the accountant's office," Mitch said after a bit, in a sort of last resort tone.

"The what?" Geoff asked.

"You know? The room on the other side of the building?"

"There are just storerooms over there," Graham said. "And the

—" He shut his mouth, cocked his head, and turned toward his brother so Aubrey couldn't see the exchange. "Right. The *accountant's* room. That's a great idea."

"Okay, that's settled," Mitch said. "Anything else?"

"My environment has to be safe and efficient. No more slipping on oil spills because someone forgot to mop them up." She shot a glance at Mitch. "Because it's too dark in the garage."

The men looked at each other and shrugged.

"Okay," Graham agreed, "whatever."

"Good," she said. "One last point. Some days, I'll need to be here twenty-four/seven. I'll need a place to sleep at those times. I don't want to be traveling back and forth between here and my lodging in the wee hours of the morning."

Mitch was out of his chair again. "You want to stay here overnight? You do know we live here, don't you?"

"No, I didn't. But I don't think that will be a problem."

"*You* don't think it'll be a problem. What a relief. Wouldn't want *you* to be troubled about *our* living arrangements." Mitch barked the words.

"I don't need a fully functional bedroom. Just a private place to catch a few hours' sleep. Maybe I could use the accountant's office?"

"Uh." Geoff mumbled. "Not a good idea."

"Surely you could find a cot or air mattress to put in there?" she asked.

"The room's not very large. And the bathroom, uh, is way across the building, over here by our offices," Graham said, tapping his fingers on the desk.

"No shower or bathtub," Geoff added. "At least down here."

She lifted a brow. "But there's one somewhere in the building?"

Mitch rubbed the back of his neck. "Well, yeah. I have one and so does Gray. But those are our private quarters."

Why were they having so much difficulty with this? Most of

the men she worked with would have offered up their own beds, let alone showers, for her. She returned a perplexed look. Who could possibly resist her request for a bed and shower? She even batted her eyelashes once, twice.

"Ah, for Pete's sake, guys," Graham said, "this isn't such a big deal. We'll find an air mattress and you can use my shower whenever you need one."

"Thanks," she smiled at him, feeling in control once again.

He merely nodded, not looking at either brother.

Mitch stood, hands on his hips. "That the end of your list? We're running out of time and patience."

Poor thing. You know you've been bested, but you're not about to admit it. She closed the folder she'd been perusing and stuck it back in her bag. Wouldn't do for them to know she'd been using her grocery list as her source of improvised demands.

~

Learn more at
BarbaraBarrettBooks.com/the-sleepover-clause-2/

ACKNOWLEDGMENTS

Thank you to The Wild Rose Press, who initially published this book in 2014.

In order for this book to take on new life now that I'm publishing it myself, it needed a brand-new, intriguing cover. My grateful thanks to my cover artist, Chris Kridler of Sky Diary Productions, for taking the few snippets of ideas I fed her about this story and bringing this catchy cover to life. I also have her to thank for the formatting.

Thank you, Harriet Sawyer, for proofing the re-edited version of this manuscript. Although many pairs of eyes have reviewed the book over its lifetime, the updates required one more look.

Thanks always to my husband, Veryl, for his continuing support of my writing career. He has seen me through more typewriters, tabletop computers and laptops than I can recall.

BOOKS BY BARBARA BARRETT

Cozy Mysteries

The Mah Jongg Mystery Series

Craks in a Marriage

Bamboozled

Connect the Dots

Beware the East Wind

Flower Power

Jokers Wild

The Charleston Challenge

The Dragon Lady Gets Her Due

Courtesy Call

also available in paperback

Nailed It Home Reno Mysteries

Measure Twice, Murder Once

Loose Screw

Death by Drywall

Homicide by Hammer

Nuts and Bolts

Snared by the Snake

Wrenched at the Reindeer Run

A LITTLE ABOUT
BARBARA BARRETT

Barbara Barrett skipped a midlife crisis by writing romance novels at night when she wasn't at her day job as human resources analyst for Iowa State Government. Her first book was published in 2012. She has now published eleven full-length contemporary romance novels and two novellas. More recently, she has published nine cozy mysteries in her Mah Jongg Mystery series and seven in her Nailed It Home Reno Mysteries series. This book is the third and final book of the Sullivan's Creek series.

Barbara is married to the man she met her senior year at college. They have two grown children, eight grandchildren and two great grandchildren.

Now retired, she spends her time in Florida, Iowa and Minnesota. She earned her B.A. degree in History from the University of Iowa and her Master's Degree in History from Drake University.

When not in front of her laptop creating her next story, she plays Mah Jongg, is learning to paint with acrylics and enjoys lunches with friends.